D0208885

Three powerhou...
offering the best in military romance!

PRAISE FOR THE WORK OF RACHEL LEE

"Lee skillfully constructs a suspenseful story—
with romance in all the right places."
—*Publishers Weekly* on *After I Dream*

"[An] outstanding thriller by the multi-talented Lee."
—*Booklist* on *Last Breath*

"Once you read *Exile's End,* you will want to find
and read all of her books about Conard County."
—*All About Romance* on *Exile's End*

READERS LOVE MERLINE LOVELACE

"Another excellent tale…[written] with an
insider's knowledge and assurance."
—*Booklist* on *After Midnight* (starred review)

"A well-paced and satisfying tale…
drawn with impressive deftness."
—*Publishers Weekly* on *Dark Side of Dawn*

"Merline Lovelace will keep you
turning pages well past midnight!"
—*Literary Times* on *Call of Duty*

RAVES FOR CATHERINE MANN

"Stark, edgy and compelling."
—*Booklist* on *Anything, Anywhere, Anytime*

"Definitely a must read."
—*The Best Reviews* on *Joint Forces*

"Terrific…four stars."
—*Romantic Times* on *Taking Cover*

A SOLDIER'S
CHRISTMAS

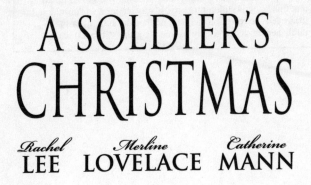

Rachel
LEE

Merline
LOVELACE

Catherine
MANN

HQN™

If you purchased this book without a cover you should be aware that this book is stolen property. It was reported as "unsold and destroyed" to the publisher, and neither the author nor the publisher has received any payment for this "stripped book."

ISBN 0-373-77014-6

A SOLDIER'S CHRISTMAS

Copyright © 2004 by Harlequin Books S.A.

The publisher acknowledges the copyright holders of the individual works as follows:

I'LL BE HOME
Copyright © 2004 by Susan Civil-Brown and Cristian Brown

A BRIDGE FOR CHRISTMAS
Copyright © 2004 by Merline Lovelace

THE WINGMAN'S ANGEL
Copyright © 2004 by Catherine Mann

All rights reserved. Except for use in any review, the reproduction or utilization of this work in whole or in part in any form by any electronic, mechanical or other means, now known or hereafter invented, including xerography, photocopying and recording, or in any information storage or retrieval system, is forbidden without the written permission of the publisher, Harlequin Enterprises Limited, 225 Duncan Mill Road, Don Mills, Ontario M3B 3K9, Canada.

All characters in this book have no existence outside the imagination of the author and have no relation whatsoever to anyone bearing the same name or names. They are not even distantly inspired by any individual known or unknown to the author, and all incidents are pure invention.

This edition published by arrangement with Harlequin Books S.A.

® and TM are trademarks of the publisher. Trademarks indicated with ® are registered in the United States Patent and Trademark Office, the Canadian Trade Marks Office and in other countries.

www.HQNBooks.com

Printed in U.S.A.

CONTENTS

I'LL BE HOME

Rachel Lee

Chapter One

The snow flurry that had begun when Seth Hardin left Casper, Wyoming, was a thick swirl of flakes by the time he was within a half hour of Conard County. In the glare of his headlights, against the backdrop of night, the snow seemed to be all that existed in the world. The black pavement of the highway was nearly invisible, its wetness soaking up the light, and only the drifts to either side delineated the road.

Little by little, however, the snow was beginning to stick. Traffic had lightened until Seth felt his was the only vehicle traveling at this late hour.

The weather and the darkness suited his mood perfectly. Coming home to Conard County—which wasn't even his real home—wasn't something he especially wanted to do. But Seth Hardin wasn't a man who avoided the hard things. If he had been, he wouldn't be a navy SEAL. He had endured things that gave him a self-knowledge far beyond most people's.

This was different, though. This was an emotional trial he was facing. The birth parents he was still coming to know were awaiting him. That was okay, he liked them both. But in that same county, in that same town, resided his ex-wife Darlene, now, by all reports, happily remarried.

He'd warned her that life as a navy wife would be brutal, with long periods of separation. It had been more brutal than either of them had anticipated, given the situation in the Middle East. And Darlene hadn't been able to handle it.

Intellectually he could forgive her, even understand it. Emotionally the scar was worse, he sometimes thought, than the one he'd gotten from the business end of an AK-47. Of course, that wound had been the beginning of the end. Or maybe it *had* been the end. Damned if he knew anymore.

As he drove through the night in a swirling cocoon of white, heading toward an unknown that might prove painful, his thoughts seemed to be on everything except the coming Christmas holiday. It had been three years since he'd last returned to Conard County, and he couldn't help thinking that this was a mistake.

But all his buddies had families, and this year he just couldn't face being the extra person at one of their dinner tables. That and the fact that Marge Tate, his birth mother, had been working on him to come until he felt that it would be downright Scrooge-ish to say no.

Oh, hell, this drive couldn't end soon enough. The quicker he was with other people, the sooner he could put all these self-pitying thoughts aside.

Bite the bullet. The thought popped into his mind the instant he first glimpsed the lights of Conard County through the thickening snowfall.

Surprisingly, though, he felt a burst of warmth in his chest, a true sense of coming back to a place he loved. Somehow, since the day he had stood on the Tate doorstep and told Marge he was her son, he had developed a deep connection to this place. For the Tate family. Much as he might have tried to deny it these past few years, it leaped up right now and reminded him that he had *family*.

As he pulled up he saw the familiar house, every light blazing. The family van, once necessary for carting six daughters around, had long since disappeared. Now the daughters had cars of their own, crowding the driveway and street. Janet wasn't coming, Marge had said, because her husband, an L.A. cop, had to work through the holiday. Seth wouldn't get a chance to see his niece or meet his new nephew.

But he believed the other five girls would be here. Certainly Wendy would, since she and her husband, Billy Joe Yuma—known to everyone except his wife as Yuma—lived here in town. And knowing the Tate family, there would be other guests as well. Nate adopted stray people the way others adopted stray animals.

It would be a madhouse, just what he needed to help him get through his first Christmas here without Darlene.

He parked as near the house as he could, two wheels in a snowdrift to make room for passing vehicles. The night wind held a vicious bite, a cold, wet sting that went right through clothes better suited for Virginia Beach than Wyoming at this time of year. He might need to buy a parka if this kept up.

There were sharp ice crystals mixed in with the soft, fluffy flakes now, promising worse to come. He pulled his duffel out of the back seat, locked the car and began to walk up the sidewalk that led to the front door. Salt, spread to clear the ice, crunched under his feet. The cold was already numbing his nose, and the wind snaked into the collar of his light jacket, making him shiver.

The curtains in the front window were open, giving a beautiful view of an undecorated Christmas tree awaiting the glory of lights. The other windows glowed with the inviting warmth of lamplight.

Bracing himself for what was to come, he rapped on the front door.

Sounds of voices came from within, sounds of laughter and music, calling him to a family gathering to which he belonged. He just wished he were in a better mood for it.

Then the door opened, and Marge's arms flew around him, hugging him and drawing him inside all at once.

"Seth!" she said with delight, holding him as close as if she had missed him every moment he'd been away. It had been a very long time since anyone had hugged him that way, and for the first time he called her Mother.

"Hi, Mom."

He dropped his bag and returned her hug, then stepped back a little, in time to see the sheen of tears in her happy eyes.

A hand fell on his shoulder and he turned his head.

"Welcome, son," said Sheriff Nate Tate.

"Dad."

The two were as alike as peas in a pod, despite the twenty-year difference in their ages. With a few more lines, some gray hair and a few more pounds, Seth would be indistinguishable from his sire. Dark-haired, tall, well-built men both, with weathered good looks.

Nate embraced him, too, then took his duffel, saying, "I'll take this up to your room. Marge, get something hot into this boy, he's freezing."

Marge touched his jacket. "This isn't nearly enough for this weather."

"I know. But it's not exactly easy to buy a parka in Virginia Beach."

She smiled, a beautiful smile, and took his hand. "Come into the kitchen and warm up before I unleash the rest of the family on you."

He was glad to follow her, not sure he was ready yet for the absolute uproar that was the Tate family and their husbands, boyfriends and family friends. It was like belonging to a small village.

His own childhood had been solitary, as the only adopted child of an older couple. Families of this sort were something he'd only seen on television programs. En masse they could still overwhelm him.

Marge sat him at the kitchen table. "Hot chocolate? Hot cider? Or something stronger?"

"Coffee, please. Coffee would be great."

There was a pot already made, and she brought him a cup. Black, just the way he preferred it. He slipped off his jacket, letting it fall back against the chair, and cupped his hands around the generous mug. Marge sat across from him, still beaming.

"I'm so glad you could come," she said gently. "We've missed you, Seth."

He didn't know quite how to respond. Surely she had to understand he'd stayed away for a reason.

Marge didn't pursue the issue. Apparently she had said all she needed to on the subject.

"Nearly everyone's here," she said warmly. "Except for Janet, of course. I think I told you she couldn't come. Mary pulled the holiday shift at her hospital. Apparently someone got sick, so she couldn't get away. She might be here the day after Christmas. Other than that, we're all going to be here. Even, would you believe it, Krissie's fiancé."

"She has a fiancé?" The thought startled him. He still thought of Krissie, the youngest of his sisters, as a child in high school.

"She's growing up, Seth." Marge shrugged. "You send your girls away to college and then next thing you know they're engaged."

A look of almost-sorrow passed over her face, and Seth asked impulsively, "Don't you like him?"

"Oh, it's not that at all," she hastened to assure him. "It's just that…my last baby is leaving the nest for good." She laughed softly. "I'm starting to feel old."

He didn't know what to say. These were all things he was utterly unfamiliar with.

"Anyway," Marge continued more briskly, "the girls are all doing well, and the men in their lives seem to be very nice—in fact, I love most of them like sons, so why am I getting all misty about it?"

"Because it's Christmas?" he suggested tentatively.

She nodded. "Probably." Surprising him, she reached out and squeezed his hand. "There's something I never told you, but I want you to know."

"What's that?"

She looked down a moment, then met his gaze straightly. "I almost died from the pain of giving you up for adoption. Don't stay away anymore, Seth. Please."

He didn't know how to answer that, either. He wasn't sure he *had* an answer just yet.

"Anyway," she said briskly, rising to get the coffeepot and top off his mug, "we also have a houseguest."

"So what's new?" he asked, drawing a laugh from her.

"It's Maria Hoskins, one of the schoolteachers here in town. She has no family here and we didn't want her spending the holiday alone."

Seth nodded. "I would have expected that."

Marge laughed. "You're getting to know us, I see."

"Some things are fairly predictable, yes."

Just then, a feminine voice outside the door called, "Marge? I was wondering…"

The words trailed off as a lovely young woman appeared in the doorway. It was as if something inside Seth suddenly hushed and went still.

She was of average height, her figure slender but not too much so. Her hair was a warm chestnut brown that caught the light and seemed to reflect fire, while her eyes were the deep blue of a calm sea. Her face was pretty, but just ever so slightly akilter, making it interesting rather than beautiful.

She froze in the doorway like a startled deer. "Oh, I'm sorry! I didn't mean to intrude."

"You're not intruding," Marge insisted. "Come in and meet our son, Seth Hardin. We managed to pry him away from the navy for a few days."

"The navy?" The young woman came into the room smiling. "Really? I've been talking to the recruiter about joining. Maybe you can give me the real skinny. I'm Maria Hoskins."

Seth, who had sprung instantly to his feet at the sight of her, a courtesy so deeply ingrained he wasn't even aware of it, took her offered hand and shook it.

Delicate bones. Skin as smooth as satin. Warm. His own hand probably felt like ice to her.

"A pleasure to meet you," he said.

"Me, too."

"Sit, sit," Marge insisted. "What did you need, Maria?"

Maria laughed. "I was just wondering where you disappeared to. Everyone is getting ready to start a game of charades."

"Well, they can go ahead without me. Go back if you like, or stay here and have coffee with us."

The vision in blue jeans and a flannel shirt decided to stay and have coffee. "I'm terrible at charades," she confided to Seth as Marge brought her a cup of coffee with cream. "At both ends of it. I can't act things out, and I can't figure out any of the clues. They'll all do better without me."

Seth felt a smile crease his cheeks, such a rare expression of late that it felt awkward.

Marge laughed and patted Maria's hand. "Feel free to hide out with us."

Nate joined them then, taking a seat at the table with the announcement, "The weather forecast is getting worse. We might have two feet of snow by morning, and the winds are going to stay strong and gusty."

Marge answered him. "In short, a blizzard."

"Sounds like it. I'm going to need to warn my men. Unless there's an emergency call, I want them all safely at home or at the office, not stranded in a drift somewhere we can't find them fast enough." He looked at Seth. "You got here just in time, son."

Chapter Two

The uproar had at last settled for the night. After being warmly greeted by four of his six sisters and Billy Joe Yuma, his brother-in-law, he had been introduced to "the boyfriends," as Nate called them. Then he had been dragged into a game of charades that played out with a lot of laughter and joking.

Finally, Yuma and Wendy went home, taking all the boyfriends with them. Everyone else headed to bed, and as the odd man out—literally—Seth was given the sofa bed in the office, a small room where Nate kept up with his paperwork and Marge handled the family finances.

The familial warmth lingered, but sleep refused to come, despite the long drive. Finally he climbed out of the bed, pulled on a pair of jeans and padded out to the family room where the evening's fire burned low. A chill seemed to come from the glass doors, beyond which snow whirled wildly, so he put another log on.

Then he settled onto the couch facing the fire and stared into the dancing red flames, hoping they would hypnotize him into sleepiness.

What he absolutely did not want to do was think about the past. It was all his fault, anyway, and having tried to warn Darlene about the hardship ahead was no excuse. He simply should never have married her. He should have listened to his head instead of his heart and spared them both a lot of misery and grief.

So much of his life was shrouded in secrecy. The wife of a SEAL would know nothing except that her husband would suddenly be gone for days, or weeks, or even months. A wife would never know where her husband was, or what he was doing. Most wives would never begin to imagine the sorts of things SEALs were called on to do. And most of what SEALs did was never traced back to them.

The strain was hard on women, harder than having a spouse gone for six months at sea. At least when your man was assigned to a specific ship, you could e-mail him. You could keep posted on the ship's condition, and approximately where it was located. All a SEAL's wife ever knew was that if he wasn't ashore with her at one of the two SEAL bases, then he was probably up to his neck in it somewhere on the globe.

He couldn't blame Darlene for being unable to live with that. But he could and *did* blame himself for letting his heart overcome his head.

Ah, hell, he was sick of the sound of his own thoughts. Coming back had been a mistake. Feelings that he'd firmly buried were bubbling up like the lava of a wakening volcano. He didn't need this crap. He needed to get his balance back.

The faintest of sounds alerted him and he twisted to look behind him. Maria Hoskins stood in the doorway, wrapped in a satin robe, a shadowy figure lit only by the firelight.

"I'm sorry," she said. "I couldn't sleep and thought I would sit out here for a while. But I don't want to disturb you."

She was exactly the kind of disturbance he needed. Something else to think about, someone to talk with besides himself. "You're not bothering me," he answered truthfully. "Come on in. I just put another log on the fire."

"Thanks." She joined him on the couch, sitting at the far end. "My room is on the corner of the house, and the wind is wailing like a banshee. It's such a mournful sound."

He nodded, though such things rarely affected him. "It's really blowing out there."

"What's a gale at sea like?"

The question seemed out of context, then he remembered she had said something about joining the navy. "Well, it depends on the gale."

She laughed quietly. "Of course."

"And it depends on the size of ship you're on," he added. "The bigger the ship, the less you get knocked around. But it can still be rough even in twenty-foot seas. A lot of times the waves get even higher. A lot higher. I was in a typhoon once and we had hundred-foot seas. That was a ride to remember."

"I thought ships avoided typhoons."

"They *try* to. But you have to remember how big a storm like that can be. You can't always get completely out of the way. But as a rule, yes, they're avoided." He smiled faintly. "I always enjoy a good gale."

"Why doesn't that surprise me?" She laughed again, the same quiet, pleasant sound. "Marge says you're a SEAL."

"Yes."

"Then you must be a remarkable man."

He didn't know quite how to respond to that. He had met near-adoration before, usually from very young men, mostly teens, who thought being a SEAL was the epitome of manliness. He'd met "groupies" before, women who sought out SEALs at bars and other places because they were attracted to the sense of danger.

But none of that was evident in Maria's statement. Her tone and expression were utterly matter-of-fact. And oddly, that embarrassed him.

"I just do my job," he said. "That's all."

She nodded, her blue eyes studying him. "Well, it's not an easy job."

"Neither is teaching," he countered.

She laughed. "It *can* be a little like guerrilla warfare at times. But mostly it's quite enjoyable."

"Then why do you want to leave?"

She tilted her head, her smile almost wistful. "Because something in me has a terrible yen to do a little traveling before I get too old to enjoy it. I can always come back to teaching in a few years if I want."

"Why the navy?"

"Join the navy and see the world. Isn't that what they say?"

He nodded, then couldn't quite contain a laugh. "Well, you'll get to see some ports, that's a fact. Assuming you get sea duty. And you'll become really familiar with your home port."

"It's more traveling than I could afford to do otherwise." She was still smiling, apparently not having taken his comment amiss. "And I've got to decide soon. I'll be twenty-seven in the spring."

"Well, you could always get a job with a cruise line. Pick one that goes to the places you'd like to visit."

"Hmm." Her smile grew crooked with amusement. "Are you trying to tell me something?"

He shrugged. "Not really. Just presenting alternatives to a four-year hitch that might take you to places you really don't want to go."

"I see." Her smile faded. "You've been there, haven't you?"

"Been where?"

"Places you really didn't want to go."

He could have laughed off her comment and said something about how he kept extending his enlistment, and you didn't put in nearly twenty years by accident. But something forced him to be straight with her. "That," he said flatly, "is part of the job."

She nodded thoughtfully. "I'll keep that in mind." Then she glanced away from him and said, "Oh! Look at the snow now."

A drift was building against the glass doors, and small white flakes were whirling in a frenzy. Rising, Seth went to turn on the outside light. Its brightness illuminated the snow, and nothing else. The world beyond had vanished in a whiteout.

"It's so beautiful," Maria breathed.

That's when Seth first realized she had joined him at the glass doors. "Yes," he said.

"I love storms of every kind. I'm crazy about thunderstorms. But this is so very beautiful. It's hard to care that tomorrow no one will be able to go anywhere."

"Was anyone planning to?"

She laughed. "Probably not. The schools are closed for the holidays, and most people have finished their Christmas shopping."

"I haven't," he admitted. "I didn't have time before I left, and I was planning to do it here."

No, he hadn't had time. He'd returned from a highly secret mission just hours before his leave began. He barely had time to jam clothes into his duffel, sign out and catch his flight to Wyoming. He certainly still hadn't enjoyed the opportunity to truly uncoil.

"I may," he said, "have to give everyone an IOU."

She touched his arm, sending a surprisingly electric tingle through him. Then she laughed. "They'll understand, Seth. The girls are grown up now."

"You laugh very easily."

Her eyes met his. "And you don't laugh at all."

It was true, he realized. He rarely laughed anymore. And when he did, it wasn't a deep, carefree laugh. More of an obligatory one. What a sorry ass he'd become.

"I'm sorry," she said after a moment. "It's none of my business."

He shrugged. "It's okay. No big deal. I've been drowning in self-pity for a while. My own company bores me."

"Because of Darlene?"

He shouldn't have been surprised that she knew. Hell, the whole county probably knew, given that Conard County boasted only about five thousand souls, and his dad had been the sheriff for nearly thirty years. Given that gossip was prime entertainment in a place this tightly knit, he'd probably been talked about from one end of the county to the other.

"Sorry," she said again. "It's just that your eyes…" She trailed off.

"That?" Now he did laugh, but it was a tight sound, humorless. "That's the thousand-yard stare, Maria. You've heard of it?"

"No."

"It's the look in a person's eyes that comes after he's been places people shouldn't go, seen things he shouldn't see." He shrugged again. "It goes with the job."

"That's sad."

"I'm a sad ass. Sorry."

She reached out suddenly and gripped his forearm. "Why do you keep putting yourself down?"

"Just being truthful."

"No, you're not." Her voice became stern. "Thank God for people like you who will do the tough jobs. I'm just sorry it costs you so much to do it."

He looked at her then, feeling every bit as hollow as his gaze. "That's right romantic."

She shook her head, frowning at him as if he were a thirteen-year-old in one of her classes. He recognized the look; more than one teacher had shot it his way. But he was past being worried by it.

"There's nothing romantic about it, Seth. But somebody's got to do it."

It was such a statement of the obvious that he didn't bother to answer. Hollow people didn't feel a whole hell of a lot, anyway…except maybe self-pity, and that was starting to drain away into anger and self-loathing. So maybe he wasn't as hollow as he'd like to be.

She let go of his arm and settled back in her corner of the couch, giving him a brief, tantalizing glimpse of silky thigh. He ignored it and turned his attention back to the fire.

"I'm glad you came home, Seth," she said after a few minutes. "I think you need it more than you realize."

Maybe, maybe not. But sitting here in the warmth of the family room, looking at a crackling fire and deepening snow, with a lovely woman beside him, he began to realize something.

He realized just how much shit he'd buried these last years behind the facade of duty and work. How he'd driven himself to avoid his demons.

God knew he had plenty of them.

Chapter Three

It wasn't much later that Maria said good night. He listened to the swish of her satin gown as she disappeared down the hallway toward the bedrooms. He'd been a boor and he knew it, but right now he couldn't regret it. Right now he had some *real* issues to deal with.

Except that his mind kept shying away from them, as if some part of him feared that if he looked into the abyss he might tip over into it and fall forever.

Time passed, the fire began to burn low, the snow had deepened into a drift well over two feet against the glass doors. He wondered vaguely if it had snowed that much, or if it was just the wind building the wall of white. Stretching, he rose to toss another log on the fire. He certainly wasn't getting any closer to sleep, or any closer to facing his demons.

When the hell had this mess begun? What had started it? As he poked the log into position, it seemed to him that the problem might have begun *before* Darlene left him. Maybe the problem was part of the reason she'd gone. Maybe he'd died inside long before.

Maybe it was just being different. God knew, Special

Ops people were different. They got to look inside themselves, know themselves, better than most folks. And what they learned about themselves wasn't pretty.

He knew, for example, that he could risk his neck to put a bomb on a ship in the middle of the night. He knew he could kill for a change of clothes to protect himself. He *knew* the stuff that most people liked to watch in movies, and he knew he was capable of the ugliest, dirtiest things in support of his mission and survival.

Maybe looking inside had started to pull him apart.

He drew the screen over the fireplace and turned. He tensed as he saw Marge, clad in footed flannel pajamas, standing near the couch.

"I thought I heard someone moving around," she said with a smile. "Can't sleep?"

He shook his head.

"I can't, either. How about I make us both a cup of cocoa."

He didn't really want it, didn't want her company. But some last bit of decency made him polite. "Sure. Thanks."

He shouldn't have come. He should have damn well stayed in the BOQ, locked himself in and faced all this crap where he wouldn't be interrupted.

Too late.

He smiled when a few minutes later Marge returned with two steaming mugs and offered him one.

"I know it's not heart healthy," she said with a little chuckle, "but I put some cream in it anyway. I come from a farm family, and I like it rich. The way my mother made it."

"Before everything in life became a threat to longevity?"

She laughed again. "You got it. The way I figure it, the human race wouldn't have survived this long if everything we ate and drank was fatal."

"Live in the moment?"

"It's the only one we have."

He nodded. "I couldn't agree more." He meant it. So why the hell was he all tangled up in his past?

"Seth…" She put her mug down. Firelight caught the red in her hair and made it blaze. "I know the divorce cut you up. I can't tell you how sorry I am. You know I was almost there myself."

He knew. The day he had showed up on the Tates' doorstep and announced to Marge that he was the son she'd given up for adoption, the son of the man she had later married, Marge's life—and Nate's, for that matter— had gone into a real tailspin. Seth had been a secret that Marge kept for twenty-seven years. And Nate had felt he could never trust her again.

"But, hon," Marge said, "it's been four years. So I have to think something else is going on. What the hell is tearing you up inside?"

Her eyes were liquid, as if she were on the verge of tears. He felt a moment of shame that it was so obvious he was messed up. "I didn't know I was wearing a sign."

"You aren't," she assured him. "But when I came in here a little while ago, and you turned away from the fire, I could see… I'm sorry, I caught you off guard."

"Forget it. No big deal."

"But it's not just the divorce?"

He shook his head and stared into the fire, not wanting to see all the sympathy and love in her gaze, neither of which he deserved. "No. I've been telling myself it was but…no."

"I didn't think so." She sighed, and he could hear her sip her cocoa. "Nate's done your job," she said finally. "You might do yourself a favor if you talked to him. He was…when he came home, it was a long time before he lost that thousand-yard stare."

Her words so closely echoed the earlier conversation with Maria that his head turned sharply toward her. But all he saw on her face was love and a kind of sadness.

"And I promise I'll leave it alone," she said. "I won't pick at your scabs."

He nodded again, for the first time wondering what it would have been like to grow up with this marvelous woman as his mother. Not that his adoptive parents hadn't been good parents. But they hadn't been the warmest or most expressive of people.

"Anyway," Marge continued, "you're probably going to feel overrun with everyone here." Deft change of subject.

Again he managed a smile. "It's fun, actually. I grew up as an only child."

"That's hard in some ways," Marge said, then added wryly, "and easier in others. Believe me. You wouldn't imagine how these girls could fight. Or what this house was like when all six of them had a pajama party on the same night. Nate and I used to say we ought to camp on the front lawn."

He nodded and managed a faint chuckle. "I can see it."

"Nowadays there's too much peace and quiet around here." She laughed. "And to think I used to wish for it."

She rose from the couch and dropped a kiss on his forehead. "Sleep, son. I'm here if you need an ear. And so is Nate."

"Thanks…Mom."

She smiled, as if it touched her that he was at last calling her that. "Good night."

Carrying her cocoa, she headed toward bed.

Outside the wind howled like a banshee, and the snow grew deeper still. It began to look as if it were going to bury the world.

Chapter Four

They were indeed snowed in. By early morning, nothing in Conard County was moving. In consternation, the Tate girls called their boyfriends over at Wendy's house and bewailed the fact that they couldn't get together. Marge, too, seemed a little upset, because they were supposed to decorate the Christmas tree together that day…and tomorrow was Christmas.

Sleepy, in an almost dreamlike state, Seth sat in an easy chair near the sliding glass doors and watched the family swirl around him as he sipped a cup of coffee. The aromas of a huge breakfast still lingered in the air: pancakes, bacon, eggs, home fries. Marge and the girls had really gone to town.

Outside, the blizzard continued, creating a whiteout that hid even nearby houses from sight. Nate had disappeared into his den to use the other phone to talk to his deputies.

"But, Mom," Krissie said to Marge, "Dad has a plow on the front of his Tahoe. He could get the boys."

Marge shook her head. "You know perfectly well that's a police vehicle and it can't be used for personal reasons. What's more, I won't have your father going out in this. He wouldn't be able to see past the front of the car."

Krissie scowled, then sighed and walked away, once again joining the other two women at the phone wanting to talk to one of the men trapped across town with their sister and brother-in-law.

Seth found himself trying to hide a smile, it was so cute.

Suddenly Krissie squealed. "The boys are coming over here!"

Marge went into action like a juggernaut. "No, they're not!" She spoke sternly and nudged her way through the girls to take the phone.

"You stay right where you are," she said into the mouthpiece. "You'd be risking your necks if you come out in this, and I'm not going to have the girls' father risking his to try to find you. Am I clear?"

Apparently she was, because she nodded, said goodbye and hung up the phone.

"Guess what," she said to her daughters. "You're stuck with your mom and dad just like in the old days."

There was a collective groan, but nobody moped or argued. Instead they turned on the TV and went to the weather channel.

"All day," Krissie announced. "We *never* have storms like this." She switched off the TV.

"It would have to happen now," Cathy remarked. "Let's go play a game or something."

"I want to sleep," Bets said. "I don't get enough sleep at school."

One by one the daughters disappeared toward their rooms, leaving Marge, Maria and Seth alone in the family room.

The wind still howled, sometimes loud enough to drown the sound of the ticking clock on the fireplace mantel.

"I guess," said Marge, "we'll have to go ahead with decorating the tree later. And I've got some pies to bake and some candy to make."

"Can I help?" Maria asked, starting to rise.

"No, you just relax. The girls always help me with this, and they're going to come out of their mopes and do it this time, too."

She looked rather purposeful as she strode toward the bedrooms.

Maria laughed quietly. "Those poor girls. All they want is their men, and now their mom's going to make them help bake."

"Better than brooding," Seth remarked. As he should well know. Problem was, he didn't take his own advice.

"Did you get any sleep last night?" she asked.

He shook his head.

"I'm sorry. I did finally. Good, deep sleep." Her smile was dazzling. "And if you don't mind, I'm going to go help with the baking, anyway. I don't like feeling useless."

He nodded, returning her smile. Then, once again, he was alone with himself. To hell with it, he thought, and went to the den to join Nate.

Nate was on the phone, but he smiled and waved Seth into the room. Seth sat across the desk from him in a wooden captain's chair. Behind him was the couch on which he'd tossed and turned too much.

"Okay," Nate said. "I agree, Micah. If it's that bad everywhere, we're shut down except for emergencies. Okay. You, too."

Nate hung up and regarded his son with a kindly eye. "No point risking my deputies out there unless there's a real need. Nothing's moving, not even on the state highway. Forecasters are calling it the blizzard of the century, for these parts at least."

"It does look wicked out there."

"Wouldn't be so bad if the temperatures weren't predicted to fall to about thirty below tonight after it stops snowing. Then we might have some *real* problems. The cold is always more deadly than the snow."

"I hope everybody has enough heating oil."

"They should. Cold is something we're used to in these parts."

Nate settled back in his chair. It creaked beneath him, but he ignored the sound as if he'd heard it so many times it had become inaudible. "Now," he said, "about you."

"What about me?"

"You're looking bad, son."

"My clock's all messed up from my last mission. I just couldn't sleep."

"Hmm." The sound implied disbelief. "You been really busy?"

"Lately, yes. All the terrorist stuff. Keeps us hopping."

Nate nodded. "I thought it might. You know, son, there aren't many who can stay in this business as long as you have."

"It's all I know."

"I know. And that concerns me."

Seth felt a spark of resentment. "My decision."

"Of course it is. And I'm damn proud of you. I'll be honest, too, and admit that sometimes I miss parts of it myself. But only *parts* of it."

Seth nodded, needing no elucidation. He knew which parts he wouldn't miss himself.

"Be that as it may," Nate continued, "maybe you ought to give some thought to a career change. Maybe you could take a training position."

Seth nearly jumped out of his chair but restrained himself, instead gripping the arms of it with white-knuckled intensity. "What is it with everyone? You, Marge…"

"Maybe we're seeing something you're not."

"You don't know me that well." It was a nasty thing to say, and he wished the words gone the instant they escaped. But they hung in the air, an accusation, a self-indictment. Nate's face creased with inexpressible sorrow.

"I wish I could change that," he said quietly.

"I'm sorry," Seth said, ashamed. "I didn't mean that the way you probably took it."

"It's all right. Too much water under the dam now, and too little time to make up for it. But you might keep in mind that you haven't come home in four years, and that makes the changes in you pretty damn obvious. That's what we're seeing, Seth."

Seth nodded. Whether he liked it or not, apparently Marge and Nate could see the internal demons he was struggling with. And it was pointless, he told himself, to get defensive about it. Absolutely pointless.

"I *am* struggling with some issues," he said finally. "I was blaming it all on the divorce, but it seems there's more to it. I'm trying to work it out."

Nate nodded. "Good. We're here if you need us for anything at all."

"Come play with me," Maria said to him when he emerged from the den.

"Play with you?"

She was smiling at him, looking adorably huggable in a navy-blue sweatsuit and white furry slippers.

"Yes," she said. "I've been banished from the kitchen. Evidently it's a family tradition, and I'm a guest, so I'm supposed to stay out of the way. So I need somebody to play with."

At that moment icy snow rattled against the sliding glass doors. Seth looked over his shoulder and realized the blizzard seemed to be worsening still. "Just don't say you want to build a snowman."

Maria laughed, tossing her head. "I want to have fun, not die of hypothermia. There are plenty of board games. Or we can play cards."

He lifted a brow at her. "Seven-card stud? Or Texas Hold 'Em?"

"Poker?" Her brow creased. "I don't know if a school-teacher should…"

He waved away her protest. "This may be a small town, but nobody here will squeal on you. Besides, I bet most of the folks in these parts play poker on cold nights."

She laughed again, her eyes sparkling. "You might be right. But I've never played."

"I'll teach you, then we'll see if we can get some of the others to join us."

"I wonder where I can find a deck of cards," Maria said, looking around.

"I'll ask Nate."

"Sure," Nate said in answer to the question. "There're a couple of new decks of cards in the drawer in the entertainment center, and poker chips if you want them. And the card table is in the hall closet."

"Which means," Seth told Maria as he set up the card table, "you're safe. If the sheriff of this town owns poker chips, who's going to say anything when the schoolmarm plays the game at his house?"

Maria laughed again. Seth realized that he really liked the sound of her laughter. Short, long, loud or quiet, every one of her laughs lifted his spirits.

"Wow," he said when he opened the large drawer in the entertainment center.

"What?" she asked, coming to peer over his shoulder.

"I was expecting a couple of boxes of plastic chips." He pulled out a long leatherette case and carried it to the table. Opening it, he said, "These are the real things. Clay chips." Pulling a black one out of the neat side-by-side stacks, he turned it in his hand, savoring the feel of it. Then he passed it to Maria.

"Like they use in casinos," he said. "Man, he's even got them marked with denominations."

"I take it this is special?" Maria asked, turning the chip over and noting the gold impression that read "50."

"Most people won't go to the expense. Nate must play a lot of poker."

"I like the way it feels."

"Yeah." He smiled at her. "Heavy. Solid."

She laughed again. "Now I really *do* think it's okay to play."

"Well, we're not going to gamble, anyway. Just play for the chips. Come on, let's set up."

Just then Nate joined them, carrying a large, oddly shaped canvas case. "Did I hear somebody say 'poker'? I've got a poker tabletop here."

He zipped open the case and pulled out the tabletop. It was folded in the middle, made of heavy fiberboard, but when he opened it there was a green felt octagonal tabletop with chip racks and cup holders. "Gotta do it right," he said.

Seth started counting out chips as Maria said, "You'll join us, won't you, Nate? But I have to warn you, I've never played before. Seth is going to teach me."

Nate winked. "I always love playing with a fish."

Maria laughed again.

"Set it up for seven," Nate told Seth. "Marge and some of the girls will join us in a little while, I'm sure. And let me warn you, Marge and Krissie are both sharks. Killer Hold 'Em players."

"So we'll play stud," Seth said with a wink to Maria. "Take away their edge."

It was Nate's turn to laugh. "That'll do it," he allowed.

They played the first dozen or so hands with all the cards faceup, so Maria could get a sense of the game.

"This is cool," she said finally. "I think I'm ready to play."

"Okay," Nate said. "My deal. Everybody ante up."

Chips were tossed into the center of the table as Nate shuffled, then dealt each of them three cards, two face-down, one faceup.

Seth glanced at his and knew he was going to fold immediately. It was more fun, anyway, to watch Maria furrow her brow as she studied her own hand.

"Remember," he told her, "that unless you already have the makings of a good hand, you probably should fold. And you can get a sense of whether or not you'll draw the card you need by looking at our faceup cards. Nate is showing an ace. It would probably not be wise to try to draw to three aces. Same for my nine. And we both have spades, so that reduces the number of spades in the deck if you're thinking about drawing to a spade flush."

She nodded. "I remember. Besides, you said not to draw to a flush unless I already had three of the suit."

"That's a good rule for beginners," Nate agreed.

Maria smiled and pushed two ten-dollar chips into the center. Seth folded.

"Uh-oh," Nate said, then laughed. "I call." He pushed twenty in.

Another card was dealt to the two of them. Maria had a pair of tens showing now, Nate an ace and a three. Maria bet, Nate folded.

"By George," Nate said, "I think she's got it."

Maria laughed and proudly showed her three tens. "I think I have it," she said.

"You certainly did," Seth agreed. His eyes met hers, and he felt a warmth somewhere deep inside. He wanted to look away, to deny the feeling, but her gaze held his and the sense of warmth continued to grow.

"Your deal," Nate said, passing the cards to Maria. Shattering the moment.

Seth sighed, feeling as if he'd been breathless for an eternity. "Ante up," he said, to cover a sense of awkwardness. This was not good, not good at all.

Chapter Five

The need for sleep finally caught up with Seth during the middle of the afternoon. Excusing himself, he headed for the couch in the den and crashed, falling instantly into a deep sleep.

When he awoke again, the world was dark and silent. Confused, he bolted upright, then remembered. The wind reminded him. The howl had diminished not at all.

He swung his feet to the floor and stretched. Night was a friend to him, and the bit of firelight that seeped beneath the door was enough to bring the room into focus. Nate's den. He could see the outlines of various furnishings by their shadows, or by the way they reflected just a bit of the orange glow.

Rising, he went to open the door and find out why it was so quiet. He was shocked to realize that the entire house was in darkness. By the firelight in the family room he could see the Christmas tree in the corner, its decorations glinting. He had missed the tree trimming.

A glance at the clock on the mantel told him he had slept for nearly twelve hours. Outside the snow continued to blow.

"It's stopped snowing," Maria's voice said from behind him.

He jumped and turned, spying her shadow on the couch.

"The wind is just blowing everything around," she told him. "The drifts will probably be deeper than ever by morning."

"Why didn't someone wake me?"

"Nate said you needed the sleep."

"But it's Christmas Eve."

"Yes." She said no more than that.

"God, I feel awful for missing it."

"Everyone understood." Her voice was gentle. "Are you hungry? Marge left you a plate in the microwave."

"Maybe later."

He stretched again and went to sit at the far end of the couch from her, resting his elbows on his knees and staring into the fire.

"We've got to stop meeting like this," she said, a tremor of laughter in her voice. "People will start talking."

He was surprised to hear his own laugh answer her. "Yeah. Can't sleep?"

"I *was* asleep. Something woke me up."

He looked over his shoulder at her. "The wind?"

"I don't know. I just know that I was suddenly wide awake. Too awake to sleep. It happens sometimes."

There was a rustle as she stirred, and firelight glinted off satin. "I was sitting here thinking about life."

"That's heavy-duty."

"Yeah." She gave a little laugh. "I'm sure you know about that. But, anyway, I was sitting here thinking about my real reasons for wanting to join the navy. The thing is, the farthest I've ever been out of Wyoming is Denver. I was born in this tiny town up north, population around three hundred. I grew up there, then went off to college in Laramie. And when I graduated, I was offered a teaching job here. By comparison to my hometown, this *is* the big city."

He nodded encouragingly, and leaned back a bit to see her. "What makes you think the world out there is better?"

"I don't know that it is. Maybe it's not. But it's *different.*"

"Very different."

"I know. At least from my trips to Denver. But I've never even seen the Great Lakes, let alone an ocean."

"You know what endless prairie looks like?"

"Yes, of course."

"Paint it blue."

She laughed. "Okay, okay."

"I'm sorry. I don't mean to make light of what you're saying. The world is full of exotic places, but unfortunately when I'm there I'm usually working. I wouldn't make a good travel brochure."

"I don't expect you would." She sighed and stirred again, unwittingly creating the seductive sound of satin against skin.

"You know where I'd like to go?" he said suddenly.

"Where?"

"Antarctica."

"Wow." She laughed. "Now, that *is* different."

"Well, it's the only place on earth where they've never fought a war."

He didn't need her silence to tell him he'd made a serious misstep. He opened his mouth to apologize, but was forestalled by the sound of her voice.

"Oh, Seth," she said, a mere sigh. Then, "You can't be sure of that." Her tone had turned teasing, as if she were trying to lift his spirits. "I've heard that some people think Atlantis is buried under all that ice."

"People have theories about Atlantis being everywhere."

"I know. My personal favorite is Central or South America."

"How come?"

"Because I don't think we've ever given those civilizations their due. Nor do I think archaeologists are willing to recognize that there's a lot of evidence for world-wide seafaring before recorded history."

"I take it this is an area of interest for you?"

"It's one of the reasons I want to travel."

"Then don't do it in the navy. Most of the places you'd want to visit are the places we're least likely to go. And when we do go there, you don't get a lot of time ashore."

"Then what would you suggest?"

The bummer of it was, he didn't have an alternative. "Go back to school? Study archaeology?"

She shook her head, her eyes glinting in the firelight. "Then I'd have to buy into the accepted theories."

"I guess so."

"You're in the navy," she said. "Why are you so dead set against it?"

Good question. One he wasn't sure he wanted to answer. Or that he could answer. "I'm just going through a bad spell," he said finally. "It happens."

"Have things been especially difficult lately?"

"I guess." But he didn't want to go into it. Couldn't go into it, anyway. Most of what he did was so damn secret he wasn't even supposed to know it himself. An old joke, but too true.

Then he heard himself say, unwillingly, "I think I'm getting tired of living my life in secrecy."

She moved a little closer to him. "That would be awfully hard, I imagine."

"You know how most people talk about their lives? I can't do much of that. I can't discuss most of what I do, and I can't even discuss the stuff with the people I do it with, because somebody might overhear. So we go out, do the job, come back, get debriefed, and it's like it never happened."

"That must have been hard on your marriage."

"Damn straight. Hard on any kind of relationship." Except with his teammates. They shared the secrets, even though they could never mention them. They trusted one another with their lives. There was an intimacy there he couldn't even achieve in marriage, and he was beginning to resent the hell out of that.

But he didn't know how to express that, without revealing too much to a woman who was still a stranger. Nor did he know if he was ready to give up the only intimacy in his life, which was with his team, in order to try to create a different intimacy with people on the outside.

He didn't even know if he *could* achieve that intimacy with anyone else.

And that, he realized, was what had been bugging the hell out of him. His life was deformed not just by ugly things, but by secrets, as well.

"But you know," she said gently, "there are lots of people who can't talk about their jobs. Lawyers, doctors, other people who do secret things for the government."

"But there *are* things they can talk about. If he doesn't mention a patient's name, a doctor can say to his wife, 'I saw a really interesting case today.'"

"Maybe he can. And how much of that is she going to be interested in?"

He didn't think it was quite the same thing, but he didn't want to argue with her. What was that perfume she was wearing? It teased and tantalized him in the same way the sound of satin slipping over her skin tantalized him.

Whoa there, man, you've been away from women too long.

But that wasn't the case and he knew it. He hadn't been away from them, he simply hadn't wanted them. Too emotionally bruised to even think about it, really. But he was thinking about it now, at the worst time possible. For God's sake, this woman was his parents' guest.

She spoke. "People can share what they choose to share. And if there are restrictions on job details, it doesn't have to be the end of the world."

He looked at her. "You think not? When most husbands come home, their wives don't have to wonder where on earth they've been for the last week or month, and what they've been doing."

"Maybe, but that's not the point, is it?"

"Why not?"

She tilted her head to one side. "Well, there *are* things you can talk about. Like the emotional climate you've been through, how you feel about it, how hard it was. A million things that don't give away any secrets."

Those were things he didn't talk about to anyone. It was understood by those who went through it with you, but never mentioned. Hell, the whole team had been there. They sure weren't going to sit down and hold a group therapy session about feelings.

No, when the job was done, it was done. Over. Finished. Put away. Nobody talked about it after debriefing. Nobody *wanted* to talk about it.

But Darlene had always wanted to know. He'd never been able to satisfy her by telling her it was all secret, and he was home now, so just forget it.

He looked away from Maria, staring into the fire's dancing flames, then over to the whirling snow in the night outside.

Maybe she was right. Maybe there was a different kind of intimacy, a kind he'd never been able to share with anyone. Most of the time, his feelings were locked up pretty tight. He didn't have room for them in his life. At times they could be a threat to his very survival. Most of the time they were simply something he didn't want to look at too closely.

But apparently they weren't going to stay safely locked up, because over the past few years he'd been growing steadily more depressed. And blaming it on Darlene wasn't cutting it.

Fact was, after four years, he didn't give a damn about Darlene one way or another, except that in a fair-minded sort of way he was glad she was at last happy. God knew, *he* hadn't made her happy.

In fact, he might as well be brutally honest with himself and admit that he'd been relieved when she packed her bags, because living with her had been a constant reminder of his shortcomings.

"Seth?" Maria's voice was gentle. "I'm sorry. Did I upset you? I didn't mean to. I only wanted to make you feel hopeful."

He turned and looked at her, feeling his eyes grow hot and feeling the hollowness in his heart. "No, it's okay. You made me realize something."

She was sensitive enough not to ask him, but for some damn reason he told her, anyway. He *needed* for once, to speak out loud to someone about what was going on inside him. And Maria was a pretty safe listener, considering he'd probably never see her again after this holiday.

"I've been lying to myself," he said. "I go around thinking I'm brutally honest with myself, but the truth is, that's just a cover. I've been lying to myself for years."

She scooted down the couch and laid a hand on his arm. "Seth…"

"Let me just say it, okay? It's time I faced up to it. The fact is, the only way I can do my job is to cut off my feelings. Oh, sure, I can laugh and joke with the guys. That's okay. I can get the hots for some woman. That's okay. But the thing is, I spend my life on the surface because I can't look down inside. I don't dare. Because I damn well know I'm not going to like what I find."

Her hand squeezed his arm gently, comfortingly, but she said nothing.

"I tell myself I know what I'm capable of. I know better than most people in the world will ever know. Better than I hope they ever *have* to know. That makes me different, sure. We SEALs like to think that makes us special. It sure as hell sets us apart. We know that our families will never understand, that we live in a whole different world."

"Yes, you do," she said quietly.

"It puts up this wall between us and our families. We know it. We even accept it. They can't go where we've been, live how we've lived, do what we've done. And we tell ourselves that what we do protects them from ever having to live the way we live."

"Don't you think it does?" she asked gently.

He looked at her again. "Yeah, it does. That part is true. I mean, if we go sink a ship that's carrying weapons-grade plutonium to some terrorist group, we're saving lives. Saving our families. Maybe even saving the world. Hell, we even pat our own backs because we do it in such a way that none of the crew dies. Hoo-ah!"

"It's true."

"I know it's true. But the thing is… We know all this stuff on the surface. We do all this stuff on the *surface.* But for the past couple of years it's like something inside me is trying to tell me that what's underneath is important, too. And I don't want to look at it. Because I know I'm going to hate myself."

"Oh, Seth…"

"I was even glad when Darlene left. I didn't admit it to myself or anyone else, but I was relieved. Just living with her reminded me of the walls. And I made her miserable, I know it." His face hardened to concrete. "The simple fact is, Maria, whatever the reason I do it, I'm not a whole lot different from a terrorist."

"Oh, my God!" Suddenly her arms were around him, holding him tight. Her voice was whispering in his ear, "No, Seth, no…"

And inside, all he could feel was glacial ice.

"It's not the same, Seth. It could never be the same. You don't set out to kill dozens, hundreds, even thousands of innocent civilians simply to make a point. You don't take people hostage and shoot them one by one to make a point."

"No."

"You don't wrap explosives around yourself, then climb onto a bus full of men, women and children. You don't hijack airliners, or grab entire teams at the Olympics. You don't encourage people to do that. You're not the same at all."

The ice inside him thawed a bit, but not a whole lot. He still had a lot of ugly memories.

"You're being too hard on yourself," she said. Her cheek was pressed to his, her lips near his ear, her voice a quiet murmur. "Yes, you've done things that are hard to live with. I'm sure you have. And I'm glad you've done them so I haven't needed to."

Through the frozen pain, the ice that filled him, he began to feel her womanliness. It was like a small candle flame of heat deep within him, and he needed desperately to reach for it, to turn it into a blaze that would melt away all the awful things within him.

But she was a guest in this house, the house of his parents. Whatever else he might or might not do, he'd never taken advantage of a woman in his life. He knew better than that.

But it felt so good to have her arms around him, to feel the soft pressure of her full breasts against his chest. To smell her perfume, rising right from the curve of her shoulder, so close to his lips right now.

He could have devoured her. He could have clung to her as if she were a life preserver. But his self-control was still intact. As always. So instead, he contented himself with wrapping his arms gently around her slender waist, returning her hug.

Thanking her for it.

They stayed that way for a long time. Little by little her fire melted away the iciness, until he began once again to feel warmth within him. It was only a small thaw, but it was a beginning.

Finally she startled him by kissing his cheek softly. Then she released him and settled back onto the couch. Reluctantly, he let her go, feeling bereft.

She sighed, as if she, too, felt the loss. "Don't do this to yourself, Seth," she said quietly. "If you're starting to hate what you do, then do something different. But don't be your own judge, jury and executioner, because you're not being fair to yourself."

Maybe he wasn't. Maybe he was just worn out. Worn down. Or maybe he just needed to take a good hard look at all the things he'd been burying. Maybe he just needed to let the emotional dam burst, so there'd be room for all the new stuff he was bound to accumulate.

And maybe he just needed to get over himself.

"So tell me about teaching," he said, shrugging off his self-pity.

He had a feeling she withdrew from him a bit then, as if his change of topic had been received as a rebuke. He didn't know how to tell her otherwise, especially when she didn't say anything about it.

"It's a rewarding job, for the most part," she answered. "It's the best job in the world when I can actually manage to instill some excitement in my classes. If it weren't for this gypsy urge in my blood, I'd probably be content to live and die a teacher."

"Sounds like a wonderful job. You know, maybe you could get a job teaching overseas. There are American schools everywhere. I bet you could get a job almost anywhere."

"I've thought about it. The problem is I'd be tied to one place again."

A chuckle escaped him. "Lady, you've got a significant problem."

She laughed in response. "Difficult to please, that's me. I want to have my cake and eat it, too. And yes, I've checked into working for cruise lines, but their in-port turnaround is so fast it wouldn't leave much time ashore. A few hours if I'm lucky."

"Travel agent? Then you'd have an excuse to go to exotic places. You'd have to check them out."

"That's one thing I haven't considered."

"Flight attendant?"

"I don't think I have the patience for that. I can tolerate misbehavior in children, but I'm not very understanding of idiocy in adults."

He laughed again, realizing that in some odd way this conversation was lifting his spirits. He turned on the couch, raising one leg and leaning against the arm so he could look right at her. "You are indeed a difficult woman." His tone was teasing.

"I know," she said mock mournfully. "I've got objections to every single thing I've thought of. I guess I'm a perpetual malcontent."

"But you don't seem discontented."

"I'm not really." Her voice grew serious. "If I have to, I can live without all the travel. But I may break down and move to a larger town, where I have a choice of more than one movie a night."

He laughed. "That *is* a good point."

"They're talking about putting in a second theater, but I may be gray before they get around to it. Besides, this is a really hardworking town. In the evenings most people are ready to collapse with their families. And

I've usually got papers to grade or lessons to plan. It's not like there's a huge demand for entertainment around here."

"No, I don't suppose there is."

"It's not like I don't have enough to do, because I do. More than enough. But I feel restless, anyway."

"Something's missing."

She nodded. "Exactly. I was even saving for a cruise to Antarctica…until I actually checked into the cost of it. So now I'm saving for a cruise to Alaska. But it won't be the same thing, and I can't quite tell you why."

He thought about it. "Maybe it's not adventurous enough."

"That could be." She tilted her head. "Maybe I'm an adventuress," she said jokingly.

He laughed at that but shook his head. "Adventur*er*. None of that diminutive stuff. I've had more than enough sensitivity training, and I can tell you, no more actress, waitress, stewardess…"

"Okay, okay! I didn't know you guys got sensitivity training."

"Mostly it's race relations stuff, but since Tailhook we've been getting stuff about dealing with the opposite sex, too. Much needed."

"Why do you say that?"

"Because I still know guys who think it would be an insult to them personally if a woman were allowed to try out for the SEALs."

"What do you think?"

"If she can do it, more power to her. But if you want my honest opinion, any woman who tries right now is apt to find herself getting twice the crap and ten times the guff."

"Isn't that always the way?"

"Sure it is."

"Well," she said, "I don't want to be a SEAL. I know

I don't have what it takes. I want to see the world from a more comfortable viewpoint."

He laughed again, and realized that he liked, really *liked*, this woman. She had humor and common sense by the bucketload, and she was beautiful besides.

And he wanted her.

Chapter Six

The silence between them grew of its own accord. It was as if, at the very same instant, their minds had had the same thought. And between them had sprung this pregnant quiet, a quiet that grew deeper and thicker with each passing instant.

Maria had never felt like this before. Oh, she'd been attracted to Seth from the instant she laid eyes on him, but that had been only yesterday. And while she'd avoided dating since coming to Conard County, largely because if she married someone here she would be here forever, she *had* had some hot-and-heavy relationships during her college years.

But nothing had ever felt like this, as if the whole world were holding its breath, waiting. Instead of growing tense with expectation and anticipation, she felt herself growing soft and languorous, her muscles relaxing as if she trembled on the very edge of sleep.

But sleep was the furthest thing from her mind. She was *yielding*. Without a touch, without a word, her entire body was readying itself to yield to this man, as if he already owned her heart and soul.

It was strange. It was wonderful. If she was still breathing, she didn't know it. She was afraid to make even the slightest move, for fear of shattering the moment. Afraid that he would touch her, afraid that he would not. Wanting and not wanting.

A yearning grew to match the softening of her every muscle, an aching tingle between her legs that superseded everything else. A heaviness that seemed to pin her to the couch.

His eyes…even in the dim, flickering light from the fire his eyes bored into her, asking questions to which she had no answers. At least not yet. He wasn't something she had planned on, or even wanted, but he was here. Now. And like an irresistible force, he held her in thrall.

Somehow, the distance closed between them. So close now she could reach out a single hand and touch him. Her breath locked in her throat, and warring signals ran through her body, paralyzing her, as they at once demanded she reach for him and wait for him.

She would never know who moved first, and in the end, it didn't matter. Suddenly they were clinging together as if they would drown if they let go. Hungry mouths met and fused, stealing and giving breath all at the same time. Hands clutched, arms gripped, skin found skin….

One of them groaned. It might have been her. Something deep inside her felt as if it were clawing its way to freedom, rising up within her to sweep her away from everything.

There was only one thought in her dazed mind…*more!*

Her hands found their way under his shirt, discovering warm, smooth skin and a ridge of scar tissue that for now she ignored. His stubbled cheeks scraped hers, burning her delicate skin, and for once she savored the feeling.

Then his hand slipped within her robe and found her breast. She sucked air with the delight of it, the feel of his roughened palm against her tender skin, his fingers playing skillfully with her nipple, feeding the ache deep inside her until her every nerve ending throbbed in time to his touch.

Another groan from somewhere...then...

She was holding her breath. He pushed her away so that she'd fallen back against the arm of the couch, and he stood over her, a shadow against the fire.

"I can't...I won't...." Then he turned and left her.

She heard the door closing, but she lay there feeling dazed, as if she'd been hit by a truck.

She *had* been hit by a truck. She'd opened herself to this man, made herself utterly vulnerable and then...he walked away.

At that moment, if she thought she could have succeeded she might have tried to kill him.

But only in that moment. Anger gave way swiftly to the pain of humiliating rejection. Burying her face in her arm, she let the hot tears fall.

For Maria, Christmas Day passed in a blur of noise and confusion and laughter. The wind had stopped, so the plows managed to clear the streets in town by 9:00 a.m. The family promptly went to church, where they met up with Wendy and Yuma and the boyfriends. Then back to the Tate house for the opening of presents while the aromas of roasting turkey filled the house.

Everyone took Seth's IOUs in good part and suggested he send them something from his military base, preferably, as Krissie said, "Something that says My Brother Is a Navy SEAL on it."

Seth laughed and teased her about sending her a Zodiak signed by all his teammates.

In fact, Maria thought with a twinge, he was in good spirits throughout the day, as if he had exorcised some kind of demon during the night. And good spirits only made him even more damnably attractive.

He and the guys cleaned up after dinner, letting all the cooks rest, then life devolved into naps and board games, and a de rigueur double feature of *The Grinch Who Stole Christmas* and *Miracle on 34th Street*.

But then the wind started to pick up again and the snow started flying. Nate switched off the Christmas carols that had been playing on the stereo and put on the TV, tuning in to the weather.

"Hell," Nate said, "it's starting again. We're going to be snowed in again tomorrow."

The three girls immediately insisted their boyfriends be allowed to stay at the house. Nate hemmed and hawed about sleeping arrangements.

"Well, someone can have my bed," Seth offered. "I'll go home with Wendy and Yuma. I've hardly had a chance to talk with them."

Nate frowned, as if he wasn't sure.

"It's okay," said Seth. "Really."

"I can sleep on the floor," one of the boys said. "Right here in front of the fire."

"Better yet," said Wendy, "Maria can come with us, too. We've got plenty of room."

Maria's heart slammed. It was the last thing on earth she wanted to do. The very last thing. Yes, she was friends with Wendy and Yuma. That was how she had become part of the Tate family circle. But if she could be at the opposite end of the planet from Seth Hardin tonight, so much the better.

"Really," said Marge, "I don't want to shove her out...."

"No shoving, Mom," Wendy said confidently. "Maria and I have been friends for years. It would be *nice* to have her stay with us."

"I can just go back to my place," Maria volunteered quickly.

"No!" and "Not in this weather!" were the answers she received from Marge, Nate and Wendy.

That seemed to decide it. The girls wanted their boyfriends, nobody was going to let Maria stay alone during this next blizzard, and so…

So. She tried to smile as if she were happy with the arrangement. And really, she promised herself, it wouldn't be so bad. Not with Wendy and Yuma there. They'd probably stay up well into the night, playing clubs or hearts and gabbing they way they usually did when they got together.

There was time for dessert, rich pies and ice cream and hot coffee laced with brandy, before it was time to go. Still, it all seemed to happen too fast.

All of a sudden she was in the back seat of Yuma and Wendy's battered Suburban, only a few inches away from Seth, while the snow whirled whitely around them, promising to bury them once again.

"Already the worst winter some portions of Wyoming have seen in recorded history," the TV weatherman was saying when Wendy switched the set on.

"Oh, goody," she said, happily. "Everybody stay home so we can stay home and drink hot toddies and enjoy our holiday."

Wendy and Yuma—nobody called him Billy Joe except Wendy—worked for the county's emergency response team. She was a flight nurse, and he a helicopter pilot. He was also a lot older than she was—nearly two decades—but it was not the first or even second thing you noticed about them when they were together. You noticed the love.

Maria's friendship with them had begun her first year of teaching in this town, when Wendy and Yuma had come in to tell her class all about their work, and later to take them out to the airport so they could see the rescue helicopter.

Somehow in the midst of all the confusion, she and Wendy had hit it off, and later over dinner, she and Yuma had hit it off as well. They'd been close ever since.

"Like family," Wendy was fond of saying.

Maria helped Wendy unload the hefty portion of leftovers Marge Tate had sent with them: turkey, gravy, stuffing, pie, yams, spinach casserole. Everything went into a well-stocked refrigerator.

"I tried," Wendy said, "to tell Mom that I'd shopped for a bunch of young males. I'm stocked to the rafters already. I figured those boys would go through this house like a wave of locusts. They made a pretty good start on it, too. Trust me, if we get snowbound for a *month* we won't starve."

Maria laughed.

"You think it's funny? Sam sat here last night and ate a whole jar of peanut butter with a spoon."

"You're joking!" Maria couldn't imagine it.

Wendy laughed. "Kid you not," she said. "I suggested he'd get fuller if he put it on bread, but he said it was better plain."

"Wouldn't I just love to have a metabolism like that. Sam's so thin and tall!"

"Me, too." Wendy patted her midsection. "I'm battling this tummy all the time."

The women exchanged looks of understanding. Neither of them would ever be a runway model or a movie star. Instead of the current vogue in female beauty, they simply looked healthy.

"On the other hand," Maria said, "neither of us is living on lettuce leaves."

Wendy laughed again. "Nor am I ever going to. I'll just keep fighting the battle of the bulge."

In the living room, Seth had helped Yuma build a fire on the hearth. The house was an older one, built around the turn of the century, with high ceilings, tall windows and ornate woodwork. It was also full of drafts.

"I keep plugging holes," Yuma said, pointing to how the heavy curtains over the windows stirred a little each time the wind gusted. "It may take the rest of my life to find them all. We're saving for some double-paned windows. Maybe they'll help."

"It's still a great house," Seth remarked.

"Oh, sure. Built to last. But leaking like a sieve right now. It's a good thing all the rooms have fireplaces or wood stoves. Otherwise we'd go broke on heating oil."

The living room was furnished in comfortably battered furniture. Yuma waved Seth into one of the easy chairs, and took the other himself.

"How have you been doing?" Seth asked Yuma. Years ago they'd discussed Yuma's posttraumatic stress disorder, a remnant of his days as a MediVac pilot in Vietnam.

"Actually," Yuma told him, "I haven't had a flashback in nearly two years now. I have the odd nightmare, but that's been it."

"I'm glad to hear it."

"But what about you?" Yuma asked. "Something's bugging you, man. You're not looking good at all."

"I'll deal with it."

"Sure. Like I did."

The words hung between them on the warming air, too insightful for Seth's comfort. Finally he said, "Damn it, everybody's looking straight through me."

Yuma laughed quietly. "Not hard to read the signs when you've been there. Listen, I won't badger you, but I'm here if you want to talk. Other than that…maybe it's time to consider a change, man."

The thought panicked Seth, although he wouldn't have expected it. But fear suddenly rose in him, grabbing his throat, stifling his breath. He knew fear. He knew its every mood and savagery, he knew what it could do *to* him and he knew what it could do *for* him. But this…this fear was something else.

And he didn't know how to read it.

"You *can* do other things," Yuma said, sounding as if he came from miles away. "You can take a training position. Switch to the Coast Guard and work in a rescue crew. Hell, you can go to work for Nate as a deputy, if you want to give up the adrenaline kick. But there are plenty of things you can do, Seth. Plenty. You've sure as hell done your part for this country."

Seth didn't reply. He couldn't.

As if on cue, the women joined them then, bearing cups of coffee and a tray of nibbles. Conversation drifted into more desultory avenues, reminiscences of the day, talk of the blizzard. Ordinary things.

Seth sat among them, half listening, saying nothing, feeling as if he were miles and centuries away.

Chapter Seven

Seth awoke during the night again. Of course he did. He was in an unfamiliar place, and when he was in an unfamiliar place, he rested with his senses on high alert. Years of training and experience had made that impossible to turn off. Besides, his job made him something of a night owl, anyway.

The wind was still blowing hard, causing the house to creak around him, singing a high-pitched note at his window. The room was warm, though, from the heat of the woodstove in the room directly below him.

Finally, too restless to stay in bed, he rose and pulled on his clothes, then reached for the parka and gloves Nate had lent him.

He needed to feel the wind on his face, and thought maybe the cold air would clear some of the cobwebs that had been stifling his brain for days. He needed to face the elements, if only briefly, because they were the only pure and untrammeled thing in his life.

He crept down the stairs as quietly as he could, then through the hallway to the front door. He could hear the sting of icy snow against the stained glass mounted in the door, and was drawn to the sound as if it held some kind of promise.

He opened the door. The wind and snow slapped his face. He stood on the porch on boards blown clear by the wind, staring into a night that was surprisingly well-illuminated by the streetlights. The snow caught their light and reflected it a million times, until the whole world was wrapped in a white, hazy cocoon.

The streets had vanished again, though, filled in between the hills left by the snowplows earlier. The snow was so dry that it formed little eddies like dust devils, and snaked across the level areas like sidewinders. All around him the night was filled with the hiss of moving snow and the whistle of the wind.

A gust whipped around the corner of the house, catching him unawares and slapping his face with stinging crystals. He closed his eyes tight, then when the assault stopped, he pulled up his hood. The parka was warm, but his thighs were rapidly registering the deadly wind, even through thick denim. It was well below zero, and he had no illusions about staying out here very long.

But the air smelled so crisp and clean, so much drier than what he was used to. Although he could only draw in small bits at a time because it was so cold, it still invigorated him and refreshed him.

God, it was beautiful!

He suddenly wished he could go cross-country skiing, just strap on a pair of boards and skim away into the darkness, into a pristine world made virginal by the snow. Maybe later in the week, he promised himself, when the weather settled and he could rent the gear.

He needed a really good workout. His body wasn't used to as much idleness as he'd put it through these last few days. Too much food, too little activity. No wonder it felt as if his brain were buried in sludge.

Finally he could no longer ignore the warning ache from his legs, and the shivering that started despite the heavy parka he wore. Regretfully, he went back inside.

The warmth of the house felt overpowering now after being outside. Still shivering, he hung the parka on a coat tree in the hall and went to the kitchen, figuring it was the room farthest from the fireplaces and woodstoves, and therefore the one in which he could warm up again without feeling quite so smothered.

To his surprise—or maybe not—Maria was already there, sitting in the near dark at the table. The only light on was the one over the stove.

"Oh!" she said, startled, when he came into the room. "I didn't know you were up."

"I stepped outside," he replied. "It's amazing out there. Beautiful."

She nodded. "I love blizzards. Can I get you something?"

"No, thanks. I just want some water."

"Glasses are in the cabinet to the right of the sink."

"Thanks."

He filled one, then sat across from her at the table. She was, he realized, rapidly becoming part of his nights.

She didn't make any jokes this night, however. Nor did she even speak to him beyond the minimal courtesies. She was upset with him, he realized, and as the memory of last night reared in his mind, he understood why.

But he didn't know what the hell to do about it. Mentioning it might embarrass her further.

"Excuse me," she said. Then she rose and carried her mug away with her.

He had hurt her, and he didn't have the words to explain why.

In the living room, away from Seth, Maria sat sipping her tea and growing angrier by the second.

Last night she had been hurt, humiliated, embarrassed. All day long she had put that on the back burner, being a courteous, pleasant guest, participating in everything and laughing as hard as anyone. But tonight, alone, the memory came back to haunt her, and hard on the heels of rejection and humiliation came a scalding anger.

He owed her something beyond "I can't...I won't...." He owed her, at the very least, an apology. But he'd come into the kitchen and sat there like a brooding sphinx, saying not a word.

Well, damn him to hell. He could sit there in his private pity party, tearing himself to pieces emotionally, letting no one even try to help.

But even as she had these bitter thoughts, she knew she was being unfair. Okay, the guy was genuinely troubled. Now he was paying the price for the last sixteen or seventeen years of his life. People did that, if they didn't deal with things as they happened. He needed some time to indulge himself and sort things out so he could bounce back.

Perfectly normal. Wendy had told her what Yuma had gone through, and Yuma himself had shared some of it.

But if he needed to be alone with his demons, why had he reached out to her in such a way, then cast her aside?

He had no right to do that to anyone. Not anyone!

But as she sat there fuming, staring into the embers of the dying fire, her anger, too, began to burn down.

She needed to be honest with herself, and honesty forced her to admit that she wouldn't have been at all happy with herself if she'd made love with Seth last night.

She wasn't the type to fall into a man's arms. She wasn't the type to give herself so readily or freely. Somewhere deep inside, she feared her attraction to him had less to do with his personality than it had to do with the fact that he was exotic in her experience. He'd traveled the world, done countless dangerous things. And even when he was struggling with himself over his past, he still had an aura of danger.

Maybe she was attracted to the *idea* of him, rather than the man himself.

But a period of reflection told her that was not the case at all. It wasn't the dangerous things he'd done that attracted her; it was the fact that he could agonize about them. That he had a heart and soul that remained unhardened despite it all.

And of course, he was just a very attractive man. Lean, weathered, muscular. Handsome, but not *too* handsome. In fact, he was very like the imaginary lover she had dreamed up in high school.

Maybe that was why she had succumbed so quickly. But whatever it was, she ought to be grateful to him for pulling them both back from the abyss. If she'd had half a brain at the time, she'd have done it herself.

But that didn't ease the sting that came from knowing she had been completely lost in his arms, but that he had not. That he hadn't been as overwhelmed by her as she had been by him.

In fact, he had left her feeling downright unattractive. And she had made herself so vulnerable to him that she still felt like a raw nerve ending.

Sighing, she sipped her tea and told herself to grow up. It was ridiculous to be both grateful that he had retained some sense and spared her, and angry that he hadn't been so overwhelmed by her charms that he'd forgotten all common sense.

She was appalled by her own inconsistency.

But, as she stared into the embers and listened to an occasional coal pop, she realized that this was about something far more significant than mere physical attraction. The simple fact was, she cared for Seth in ways that had nothing to do with his attractions as a man. She had known him for such a short time, and yet she yearned for his companionship. Yearned to sit in the quiet dark with him and just *be*.

It didn't matter whether or not they spoke a word. What *did* matter to her was that they be together. Near enough to touch, even if they didn't.

What was growing inside her was far more dangerous than mere physical attraction, and had far less of a basis. She hardly knew the man.

Yet she felt as if she'd known him all her life. How silly. How…scary.

And now, strangely enough, she was beginning to wish she hadn't given him the polite cold shoulder in the kitchen. Began to think of ways she might go back in there and apologize, then wondered what exactly she needed to apologize for? For not being chatty? He hadn't exactly been chatty himself. She'd been polite, asked him if she could get him anything, then when he sat there in silence, she'd gotten up and left.

That didn't call for an apology. She wasn't his hostess, for crying out loud.

And what's more, she didn't need another rejection. There had been too many rejections in her life.

"Maria?"

His voice, so close when she had thought herself all alone, startled her and she jumped. Her tea sloshed dangerously close to the edge of her mug.

"Sorry," he said. "I didn't mean to startle you."

"It's, uh, not a problem," she said, hastily setting her cup on the end table so the tremor of her hands wouldn't give her away.

She didn't want to look at him, didn't want to see his tall, powerful shape highlighted by the dim red glow of the fire's embers. It was scant relief, however, when he sat on the couch beside her.

"Look," he said quietly. "I want to apologize."

She kept her gaze firmly fixed on the fire. Her hands knotted together, and her heart climbed into her throat. "For what?"

"For the way I behaved last night."

It appalled her to realize that if he apologized for making a pass at her, she was going to feel even more crushed than she did now. "No…" She had to find some way to forestall those words.

"No, really," he insisted. "I'm sorry. The way I…"

She was going to knock his block off if he said he was sorry for kissing her. He was going to find out just how much fury a scorned woman could produce. Her fists clenched until her nails bit into her palms.

"I'm sorry," he said again, "for the way I…pulled away from you."

For an instant, she wasn't sure she'd heard him correctly. He couldn't really be saying…

"I've been thinking about it since," he continued. "I had no right to…make a pass at you. But when I did…well, the reason I left was because I didn't have the right to do what I was doing. You were the guest of my parents, you hardly know me…."

Relief flowed through her. The reasons he had just given her were valid, reasons she would have chosen herself. They weren't a rejection of her, but of the situation they were in.

"It's okay," she said, smiling at him. Her insides still had a severe case of the jitters, but the smile came naturally.

"Well, I'm still sorry. I can imagine how I made you feel."

Which surely put him on the list of the world's most sensitive men, she thought. Still smiling, she shrugged. "You did what was best. I'm not sure that either of us…was ready for where we were heading."

"Probably not." He sighed and sank farther down on

the couch, crossing his long legs at the ankles, then folding his hands on his flat belly.

"Are you feeling any better?" she asked him.

"You know, I think I am." He glanced at her and smiled. "I've been drowning in self-pity for so long I think I almost forgot how to climb out of the pit."

"And you've remembered?"

"A bit, anyway. Because it struck me a little while ago, as I was sitting in the kitchen, that yesterday doesn't matter nearly as much as tomorrow. I can't change the past. But I can change what I do from here on out."

"Will you?"

"I don't know. Because the truth is…I'm honestly not sure I've been such an awful person. I don't like some of what I've had to do, but someone had to do it. And I'd like to think more good has come out of it than bad."

"I'm sure it has." She hesitated, then offered, "Unfortunately, life isn't black and white. It's all kinds of shades of dirty gray. It's rare that we get to do something purely noble."

"If ever." He sighed and leaned his head back against the couch, turning it so he could look at her. "I was being purely noble last night, or so I thought. Then I couldn't get your face out of my head. I wounded you."

She could feel her cheeks redden and was grateful he couldn't see it. Bad enough that he had read her so well last night.

"Maria?"

He was asking, but she wasn't sure she wanted to tell him. Then she remembered how forthright he'd been with her, and the painful things he'd been willing to share. This was the very least she owed him.

Her voice muffled with shame, or possibly embarrassment, she said, "I felt…rejected. It's just…I've been rejected too often."

"I'm truly sorry. Because I wasn't rejecting you. Not at all."

"I understand that now."

"But what do you mean, you've been rejected too often?"

Did she really want to go into this? She hesitated for a long time, then finally plunged in. "I knew I wasn't the prettiest girl in school, and I was too smart, or so people kept telling me. No big deal."

"Maybe it was a big deal."

"Maybe," she admitted. "I never even got asked to the prom."

"Ouch."

"Exactly. So off to college. And I met this guy in my Bible study group and we started dating, and he hardly ever touched me. I figured he was being a good Christian, you know. We had all promised to abstain, and so on. So I didn't let it bother me until I found out he was sleeping with my best friend."

"Oh, Maria…"

She shrugged again. "I was young, and unfortunately it messed me up a bit. So I got involved with this guy who was different. You know what I mean? He was on some kind of edge, he was different from the people I usually hung around with and his attention was flattering. I got suckered right in. So one night I gave him my virginity, and the next morning he tossed me out and never spoke to me again."

"Oh, babe, I'm so sorry."

"Hey, a lot of women could tell you the same stories. I'm not special."

"I think you *are* special, and you're also a very pretty woman."

She gave an embarrassed little laugh. "Well, all the pieces finally grew together in proper proportion."

"I'll say!"

The obvious admiration in his voice caused her to blush again, and once again she was grateful the light was both dim and ruddy.

"You don't have to perjure yourself," she told him jokingly.

He laughed. "I'll swear it on a stack of Bibles. You're a *very* attractive woman. And if nobody else has noticed that, the world must be blind."

"I don't know if they *have* noticed. I've been here since college, and I've made it a point not to date."

"How come?"

"Because I don't want to spend the rest of my life here. Crazy, I know. It's the kind of place most people would love to live. But…"

"But you're a gypsy."

"Yes, at heart I guess I am. At least until I've seen something of the world."

"Well, it's a good idea to do the things you want before you tie yourself down."

"Exactly," she said. "What about you, though? Don't you ever want children?"

He sighed again and turned to stare up at the ceiling. "Yes, I do want kids," he said quietly. "But it would probably be best to wait another few years, until I can retire."

She looked at him, feeling surprised. "You're going to retire?" The idea seemed amazing.

"Sure, when I get my twenty in. I'll be thirty-eight, plenty of time to start a new life."

"Well, of course, but…"

"But what?"

"You balk any time someone suggests you do something else with the rest of your navy career. I guess I just assumed you'd never retire."

"There was a time I figured I'd go for thirty. But I've got to be honest, Maria. I won't be fit to be a SEAL much longer. Age catches up with the best of us, you know. In fact, statistically speaking, there's a good chance over the next few years that I'll display a cardiac anomaly that will ground me. It happens to folks like me all the time. Nothing to really worry about, but enough to get you pulled off special duties. Anyway, nobody can do this job forever."

"I wouldn't think so. But a training position…"

He shook his head. "I think I'd be better off making a clean break. I don't want to feel as if I'm on the outside looking in."

She nodded slowly. "I guess I can understand that. But what will you do then?"

"I've got plenty of time to decide. But I've been thinking about going back to college. I didn't have the chance to go when I graduated from high school, and over the years I've taken some correspondence courses. I think I'd like to get a degree."

"In what?"

He smiled. "Who knows? All the possibilities are still open to me."

She smiled. "I remember feeling like that once. It was my sophomore year in college. A glorious fall day, with cool dry air and lots of sunshine. And I remember this elation just bubbling up to fill me because I stood at a cusp, I could take any direction I wanted. It was a feeling of such sheer freedom."

"Exactly," he agreed. "And you know what? Just thinking about it gives me that feeling. Thank you."

"Me? For what?"

"For talking with me last night and tonight. For giving me something to think about besides my own misery. I still have a future. And damn it, I'm going to make the best of it!"

Chapter Eight

The change in him was so radical that Maria found herself wondering if it were real, or just some kind of manic episode.

But he didn't sound edgy or hyper; he just sounded as if he'd made some kind of peace with himself. God knows he needed to. He'd been beating himself up something awful last night.

He rolled his head and looked at her again. "You're wondering if I've lost my marbles."

"Yes. No. Well, not exactly. It's just such a change."

"Yeah, I know. Thing is, I've been sick of myself for some time now. But it was like I was caught in some kind of whirlpool that just kept sucking me down no matter how hard I fought it.

"But I've been thinking about a lot of things today. About Nate—Dad—and Yuma. And about *why* I do the things I do. And I realized I've been making it far harder on myself than I need to. And after talking with you last night I realized…if I'd ever talked to Darlene the way I talked to you, she might not have left."

"Which means?"

"Which means I've crossed the Rubicon, and someday I might actually be good at building a relationship. Like you said, not everything is classified."

He closed his eyes, savoring this moment of peace. He knew that he still had stuff to deal with, but it was as if he'd at last been released from the hell he'd been steadily sinking into because of his sense of failure after Darlene left him.

He'd finally worked his way to the core of the problem, and with a small nudge from Maria had figured out exactly where he'd gone wrong.

There were still problems he needed to address, of course, and he knew it wasn't going to be easy to stay on this side of the Rubicon. Old habits died hard. But Maria was right. There *was* another kind of intimacy.

And he needed to explore the twists and turns that had led him to this point. He needed to talk about them to get them perfectly clear in his own head.

He opened his eyes and found that Maria still appeared to be wide awake and attentive. "Can I bend your ear?"

"Be my guest."

And she smiled, that smile that did crazy things inside him. That made his heart skip a beat. There was something else here that was going to have to be dealt with one way or another, but he wasn't anywhere near ready to get to that.

"I think," he said slowly, "that I got into this mess because I was alone for so long."

She nodded encouragingly.

"I don't know if you're aware of it, but I was adopted."

"Marge told me. She said she and Nate weren't yet married, and he was in Vietnam when she learned she was pregnant with you. Apparently her father disapproved of Nate and was stealing her letters to him, and his letters to her."

Seth nodded. "And when she learned she was having me, she was sent away. She thought Nate had abandoned her, thanks to her father, and gave me up for adoption."

Maria nodded. "It's such a sad story, Seth."

"Sadder for them, I think. I had a good family. It wasn't a demonstrative family like the Tates, though. And I was an only child. So I kind of developed a tendency to keep things inside."

"I can see that. You must have needed to depend on your own resources a lot."

He nodded. "For almost everything except food and shelter. Don't misunderstand me. My adoptive parents were good to me, and they loved me. But we never did find a really good way to relate."

"I'm sorry."

He shrugged. "A lot of kids have it a lot worse. I was lucky. But, anyway, at eighteen I joined the navy to see the world. Sound familiar?"

She gave a little laugh. "Yes, it does."

"And being eighteen, as soon as I could, I volunteered for the SEALs. Looking back, I'm not sure if I needed to prove myself in some way. I *do* know that I wanted to be the biggest, baddest dude on the block." He gave a small snort of laughter. "Not unusual at that age."

"No, it's not."

"Anyway, I actually made it through BUD/S, the training program. And I discovered something I'd never really experienced before. The kind of companionship that men can have when they undergo hardship together. When they depend on one another for their lives. We grew up together, Maria, in those six months. And we were cemented in ways I can't really put into words."

"I can imagine it, though, Seth. It must have been really intense."

"'Intense' doesn't begin to cover it. They force you to realize that you are *not* going to make it without your buddies. No way. They force you to realize that each of us holds the lives of our teammates in our hands. I don't know of much else like it.

"Anyway, by the time you go through that, you've changed. Significantly changed. I certainly wasn't a kid anymore. I was acutely aware of my limits, my abilities, and more important, my dependencies on the rest of the team. And what I didn't know by the end of BUD/S, I sure as hell knew after a couple of missions."

He fell silent, still sorting through his thoughts. She waited patiently. He liked that about her. Darlene, frankly, had never been one to sit quietly and wait for anything. She'd had a vitality that had kept her talking and prying, and seldom quiet. Until the end.

"Well," he said after a moment, "I think I'm getting a little sidetracked here. The point I'm trying to get to is that I was used to being solitary, and suddenly I had a sort of family with truly intense connections. But it was another undemonstrative family, another family where things weren't talked about. I mean, we did our missions, got debriefed, and basically forgot about them because they were secret and we couldn't discuss them. So while we were closer than brothers, it was an…unspoken closeness. And the more we did, the more was left unsaid. We got quieter, steadier, tougher, more cynical about some things. And we felt increasingly separated from the world around us, because of our experiences."

"That's…unfortunate."

"In a way, yes. It's necessary, but it has its down side. Maybe more so for me than others. I don't know. Plenty of SEALs actually are married, although I have to admit there are a lot of divorces, too. It's hard on wives. Very hard. We have a closeness they can't be a part of. You know, I just realized that."

"How so?"

"That our wives are shut out. It must be really hard for them. We have this bond, and they're always outsiders to it. They can never, ever be part of it. Damn, I wouldn't be surprised if they get jealous of it."

"Maybe some do."

"Maybe." He sighed and rubbed his eyes. "So, bottom line is, I'm probably more closed than most. And maybe because of that, I didn't make enough room in my life for anything except the team bond. It was the most intimacy I'd ever known in my life."

"Oh, Seth." Her voice didn't sound sad, exactly, but it did sound very sympathetic.

"I think," he said finally, "that I kept Darlene on the other side of a glass wall. I put a huge barrier between us, instead of bringing her to the other side with me. You know, I think I need to call her and apologize."

"That might be a very good idea, if you don't think it'll just upset her."

He looked at her. "It might do her some good to know none of it was her fault. I know when she left she was blaming herself, saying she wasn't the right person, that she'd failed me and she couldn't live with it anymore. God, I messed her up."

Maria went to the kitchen to make them both some hot chocolate, leaving Seth to think in solitude for a few minutes. She had to admit she was pretty impressed with him. Few people could sort their way through their own psyches as well as he seemed to be doing.

She put the kettle on and turned on the flame beneath it. The brief whiff of the gas suddenly transported her back to her grandmother's as a small child.

Sitting in her grandmother's kitchen at the big round oak table perpetually covered with oilcloth, was one of her happiest childhood memories. Grandma would give her a brown sugar lump as she puttered around making tea for herself, or dinner for the two of them.

On warm summer evenings, they would sit in rockers on the front porch and drink homemade lemonade while the breeze ruffled the vines on the trellis. Trips to the pond to feed the ducks stale bread. "Picnics" of graham crackers and strawberry jam mixed with powdered sugar to frost them, taken on long walks along the train tracks until they found a place where Grandma felt they could settle and have their delightful snack.

As the kettle whistled, Maria started back to the present, and wondered why she had traveled down that particular memory lane. It had been a long time since Grandma had passed on, a long time since Maria had felt utterly safe and happy.

Maybe it was because she didn't feel safe now. Not simply because she was contemplating a major life change, a change so drastic she could barely begin to imagine what it would really be like. But, perhaps, because of the man in the living room, who was waking yearnings she thought she'd put aside a long, long time ago.

Busying her hands, she dumped packets of cocoa mix into mugs, then poured boiling water into them. When she picked up the spoon and began to stir, however, her thoughts drifted again.

Drifted to her grandmother, drifted to Seth. Somewhere inside her there was a connection, but she couldn't find it. Two more disparate people she couldn't imagine.

Yet perhaps that wasn't true. Grandma had been tough, tougher than Maria hoped she'd ever have to be. The woman had survived homesteading in the wilderness of Wyoming, had survived droughts and blizzards, the deaths of some of her children, the loss of her husband...so many sorrows and hard times. Yet Grandma had persevered, moving forward into each new day with a peace that seemed to bless those around her, as if hardship had taught her she could survive whatever life brought. Maria admired her strength—and maybe envied it a little.

Seth, too, had survived unimaginable difficulties. He took them on willingly. Maybe that was the connection. Didn't that make him pretty damn special, too?

By comparison, Maria felt untested and untried. Maybe that was why she was thinking of joining the navy. Maybe she sought tests and trials of her own. Maybe the journey she really needed was not so much one of seeing exotic places as it was of finding herself.

Or maybe it wasn't even that. Maybe it was just that there was a huge void in her life she needed to fill, and she was casting about for a way to do it. But was joining the navy the right way? Or just running away?

Sighing, she gathered up the mugs and went back to the living room. It seemed Seth wasn't the only one who needed to do some soul-searching.

Chapter Nine

The wind kicked up with renewed force. Mug in hand, Seth wandered to one of the tall windows and drew the drape back so he could look out.

"The whiteout's even worse now," he remarked.

"This is certainly the longest storm I've seen since moving here," Maria replied.

"It's rugged, all right. I'm not sure it isn't mostly just the wind, though. When I was outside earlier it was so dry the snow was blowing over itself."

"That happens sometimes," she agreed.

"I didn't see much of it when I was growing up in Denver."

"Well, heck, haven't you heard? That's a tropical climate."

He laughed and let the curtain fall so he could turn and look at her. "So it seemed. People were forever driving as if they couldn't believe that snow had fallen overnight. It got pretty bad sometimes."

"Once a bunch of us from college, over semester break, decided to pile into a friend's car and take a trip. We hit Denver first, soaked up a little nightlife, then headed up into the mountains after a snowfall." She laughed and shook her head.

"And?"

"Well, it wasn't too bad in Denver. The roads were starting to clear by about nine in the morning, so we packed up and headed west, figuring we might spend a few hours in Vail, maybe do some skiing there or at Copper Mountain. Anyway, the higher we got into the mountains, the worse the roads got, so we were moving at a pretty steady thirty to thirty-five. And all these cars were zipping past us at sixty, skis on the roof racks, wanting to get to the slopes as early as possible."

She shook her head and laughed again. "We cracked up laughing later, though, because as we approached the Eisenhower Tunnel, most of these cars had skidded off the road. I mean, the shoulder and the median looked like a parking lot. And we just kept chugging along at thirty."

He chuckled. "I've seen that a few times myself."

"Of course, anywhere you live, every winter you have to learn to drive again at the first snowfall."

"But in Denver it's like every snowfall is the first one."

"For some people, anyway," she laughed. "I'm sure it's only a handful. But an amusing handful."

"A dangerous handful." He smiled over his mug at her. "I like your laugh."

She froze, feeling embarrassed again. "It's just a laugh."

"No, it's a nice laugh. Infectious. Makes me grin just hearing it."

"Well, thank you."

"You're welcome," he said with mock gravity.

But as he lifted his mug to his lips, his gaze held hers, and even in the dim, ruddy light she could tell that something had changed.

His stare made her feel self-conscious, and she looked down at herself, wondering if she was still decently covered. Satin wrapped her like a cocoon. So she looked into the fire and cast about for some way to change the mood. Because if he came on to her again and then pulled away, she'd probably be scarred for life.

As if she wasn't already.

"I should put another log on," she said finally.

"I'll do it."

He crossed the room, set his mug on the mantel and squatted before the fireplace to open the screen. The view, she thought, was a nice one. Narrow hips, tight rump...

Oh, heavens, she had to stop thinking this way!

She wasn't built for flings, and a fling was all this could ever be. In a week or two, whenever his leave was up, he'd return to Virginia Beach and they'd probably never meet again. Not after she joined the navy. There was no reason to believe she'd ever be stationed anywhere near his SEAL team. And even if she was, who was to say that he'd ever want to see her again?

But she couldn't drag her gaze away from him as he poked at the fire, stirring up the embers, then placing another two logs on it. He waited, squatting, until they caught, then put the poker back and closed the screen.

She pulled her gaze away just in time as he straightened and turned toward her. "There," he said. "You'll keep warm now."

Warmth wasn't her problem. His mere presence was keeping her warm enough to have withstood the cold outside. "Thank you."

"Maybe," he suggested, "after this blows over, if it warms up some, we can go cross-country skiing together."

She wished her heart would stop doing little flops in her breast. "I'd like that."

Skiing, at least, was safe. They'd be busy having fun, and it would be too cold out there to get into any trouble. Safer then sitting alone together in this dimly lit living room while the wind howled outside.

She really ought to go back up to her room. But she couldn't make herself move. It was as if her body didn't want to be any farther from Seth than it was now. In fact, it wanted to be even closer.

Floundering for some self-control before she hurled herself into this man's arms in a blind need to satisfy the growing ache within her, she said, "I imagine it's been difficult to get used to a new family."

He had returned to his post by the window, holding the curtain back and watching the snow whirl like dervishes. "Difficult? I don't know that I'd say that. They've all made it as easy on me as they possibly could. Although I felt like hell when Marge and Nate separated after I showed up."

"What made you come looking for them?"

He dropped the curtain and turned toward her. "My adoptive parents had died. While I was going through their papers, I learned about Marge. And…well…I didn't have any family at all. I don't know whether I just needed to satisfy my curiosity or if I needed something deeper. I know it never entered my head that she was married to my real father, or that her husband didn't know about me. God, did I feel like hell."

"You weren't responsible."

He shook his head. "I was responsible, all right. I should have thought it through better before I just popped up on the doorstep."

"I think the outcome would have been the same. Marge told me that after all those years, not telling Nate about you was in large part because she didn't want to disrupt *your* life. And she knew Nate would want to find you. She felt she was sparing you both. But once you contacted her in *any* way… Well, I honestly think the same thing would have happened. And from what I see, I think the breakup actually strengthened them."

He nodded slowly. "Nate told me it made him a better husband."

"So it all worked out for the best. Still…"

"Still," he agreed, "it's not the same as a family you grow up with. Especially since I'm away so much. But I love them all, don't misunderstand me."

"I could see that." She smiled. "They're pretty fond of you, too."

He chuckled. "They were even good about my IOUs. Maybe you can help me do some shopping for them. I'm not as in touch as I ought to be."

"I'd be glad to." Maybe this was getting just a little too cozy? Yet not even her emotional survival instinct could pull her away.

"What about your family?" he asked. "Where are they?"

"My two brothers are in computers, and they travel all the time. Right now, Sam is on a job in Germany, and Frank is in Japan. And my parents are still in the little town I grew up in. Except this year they went to Hawaii for Christmas. They've been saving for years. Mom says she's wanted to spend a Christmas there ever since the first time she heard Bing Crosby sing 'Meli Kalikimaka.'"

"I bet they're sitting on the beach right now."

"Probably. Soaking up sun. It'll be good for both of them. They hardly ever get away because they own their own business. It's practically a twenty-four/seven job."

He nodded. "More power to them, then."

"That's what I say. And that's why I'm spending the holidays at the Tates'."

"No wonder you want to be a gypsy. You must be dying of envy."

"Sometimes." Then she laughed. "But I also hear my brothers complain about their travels. Never home, no time for dating, why rent an apartment when they're hardly there…that kind of thing."

A sudden gust of wind rattled the windowpanes and stirred the curtains just a little.

Maria couldn't repress a shiver. "I hope to God no one is out in this."

As if in answer to her thoughts, the phones all over the house started shrilling. Someone picked it up on the second ring.

Seth looked at the clock. It was 3:00 a.m.

"This isn't good."

"I'm going with you," Seth insisted as Wendy and Yuma climbed into their cold-weather gear. "It's too dangerous for you two to go out there alone. Hell, you won't be able to land in this. I have plenty of experience rappelling in worse conditions."

"I don't know," Wendy said. "You're not medical personnel."

"I know plenty of first aid. Plus I know how to go down, get someone in a basket. Do you?"

Wendy and Yuma exchanged glances. "We're trained for mountain rescue," Yuma said.

"Yeah, but I bet you don't go out to do that with just the two of you."

"He's right," said Wendy, looking at Yuma.

"Okay, okay, but borrow my extra boots, man. You'll freeze your feet off."

"I'm coming, too," Maria announced. She was descending the stairs in jeans and a sweater, and boots. "At least as far as the hangar. If you get stuck in a snowdrift, you're going to need help digging out."

And that was how the four of them came to be sitting in Yuma and Wendy's Tahoe with the snowplow on the front.

"Damn," said Yuma, "time's awasting." Lowering the plow, he hit the accelerator and roared down the driveway and onto the road, with only a small skid or two.

Seth was convinced that the only reason they were going to get through this to the airstrip was because of the tire chains. He could feel the snow pushing back at them, reluctant to give way even before the plow. And when it did give way, it blew back at them, obscuring their view.

And Yuma just kept going faster and faster, driving more by memory than by sight.

It was going to be a hell of a trip.

Chapter Ten

The MediVac helicopter was safely tucked in its hangar. Yuma had to plow away enough snow to haul it out and bring it to the helipad.

As he was pulling it out with a small tow truck, Wendy was inside with Maria and Seth, starting up the radio, telling Maria how to operate it. "We're probably going to have to take the patient to a hospital in Laramie," she told Maria. "But when we come back, we're going to need someplace to land. Do you think you can manage the plow?"

"Of course," Maria said. "You can count on me."

"Thanks." Then Wendy turned to Seth. "And thank *you*. Frankly, I don't think I could do this by myself."

"That's what brothers are for."

She smiled at him, a huge, warm smile. "I always wanted one just like you."

Impulsively, Seth turned and hugged Maria, whose eyes were showing strain. "We'll be back before you know it. Honestly, Maria, for what we're going to do, these conditions aren't as bad as they look."

She nodded, returned his hug as if she never wanted to let go. Then, with evident reluctance, she stepped back.

The helicopter was on the pad now, and the rotors were beginning to turn as the engines whined. Seth and his sister ducked under them and climbed aboard the Huey. Old but well maintained, she was a great bird. Once the door closed behind them, the noise was dampened, but only a bit. Wendy handed Seth a headset.

"Okay, can everyone hear me?"

"Yo," answered Yuma.

"Yo," replied Seth.

"Seth, we're going out to a ranch about twenty miles from here. A woman called and said her husband had gone out to the barn to check on the livestock, and hasn't come back. We don't know exactly what we're going to find. The patient is young, maybe thirty-five, but with this cold…well, he might have had a heart attack. Or he might simply have grown hypothermic and be lying out there somewhere in the snow. If it's the latter, we have a good chance."

She didn't give the odds on the former, but Seth could read between the lines. "The cold," he said after a moment. It would reduce his brain's need for oxygen. "Right now it might be his best friend."

The trip was rough; the wind was stronger at higher altitudes than it was on the ground. Still, Seth had taken far rougher helicopter rides, rides with serious danger at the other end. Seth spent the time checking the rappelling equipment and the retrieval basket.

"Are you sure you want to do this?" Wendy asked over the headset. "I can do it."

"I bet I've had a lot more experience with this than you…under far worse conditions."

A staticky laugh reached him. "I don't doubt it."

The flight was mercifully short. Even with the headwind they made good time, and after only ten minutes they were over the ranch.

"I'm going to put you out between the house and barn," Yuma said, his voice crackling over the radio. "The wife said her husband had a safety rope running between the two buildings, so he shouldn't be too far from it. She may already be out looking for him herself."

"Not good," Wendy remarked. "I told her to stay inside."

"Well, if she didn't, we may have two victims out there. I'll get in touch with Maria and see if she can raise the wife on the phone. Meantime, Seth, I can't go too low or I'll blow up so much snow you won't know where you are."

"Roger that," Seth said. "We have fifty feet of rope."

"Winch and basket ready?" Yuma asked.

"Yes," said Wendy. "All set back here."

"Then it's all yours, Seth. Switch to mobile for comm check."

Seth changed over to the lightweight radio headset that was attached to the transmitter in his pocket. The headset itself fit into his ear with a mike that reached to his mouth. He pulled a ski mask over his face.

"Comm check," he said. "One, two, three…"

"I've got you," Yuma answered.

"Me, too," said Wendy.

"Okay," Yuma said, "we're right over the spot. I don't see any movement, but the rotor wash is stirring the snow some. You've got ten minutes, Seth. Any longer and you'll be a casualty, too."

"Roger. I'm going now."

He pulled open the side door on the Huey, attached the rappelling gear to the rope, then eased himself backward out of the chopper.

The drop was easier than a lot he'd made; it wasn't even the coldest. The stinging snow couldn't reach him through his ski mask, and he was on the ground and up to his knees in snow in only a few moments.

"I'm down," he said. "Releasing rope now." He detached his gear, and an instant later Yuma pulled the chopper up and away, so the wash wouldn't kick up the snow more than it already was. Then the chopper turned and the floodlamps came on, illuminating a large swath of the area in question.

Seth saw the safety rope between the house and the barn almost immediately. He slogged toward it, grabbed hold and began to make his way toward the barn. There was still evidence that someone had walked this way, a depressed path through the snow that was already starting to fill in.

As he walked, he checked around him for any signs of another depression, one that might have been made by someone who fell. Nothing.

Then he reached the barn.

"I'm checking inside before I head back to the house."

"Roger," Yuma replied.

The rope led straight to a small door. Marks in the snow testified that it had recently been opened. Seth pulled at it, fighting the wind, then stepped into the relative warmth and the utter darkness of the building. The smell of hay and horses was strong. A nicker greeted his entry, and the stirring of hoofed feet.

Pulling a flashlight off his belt, he switched it on and hunted for a light switch. When he found it, near the door, he flipped it on. Nothing happened. All he would have was the beam of his flashlight.

"Oh, God," said a woman's voice from a few feet away. "I think he's dead."

The husband did indeed seem dead as Seth dragged him outside and loaded him into the basket. "Go," he said, and the basket began its climb.

But the wife was in little better condition. He knelt beside her while her husband was being pulled up, and felt her violent shivering. She'd dressed to come outside, but not well enough. Worry about her husband had caused her to rush and cut corners. She wore mittens, but they were frozen stiff from the moisture released by her body. She had pulled up the hood on her parka but hadn't zipped the snorkel all the way, probably for fear of not seeing him. Her head was tucked down into her chest, and all he could see of her by his flashlight was the top of a hood edged in fur.

"I found him outside," she said, shivering so hard her voice kept breaking. "He was in the snow. I dragged him in here...."

Two minutes later he sent her up on the basket, too. Five minutes after that he followed her.

Wendy put the rancher and his wife on bunks along one side of the Huey and covered them with blankets. They were going to the Community Hospital, she told Seth. The rancher was still alive, although his heartbeat was so slow it was hard to detect.

Then she returned her attention to her patients and to radioing the emergency physician and the hospital. Out of the loop now, Seth pulled off his headset and settled into the bucket seat, watching his sister work.

Even in the bouncing helicopter, her movements were swift and efficient, her touch always gentle. He admired her dedication to saving lives even under dangerous conditions.

"Where's your baby?" Wendy asked the woman.

"M-m-my s-s-sister's."

Then he looked at the rancher's wife, still shivering as she lay in the top bunk, and wondered if the rancher knew what a lucky man he was to have a woman like her in his life. A woman who would go out into a deadly night to try to save him was pretty damn special. He finally caught a glimpse of her face as she turned toward Wendy.

His heart stood still.

The woman in the top bunk was Darlene.

* * *

"How's the pad look?" Yuma asked Maria over the radio.

"Some snow has blown over it," she told him, peering out the windows. "But it doesn't look too bad."

"Rotor wash is going to kick up a mess," he said, his voice crackling on the radio. "Okay, we'll be leaving the hospital in just a few minutes. There's a switch on the panel behind you as you face the radio. Yellow, and it reads 'lights.' I forgot to hit it before we left. Flip it, will you?"

She did as asked, and through the swirling snow saw the landing pad light up. "On," she told Yuma. "The pad's lit."

"Thanks, Maria. Be there in ten."

She sat back in her chair, listening to dead air on the radio, waiting. It was a long wait. She'd been on the edge of her seat with fear earlier, knowing that Seth was rappelling down into the storm. She'd nearly jumped for joy when she heard he'd found the couple. She listened as they were raised to the chopper, and then as Seth followed them up. Relief had washed over her, leaving her weak.

Then she'd listened as Wendy talked to the hospital about her patients. And she'd heard their names.

Seth's ex-wife.

She sat there, waiting for the chopper to return, wondering if her world was about to shatter around her.

When the chopper landed, it swirled up so much snow that it nearly vanished in the whirlwind. But moments later, the rotors began to slow, and the snow began to yield again to the wind, blowing away.

Seth and Yuma stayed outside to tow the chopper back into the hangar, but Wendy came directly into the office. She took one look at Maria's face and said, "You heard."

"His ex-wife." Maria nodded, trying to look as if it didn't matter.

"He's going back to the hospital to see her."

"He probably should."

"Yes." Wendy sat beside her and looked out the windows. "Look…"

"Please," Maria said. "It's no big deal. But if you're taking him to the hospital, could you drop me at my place? It's on the way."

She felt Wendy look at her, but she kept her gaze fixed elsewhere.

"Of course," Wendy said finally. "But you'll come over again later today?"

"Sure." Maria managed a bright smile. But she didn't mean it.

The plows were out, working steadily to try to clear roads. The return trip was far quicker and easier than the outbound trip. The first stop was Maria's house. It was then that Seth spoke the only words he'd spoken in her presence since his return.

"See you later," he said.

"Sure," she answered, then climbed out.

Yuma, ever safety conscious, waited until she was inside her front door before he drove off. The night was still cold enough to kill.

Then she was alone inside her tiny house, alone with her thoughts, alone with her feelings. Alone with the realization that she had become far too involved with a man who had entered her life two short days ago.

Chapter Eleven

"Seth!" Darlene's eyes widened as he entered her hospital room. "I thought I'd imagined you. You saved us."

He brushed that aside. "Your husband's going to be okay."

"Yes, they told me. He should be in that bed right there soon. It's nice that they put couples together now."

"Yes." He stood awkwardly at the foot of her bed, looking at her familiar, yet somehow unfamiliar, face. Feeling the need to say something but not quite sure how to begin.

"How are you doing?" she asked him. "You look a little thin."

"I had some growing to do."

"Oh." Her eyes shifted away from him, then came back. "I'm sorry I failed you. You warned me I wouldn't be able to handle it."

He shook his head hard in denial. "You didn't... You didn't. *I* did."

"No..."

"Darlene, I didn't come here to argue. I don't want to upset you. I just want you to know..." He hesitated, seeking the words. "I was the one who failed. Because…because…I didn't ever let you into my life. I kept you on the outermost edge of it. And I'm ashamed to admit it took me all this time to figure it out."

"Oh, Seth…" Her eyes filled with tears.

"I'm sorry. I swore I wasn't going to upset you. But… You're the kind of woman who'll go out into a deadly blizzard to save her man. I wasn't good enough for you. I never appreciated just what a jewel you were. And I kept you away from me. I'm sorry."

"Seth…"

"I'm happy for your new life. I hope you've found all the things I couldn't give you. Godspeed."

Then he turned and walked out, ramrod straight, feeling that finally, finally, he'd gotten his head and heart in order.

Wendy and Yuma had waited for him. And when he asked them to drop him at Maria's house, they said not a word.

Thus it happened that a half hour after they'd dropped Maria off, he was hammering on her door, not caring if he woke the entire neighborhood.

The hammering frightened Maria. She had just finished changing into her nightclothes, a somewhat less-fancy outfit than she'd taken with her to be a guest. She was wearing a knee-length T-shirt, fuzzy slippers and a warm flannel robe.

And now someone was banging on her door as if the world were about to end.

Concerned, she pulled back the curtain over the window in her front door and saw Seth standing out there in the cold. On the street behind him was Wendy and Yuma's truck.

At once she opened the door, letting in a blast of cold and stinging ice crystals. "What's wrong?"

"I need to talk to you."

"Sure," she said, but not at all certain she should let him in. She stepped back, anyway, and he turned to wave the car away. Yuma and Wendy drove off into the night and Seth stepped into the warm quiet of her home. She closed the door behind him, shutting out the night.

"What's wrong?" she asked again.

He faced her and startled her with a smile. "Not a damn thing."

He threw aside his jacket. It landed somewhere on the floor. Then he kicked off his boots and tossed his gloves in the same general direction.

"Seth?"

Then, oh, then, he took her into his arms and kissed her as if he were dying of thirst and she was the water of life.

He felt her instant of resistance and almost pulled away, but then she melted into his arms as if she wanted to fill every crack and crevice between them with her body. Her mouth answered his kiss, just as hungry and needy, just as rough and passionate, as if she, too, had waited forever for this moment.

Along with his rising, unstoppable passion he felt wonder and awe that she was welcoming him so readily. With his hands he sought to give her wild pleasure, stroking her back and hips over and over, pulling her closer and closer to his throbbing manhood.

Her need suddenly seemed to meet his, for she arched against him, pressing her pelvis to his, causing him to groan with unbounded delight and need.

His hands slipped within her robe and found thin cotton, sensuous in its softness. With his thumbs he traced her ribs gently as he held her close, as his mouth plundered hers and hers plundered his in return.

All he could hear was the hammering of his heart and the gasps they both made. Finally one hand lifted, finding her breast and kneading.

The touch electrified her. She arched her hips hard against his and groaned, a sound from deep within her. It was the most exciting sound he had ever heard.

Her breast was firm, full, its nipple already hard and begging. Impatient now, he wrapped one arm around her waist to hold her, then bent her back until his mouth found that nipple through the fabric. He sucked, hard, then nibbled gently, feeling the tremors run through her, feeling her nails dig into his shoulders. Hearing her groans.

Her hands were suddenly tearing at his shirt, pulling it open, then pressing warm to the skin of his chest, finding his own nipples to pinch. The surprise of it shocked him just an instant, then the pleasure of it kicked him into overdrive.

Her robe and shirt vanished. He barely spared a moment to take in her lush beauty before he tore off his own shirt and unfastened his jeans so they fell to his knees.

Then he swept her onto the couch and settled himself between her welcoming thighs. She was wet and open and welcoming, and as he plunged into her he thought he heard her say, "Yessss...."

But the driving need of his body was in control and he plunged again and again into her soft, hot depths, feeling the indescribable pressure building within him.

Distantly he heard her cry out. Then his own shout joined hers as with one last thrust, he emptied himself into her.

Sweat-soaked skin clung. Breaths rasped quickly, gradually slowing. The world returned, dim, quiet, a counterpoint to all that had happened.

With some surprise, as he lay on her, Seth realized his jeans were still tangled around his knees. It could have been embarrassing, except that he couldn't feel embarrassed with this woman. Not when she still clung to his shoulders, not when her lips were pressing tiny kisses along his collarbone.

Slowly, he lifted his head, daring to meet her eyes. Daring to learn her reaction.

She smiled as she met his gaze. A smile filled him, too, and emerged at last on his face.

Sighing, happier than he could ever remember feeling, he touched his forehead to hers. "I must be crushing you."

"I'm loving it."

But reluctantly he withdrew from her. He had to struggle a bit because of his jeans, which made her giggle. He pretended to scowl at her as he fought the twisted denim and finally freed himself of it.

Then he lifted one of her feet and pointed to the fuzzy slipper. "I'm not the only one."

She went off into a peal of laughter, surely the most beautiful sound he'd ever heard.

"I'm thirsty," she said suddenly. "Want something?"

All he wanted was her. Again. Right now. But he was more than rewarded for his patience when she rose from the couch and padded naked to her kitchen.

"Something warm?" she asked over her shoulder.

"Right now I'm as warm as toast. Maybe warmer."

She laughed. "You're naughty."

"I can get naughtier."

"Good." With an impish smile she disappeared.

But when she was no longer in view to distract him, he realized reluctantly that they needed to talk. So he pulled on the jeans he had just struggled out of and picked up her robe.

He followed her to the kitchen, where she was putting the kettle on. She turned with a smile that faded when she saw his jeans and what he was carrying.

"You're leaving?" she asked.

"Absolutely not. But, Maria, we need to talk. We really do."

She nodded slowly. "Okay." She sounded frightened.

Hell, he realized he was feeling frightened, too. He helped her into her robe, then sat at the dinette until she had finished making two cups of tea. He noticed that she sat across from him, not beside him.

"I'm listening," she said.

"I guess," he said slowly, "I should start with Darlene."

Her heart slammed and her hands tightened around her mug. She didn't think she wanted to hear this at all. "What about her?" she asked, then winced at the belligerence of her tone.

"Just that…" He sighed and ran his fingers through his hair. Then he looked straight at her. "I saw her tonight. I talked to her."

"I know." She waited, suddenly fearful that now that he'd settled his business with Darlene, he'd leave.

"I said goodbye to her. I mean *really* goodbye."

"Goodbye?"

"Yes. I went in there and told her how I'd failed her. I apologized for keeping her on the edge of my life. I was able to do that because of *you,* Maria."

She wanted to wave that aside, but something told her to remain perfectly still and quiet for now.

"I was able to face up to who I was back then, and all the things I'd done wrong. And I told her I was sorry. And I walked out of that hospital feeling like I'd shed a hundred pounds of dead weight."

"I'm glad."

He smiled at her. "It was because of you. You made me see what the problem was. And more than that, by talking to you, I realized I could overcome it. I've shared things with you that I've never told anyone."

She didn't know exactly how to reply to that, mainly because she didn't know where he was heading. Was he about to say, *Now that you've helped me figure it out, I'm going back to my life. Thanks, it's been swell?*

She tightened her grip on her mug even more.

"The thing is," he said, "I've become intimate with you in so many ways I thought I never could. And I realized tonight…well… I love you."

Shock froze her tongue. Her eyes were huge, but she couldn't speak a word.

Finally he asked tentatively, "Did I upset you?"

Mute, she shook her head.

"Maria?"

Finally it burst out of her, too. "I love you, Seth."

An instant later they were in each other's arms, laughing, and maybe crying a little, too.

A long time later they lay in her bed holding hands, staring up at the darkened ceiling while the wind keened outside.

"I wanted to ask you," he said. "About our future. You want to travel. But I've got nearly four years left. Can we compromise so we don't have to be apart?"

"Compromise how?" she asked.

"Well, I could take a training position at Coronado. That's in California. Would you mind living in California for four years? Then we could travel the world. Together."

"Oh, Seth…" She rolled into his arms, amazed that all her dreams could come true in one night because of this one man.

"Could you handle it?" he asked. "I'd rather you not enlist, because we might not be stationed together."

"Oh, Seth," she said again. "Of course I could handle it. I'd love it!"

He sighed, then snuggled her closer. "I love you, Maria. I promise I'll do whatever it takes to make you happy. And if I slip, tell me. Promise you'll tell me."

"I promise," she said. "Just keep being you, Seth. The man I fell in love with."

"Will you marry me?"

"I wouldn't think of doing anything else."

He laughed. "I guess I finally found my way home."
She knew exactly what he meant. Home was in his arms.
Forever.

A BRIDGE
FOR CHRISTMAS

Merline Lovelace

To the men and women I served with and who now serve. May the joy and peace of Christmas find you, wherever you are.

Chapter One

"Yo! Captain Trent!"

USAF Captain Abigail Trent barely heard the shout over the hip-hop version of "Santa Claus Is Coming to Town" blasting through the boom box hung from the center pole of the mess tent.

"Over here."

A tall, rangy non-com motioned her toward the group clustered around a scrawny pine stuck in a barrel of sand.

"We finished the tree," Sergeant Davis announced. "What do you think?"

Abigail eyed the decorations hanging from the branches. Her Red Horse troops had gone all out. Highly skilled combat engineers and world-class scroungers, they'd strung red runway warning lights, shredded wire-thin copper tubing into tinsel, and hand-painted Christmas scenes on fat, round globes.

Abby's brows snapped together. Bending, she took a closer look at the globes. "Please tell me those aren't what I think they are."

Davis flashed a wide grin. "I told the guys we might as well get some use out of that carton of condoms headquarters sent in with our medical supplies. We sure won't be using them for recreational purposes."

He had that right. When Abby's sixteen-person combat engineering team had choppered into this remote site high in the Taurus Mountains eight days ago, they'd found the village nestled along the river below deserted. Located in the hot zone between Turkey, Iran and Iraq, the area had been fiercely fought over in past years. Only the village priest remained, stubbornly refusing to leave his near roofless church and the band of ragtag orphans in his charge. The children had nowhere else to go, the bearded Greek Orthodox priest had explained. Father Dominic intended to keep them here, under his watchful eye, until the vicious guerrilla fighting in the area subsided and the scattered residents returned to the village that had straddled the banks of the river since ancient times.

Abby suspected the fighting wouldn't end anytime soon. There were too many factions, too many lingering hatreds. Greeks, Romans, Turks, Persians, Syrians, Russians—all had tramped through the high mountain pass on their way to conquer one another. The Republic of Turkey claimed the area at present, but the fiercely independent local tribes waged war against the central government almost as fiercely as they did against one another.

Now the Americans had arrived. Or would arrive, once Abby's Red Horse team finished its prep work for the Special Operations forward detachment scheduled to deploy in here just after Christmas. Dubbed Chargin' Charlies after the stomping, snorting stallion that was the unit's mascot, her sixteen-person Red Horse crew had hit the ground running. Working day and night, they'd completed their initial survey. Now they were laying out the site for the second-echelon construction team. This was their first break—a stand-down for Christmas Eve. To celebrate the occasion, they'd decided to throw a party for the orphans.

"Just don't tell Father Dominic those decorations are, uh, medical supplies," Abby begged the still-grinning Sergeant Davis. "He has his doubts about us as it is."

"Not to worry, Cap."

Leaving Davis and his committee to admire their handiwork, Abby checked on the mess sergeant. When in the field, her team subsisted primarily on MREs—Meals Ready to Eat. But Christmas called for turkey and all the trimmings. Since the weather was expected to turn nasty later tonight and preclude flights, headquarters had choppered in special containers of real food earlier this afternoon. Abby's troops had taken a vote and decided to share their feast with Father Dominic and his charges this evening instead of waiting for tomorrow. The tantalizing aromas emanating from the containers had set stomachs growling all afternoon. Abby's added to the chorus as she peered over the shoulder of the lanky Texan who doubled as their mess sergeant.

"Everything under control, Oakes?"

"Roger that, Captain." He pried the lid off another container. The tangy scent of cranberry sauce joined the other delicious aromas. "Those kids are really gonna chow down tonight."

Nodding, Abby hitched up the collar of her field jacket, tugged her knit stocking cap down over her ears, and braced herself. The moment she stepped outside the heated mess tent, a blast of frigid mountain air hit her like a slap to the face. The wind caught a loose strand of her auburn hair and whipped it free of her cap. She hooked it behind her ear and stood for a moment, drinking in the scene.

The Taurus Mountains rose all around her, jagged peaks of granite capped with snow. Far below, the river that had carved a gorge through the mountain untold millennia ago glinted under a thick crusting of ice. Only a small channel remained open in the river's center, the current fast flowing and clogged with chunks of ice that had broken free upstream.

Hunching her shoulders against the wind, Abby peered down at the ancient Roman bridge spanning the river. Its two square support columns still stood, as did the arch connecting them, but the causeway had taken a direct hit in the recent fighting. The engineer in her wanted to weep at the sight of the gaping hole smack in the center of the causeway. That bridge had stood for more than two thousand years, a monument to Roman engineering and the durability of the voussoir arch.

The Romans weren't the first to utilize the arch in construction, of course. They'd stolen the concept from the Etruscans. But they'd perfected the art of distributing weight and stress across a geometric half circle capped with a center keystone. That technique had allowed them to build such glorious structures as the many-arched Coliseum in Rome and the Pont du Gard in southern France. The same technique had led eventually to the vaulted medieval cathedrals that stole Abby's breath every time she walked into one.

She was still mourning the damage to the bridge when the raucous hip-hop blasting through the speakers inside the tent gave way to the far more mellow strains of Bing Crosby's "White Christmas." Instantly, Abby's thoughts veered away from Roman architecture. A wave of homesickness hit her, so swift and sharp she almost doubled over.

Like bright shining ornaments, vivid images tumbled through her mind. Pine garlands festooning the windows of the town house in Philadelphia's historic Chestnut Hill district where she'd grown up. Her mom, elegant in red wool and pearls. Her dad in the plaid smoking jacket he wore only on Christmas Eve, when the family gathered around the tree. Her sister and brother-in-law and two lively nieces, their eyes round with wonder and delicious anticipation.

And Eric, Abby's would-be fiancé. The handsome architect had attended the Trent family gathering last Christmas Eve. He had fit right in. He'd also joined the chorus of dismayed protests when Abby announced her decision to join the Air Force Reserves. She'd tried to explain that she needed to do more than sit behind a desk. That 9/11 had stirred a desire to serve her country and help in the war against terrorism in her own small way.

Of course, Abby didn't know then her reserve unit would be called up for active duty a few short months after she joined. Or that she'd spend her next Christmas thousands of miles away from Philadelphia, sharing an airlifted turkey dinner with sixteen rough-and-ready combat engineers.

Correction, she thought, catching sight of the tall, square-shouldered figure making his way toward her. Make that sixteen combat engineers and one hardheaded Special Operations pilot.

Squaring her shoulders, Abby braced herself for the next skirmish in her private, ongoing war with Major Dan Maxwell. Maxwell had been on her case almost from the day they arrived. As Special Ops liaison, he was here to advise Abby on his unit's operational needs while her team laid out the site. Unfortunately, the major tended to confuse "advise" with "do it my way."

Like Abby, the pilot was bundled up against the biting wind. Instead of camouflage BDUs and a heavy, hooded field jacket, though, Maxwell wore his Nomex flight suit and a fleece-lined bomber jacket. The wind ruffled his short black hair and put blades of color in his lean, tanned cheeks.

"I understand your troops are standing down for the rest of the day," he said by way of greeting.

"That's right."

"I also heard you invited the village priest and his charges up to the site for chow."

His tone implied she should have consulted with him first, or so it seemed to Abby. Bristling, she lifted her chin.

"Yes, I did. Do you have a problem with that, Major?"

His eyes narrowed. She felt the impact of that ice-blue laser stare all the way to her boot tops.

"No problem," he answered after a long moment. "I just wanted to contribute to the festivities."

"Oh." She couldn't quite bring herself to apologize. Shrugging, she offered an olive branch of sorts. "All contributions gratefully accepted. What do you have?"

"Over here."

Curious, she followed him to the pallets stacked outside the tent that sheltered their supplies and equipment. Her troops had stowed all the controlled items, but hadn't had time to stash the rest of the stuff airlifted in with their Christmas dinner earlier. Shifting from boot to boot in the cold, Abby waited while Maxwell pried the lid off a crate stenciled Special Ops—Priority.

"I radioed base when I heard about the party," he informed her. "They scrounged up toys and candy for the kids. Also some warm clothing."

Well, darn! Here Abby had cast the major firmly in the role of Scrooge. Why the heck did he have to go and spoil the image?

Not that he looked anything like a Scrooge, she admitted silently. With his jet-black hair, to-die-for blue eyes and linebacker's shoulders, he came closer to a hulked-up Pierce Brosnan.

She wasn't the only one who'd noticed the resemblance. Senior Airman Joyce Carmichael, the only other female on the team, swore her temperature spiked every time Maxwell came within ten yards. Abby had been forced to remind the irrepressible Joyce that there would be no fraternization or fooling around in the ranks.

Although…

There were moments when Abby had glanced up, met Maxwell's gaze and felt her skin go all prickly.

Moments just like this one.

More than a little annoyed by the sensation, she masked it behind a cool smile. "Thanks for getting into the spirit of things. I'll send Sergeant Davis and the guys out to haul this stuff into the mess tent. They might be able to scare up something to use as wrapping paper."

"Good enough."

Folding his arms, Dan leaned a hip against the crate and let his glance linger on the captain's backside until it disappeared around the corner of the supply tent. Not even the baggy BDUs could disguise her trim curves.

Grimacing, Dan tried to loosen the kink the woman put in his gut every time he laid eyes on her. He was here to do a job. So was Trent. Neither of them had time for distractions. Or they hadn't until this afternoon.

It was the stand-down, he thought wryly. That, and the Christmas music pouring out of the boom box. With a few hours of unexpected time on his hands, Dan had started thinking all kinds of crazy things—like finding Captain Abigail Trent under his tree Christmas morning, wrapped in a big red bow and nothing else.

Yeah, like that was going to happen! Rumor had it she was all but engaged to some high-priced architect back home. Word was she intended to finish her reserve hitch and scoot right back to Philadelphia, the boyfriend and the six-figure job she'd left behind.

Dan, on the other hand, was in for the duration. Raised by a drunk of a father, he'd worked his way through high school and college, then joined the air force at the start of the first Gulf War. A brief, disastrous marriage had convinced him the military was the only family he needed.

And it had been, until he'd climbed out of a chopper to join Captain Trent and her Red Horse team eight days ago. With some effort, he worked his mind around the acronym. Red Horse—Rapid Engineer-Deployable Heavy Operational Repair Squadron, Engineer. A fancy name for a highly mobile team that could perform such varied tasks as bare-base site surveys, demolition operations, well drilling, power generation, and construction of everything from runways to mobile aircraft hangars. Abby Trent, Dan had discovered in the past eight days, knew a little about all of those engineering functions and a whole lot more about leadership.

She led instinctively, by listening to her people when they came up with ideas and guiding them to find a solution when they didn't. What's more, she did it with a breezy, no-nonsense competence that had earned her troops' fierce, unrelenting loyalty.

Her leadership skills alone would have made Dan sit up and take notice. Throw in misty-green eyes, hair as fiery as the sunset off Malibu Beach and a killer set of curves, and he'd had to force himself to keep his mind on the mission these past eight days.

Oh, well. The captain and her team would finish their site survey and depart the area soon. Dan would remain behind with his Special Ops unit. Time and distance would kill his craving for sexy Abigail Trent.

Or so he thought, until the woman walked into the mess tent later that evening.

Abby paused in the doorway, her eyes lighting up at the scene inside.

Father Dominic and the children had already arrived. Sergeant Davis had glued rolls of cotton to his cheeks and was booming ho-hos as he passed out presents. "Feliz Navidad" blared through the speakers. Brown-paper "Christmas" wrapping flew. Kids shrieked with delight.

The Americans appeared to be having as much fun as the children. The long, tall Texan, Steve Oakes, was down on his knees winding up a spring-driven dump truck. Joyce Carmichael cuddled a wide-eyed little girl on her lap, showing her how to comb the mane of a fluorescent pink pony. Dan Maxwell stood just inside the entrance, engaged in an animated conversation conducted via hand gestures with a towheaded youngster of seven or eight.

He glanced up at Abby's entrance and his smile took a sardonic twist. Wondering what the heck she'd done now, Abby bristled. Before she could say anything, though, Sergeant Davis paused in his ho-hoing to call a warning across the heads of the youngsters.

"Yo, Cap! Better watch where you're standing."

At her blank look, Davis hooked a thumb upward. Abby craned her neck, spotted the twig dangling from a string and swallowed a groan. She lowered her gaze and locked glances with the man standing a few feet from her.

"Mistletoe," Maxwell said, his eyes glinting.

"Mistletoe," she echoed, annoyed at the breathy note to her voice.

The glint in his eyes deepened. "Guess we'd better follow tradition."

Abby didn't see any way out. Her troops were watching with expressions of mischievous glee. She didn't have the heart to spoil their fun.

"Guess so," she replied with, what she hoped was a credible nonchalance.

Her pulse did not leap in anticipation as she lifted her face to his. It was just thumping along to the joyful beat of "Feliz Navidad."

That didn't explain why her knees went wobbly when he bent toward her, however. Or the sudden catch to her breath when his mouth brushed hers. Or the guilt that stabbed through her when she remembered how Eric had kissed her under the mistletoe at her parents' house last year.

The memory jerked Abby's head back. Flushing, she tried to cover her reaction with a laugh. "Leave it to the combat engineers to rig a booby trap."

"Yeah," Dan muttered under his breath as she wove her way through the crowd. "You Chargin' Charlies are good at that."

Damn! He hadn't felt a kick like that since...since... He searched his mind, thoroughly disgruntled by the fact that he couldn't remember *ever* getting such a jolt from a single kiss. What *was* it about Abby Trent that revved his engines so fast and so hard?

Still feeling the aftershock, he looked around for the kid he'd cornered just before Abby appeared. He'd caught the boy at the food table, stuffing apples and bananas into his pockets. Dan had tried to convince him he didn't need to stash away a secret hoard, that they'd send the leftovers back with Father Dominic. The kid either hadn't understood or didn't believe there would be anything left after the others got to the table. Jutting out his chin, he'd crammed another banana into his pocket. Now, apparently, he'd disappeared.

He must have slipped outside while Dan was otherwise engaged with the delectable Captain Trent. Worried that he'd scared the kid away from the party, Dan tugged on his leather bomber jacket and went out into the night.

As predicted, the weather had taken a serious hit. Thick, icy fog obscured the moon, the snow-capped peaks, even the valley below. Skirting the dilapidated bus Father Dominic had driven up to the site, Dan searched for the AWOL boy.

He found him crouched beside the pallets stacked outside the supply tent. In the dim glow of the floodlights rigged around the site, Dan saw he'd pried up the lid on a crate marked with a Red Cross emblem and was pawing through the contents. Looking for drugs or other substances to peddle on the black market, Dan guessed.

The kid couldn't know Abby's troops had secured all controlled items. That crate contained only bandages, aspirin, antiseptic ointment and other over-the-counter items. Even those items, though, would fetch a hefty price in this war-ravaged area.

Dan approached slowly, his footsteps muffled by the dense fog. "Sorry, kid, that stuff stays here."

Startled, the boy sprang up. Dan whipped out a hand and snagged his collar before he could take off. His skinny arms thrashing, the boy twisted and jerked and poured out a passionate defense in his own language.

"Hey, it's okay! I'm not going to… Ow!"

At the solid whack to his shins, Dan instinctively tightened his grip. The boy's jacket hitched up around his neck. Panic added volume to his protests. His cries cut through the fog, carried over the mellow rendition of Elvis Presley's "Blue Christmas" now drifting from the mess tent, and brought Father Dominic running.

Abby was right behind him. "What's going on?"

Dan wasn't about to rat on the kid. With his country ripped apart by war, his village in ruins and his parents either dead or missing, the boy had it tough enough as it was.

"Just a little misunderstanding. Not worth disrupting the party over."

More than a misunderstanding, it turned out. After a fierce interrogation, Father Dominic disclosed that the boy—Constantine—hadn't been pilfering food and supplies for himself, but for his older sister.

"Maria, she goes away to look for their father," the priest explained in his halting English. "The rebels take him. They take all the men and force them to fight."

The men and many of the boys, Dan knew. Word was, all males strong enough to tote a rifle had been rounded up and marched off at gunpoint. With no help to work the fields hacked out of the rocky, barren slopes, the women of the village had scattered soon after that.

"Maria comes back a few days ago," the priest said. "She hides in the village."

A frown creased Abby's brow. "Why is she hiding?"

"Constantine, he says she is afraid."

"Of us?"

"Of anyone who wears the uniform."

Abby bit her lip. She was so used to thinking of the military as the good guys, it had been a shock to discover how many people feared soldiers of any stripe in this corner of the world.

The boy tugged on Father Dominic's sleeve to get his attention.

"Constantine says Maria is sick," the priest translated, frowning. "I must gather up the children and go to find her."

"You can't drive the bus back down the mountain in this weather," Abby protested. "Why not leave the children here? I'll drive you down in the jeep."

"You stay with your troops," Dan countered. "I'll drive him."

She didn't waste time arguing. "We'll both go."

They started down the mountain less than fifteen minutes later. Dan was at the wheel of the jeep, bundled against the cold in his flight suit and heavy jacket. Father Dominic huddled beside him. Abby and the boy sat in the back, wedged between a box of food and medical supplies.

She'd tugged her stocking cap down over her ears and pulled up the hood of her field jacket for added protection against the icy wind. The boy was almost lost in a black-and-orange Detroit Tigers jacket, one of the items of clothing shipped in by Dan's unit.

The haunting strains of "Silent Night" followed them until the fog smothered every sound but the hiss of the tires on the narrow mountain track.

Chapter Two

The twenty-minute drive down to the village took an excruciating hour and a half. Thick, swirling fog shrouded the mountain, making every turn treacherous. Slushy snow and ice added to the hazards.

By the time the jeep's headlights picked up the Greek Orthodox cross adorning Father Dominic's church, the muscles in Dan's neck had torqued tight and his palms were sweating inside his gloves.

A mere handful of buildings, the village straddled both banks of the river. The houses and barns stood dark and silent. The roofs of some had caved in. Shell holes pockmarked others.

"The fighting here was fierce," Father Dominic said sadly as Dan navigated the cobbled lane that constituted the village's only paved street. "The last battle…" Sighing, he shook his head. "It was very bad. The rebels, they bomb the bridge, even the church."

Following his directions, Dan drove the length of the narrow street. The eerie stillness raised the hairs on the back of his neck. He'd slipped extra ammo clips for his sidearm into the pockets on his webbed belt. He'd also confirmed Abby had clipped on a radio and packed an assortment of emergency gear with the food and supplies she'd loaded into the jeep. Still, he found himself wishing he'd strapped on a little more firepower as the vehicle's headlights picked a path through the swirling haze.

When the lane began to slope down to the ramparts of the ancient Roman bridge, Dan slowed to a halt and turned a questioning look on the priest.

"Where now?"

Father Dominic slewed around in his seat and conducted a brief conversation with the boy. Facing front again, he waved a hand in the general direction of the river.

"Constantine says his sister is hiding there."

Dan squinted through the swirling fog. "Where?"

His passenger stabbed a finger at the cluster of buildings barely visible on the far side of the river. "There."

"How do we get across?"

"We must take the bridge."

"You're kidding, right?"

Perplexed by the question, the priest lifted his shoulders. "It is the only way."

"I hate to be the one to break it to you, Padre, but your bridge has a hole in it."

"This I know."

"So how do you figure we drive the jeep across?"

"We do not drive. We walk there, on the wall. Constantine says he does this to reach his sister."

Dan eyed the narrow stone ledge for several moments before twisting around in his seat. His gaze locked with Abby's as she squinted through the hood of her field jacket.

"I'm not liking the look of this."

"Me, neither."

She leaned forward, peering through the jeep's windshield at the stone bridge. Despite the fog, the gaping hole halfway across was clearly visible. She clambered out of the vehicle and shoved back her hood.

"I want to take a closer look."

Dan fished out a high-powered flashlight and joined her. They walked upriver a few yards and aimed the beam at the damaged side of the bridge. Chewing on the inside of her cheek, Abby studied the crumbled stone and masonry.

"Judging from the damage pattern, I say it took a mortar hit."

That didn't sound good to Dan, but he kept his thoughts to himself until they retraced their steps, walked downriver and examined the bridge from the other side. From this perspective, the structure appeared undamaged. The two stone support columns stood solid and square against the night. The low wall edging this side of the causeway stretched unbroken from one bank to the other.

"Think it will take our weight?"

"It should," Abby replied after a moment. "The load-bearing arch and keystone are still intact."

"You sure about that?"

"As sure as I can be given the circumstances," she returned dryly. Her gaze swept the ancient structure once more. "That arch has withstood two thousand plus years of spring floods, winter freezes and war. The centurion who designed and directed its construction was some kind of engineer."

"So are you."

She jerked her head around. Her face was a pale blur in the diffused light, but Dan saw the startled surprise that lifted her auburn brows.

"Am I hearing right? Did you just give me a positive stroke?"

Not the kind of stroke he'd like to give her, Dan thought wryly. "Look, I know I've been riding you a little…."

Her brows soared again.

"Okay, I've been a pain in the butt."

"Make that a *major* pain."

Grinning, he acknowledged the pun. "But you got the site laid out. Better and faster than I thought it could be done."

"Almost laid out," she corrected, although she couldn't help preening a little. "Two more days and my team is outta here."

The reminder rubbed Dan the wrong way. His grin disappeared. In its wake came something close to a scowl.

What was with him tonight? So he had a bad case of the hots for the captain? So that kiss under the mistletoe a while ago had come close to short-circuiting his entire system? He'd known all along Abby's team would roll out when they completed the site prep. A heavy construction team would roll in behind them, and Dan's Special Ops detachment would follow. That was how it happened in the military.

That was also why his marriage had broken up, Dan reminded himself as he and Abby walked back along the riverbank. Special Operations personnel never stayed in one spot for very long. Dan's frequent temporary-duty assignments to hot spots around the world had made for steamy homecomings the first year or so. After that, the lengthy absences had worked against a union based more on physical attraction than love. He'd discovered later his ex had consoled herself with a number of men during his frequent absences, including the real estate agent she'd married two days after their divorce went through. Dan hadn't blamed her.

Even now, the memory of his broken marriage didn't bother him half as much as the realization that he and Abby Trent would go their separate ways in a few days.

"Here's the plan," he said brusquely, shoving the thought aside to focus on the immediate problem. "You wait with Father Dominic and the boy in the jeep. I'll boogie across the bridge and find the girl."

Abby didn't bat an eye. Ignoring their difference in rank, she asserted her authority as officer in charge of the project that had brought them both to this remote mountain site.

"Wrong."

"'Scuse me?"

"I'm the one with the working knowledge of stress fractures and load distribution, remember? I'll go across the bridge. You wait with Father Dominic and the boy."

"No way."

"I also weigh less than you do," she reminded him— unnecessarily, Dan thought. "We know the wall will hold Constantine. He says he's crossed it several times. It should hold me."

"He *says* he's crossed it several times. He could be lying."

"Lying?"

Dan flicked a glance at the two figures waiting beside the jeep. When he turned back, a muscle ticked in the side of his jaw.

"It wouldn't be the first time a pint-size guerrilla has lured Americans into a trap. The bridge could be mined and set to blow apart under us. I lost a friend exactly that way in Afghanistan."

Abby's lips thinned. She knew they had to consider the possibility of a booby trap. Unfortunately, they were a fact of life in this war-ravaged corner of the world. And all too easy to plant.

Dubbed antipersonnel devices by some Pentagon wag, landmines had been integral to military operations since first introduced in World War I. They'd become so much a part of modern warfare, in fact, they now constituted an international scourge.

The thought that the rebels might have mined what remained of this ancient stone structure started Abby's stomach churning. The idea that kid in the jeep could be luring them into a trap only added to the sick feeling.

This was Christmas Eve, for pity's sake! A night when they should be celebrating peace, not worrying about ambushes.

With the sick feeling came another fierce wave of homesickness. What the heck was she doing in this war-ravaged country, thousands of miles from home? She could be sitting beside a roaring fire right now, sipping eggnog and singing carols with her family.

The swamping sensation disappeared almost as quickly as it had come. She was here because she'd volunteered to serve her country. No one had twisted her arm. No one had put a gun to her head and forced her into the ranks of a ragtag guerrilla army, as had happened to the men in this village.

Wrenching her thoughts back to the task at hand, Abby reminded Dan her team included a demolitions man.

"Senior Airman Perry swept the area for antipersonnel devices when we first arrived."

"Did he sweep the bridge itself?"

"Just the road leading down to it and the buildings on this side of the river."

She chewed on the inside of her cheek.

"Let's talk to Father Dominic again," she suggested after a moment. "He should have a feel for whether the boy is telling the truth about his sister."

The very suggestion that his charge might be lying shocked the priest to his core. "No! No! Constantine would not send us into harm."

The boy echoed his sentiments, his young voice strident and urgent. Although neither Abby nor Dan could understand his words, they grasped his intent quickly enough when he hopped out of the jeep and started for the bridge. Dan caught him by the back of his Detroit Tigers jacket.

"Hold on, kid."

The boy gestured furiously toward the bridge and launched another passionate appeal. His sister's name came up so often and so desperately he convinced Abby.

"I'm going across."

Her terse pronouncement cut through Constantine's urgent pleas and earned her a rapier look from Dan.

"*We're* going across," he countered grimly. "Slowly and carefully."

One look at his face told her it would be a waste of breath to argue. Shrugging, Abby checked to make sure her radio was clipped securely to her shoulder, then stuffed several packs of Meals Ready to Eat and the first aid kit into her pockets. She didn't have any idea what they'd find on the other side of the bridge, but she'd learned to go into every situation as prepared as possible.

"Wait here," she instructed Father Dominic. "Keep Constantine with you until the major and I make sure the bridge wall will bear our weight."

Arguing her fewer pounds, Abby insisted on taking the lead. Dan would follow a few paces behind. Close enough to grab her if she slipped on the slick stone. Far enough back that his weight wouldn't combine with hers to overstress the damaged area.

That was the plan, anyway.

Her heart in her throat, she walked onto the bridge ramp. She kept the flashlight aimed at the stones. Despite Father Dominic's assurances and the boy's vociferous protests, she found herself searching for the glint of a trip wire or a loose stone that might hide a pressure mine.

Sweat pooled under her heavy fatigue jacket. The misty fog stung her cheeks and formed tiny icicles on her lashes. Step by cautious step, she approached as close as she dared to the gaping hole in the center of the bridge.

"Time to take to the wall," she muttered to the man behind her.

With Dan gripping her hand, Abby climbed onto the stone ledge. It was only about six inches wide. Her fingers locked in Dan's, she leaned over and looked down. Way down. Below the bridge, a thick coat of ice crusted the river close to its banks. Dark water coursed through the narrow center channel. The swift, rushing current looked all too eager to suck her in.

"Got your balance?"

As much as Abby wanted to hang on to the lifeline of Dan's hand, she loosed her clawlike grip.

"Yeah," she answered, in something too close to a squeak for her liking.

Gulping, she planted one boot in front of the other. Inch by inch, stone by stone, she began a slow, shuffling walk.

Dan climbed onto the wall behind her and followed her into the swirling mist.

They had inched their way past the damaged support column and were more than halfway across when a sharp crack rifled through the night.

Abby just about jumped out of her boots. It took every ounce of willpower she possessed not to dive for that skimpy six inches of stone. She dropped into a crouch instead, hunching her shoulders up around her ears.

"Was that a shot?" she screeched to Dan.

Before he could reply, another crack spilt the night. A desperate shout from Father Dominic rode the echo of that awful sound.

"The ice!" the priest yelled. "She breaks!"

Her pulse pounding, Abby shot a look downward. The sight of a great chunk of ice ripping away from the river's crust sent her heart plunging to her boots. The swift water in the channel picked up the mini-iceberg and sent it straight for the damaged support column.

Abby didn't have time to calculate the speed or the force of that swift-moving projectile, but she had a good idea of its impact on a structural support already weakened by a mortar strike.

"It's going to hit the support behind us!" she shouted to Dan. "We have to go forward. Fast!"

Like a tightrope walker with the rope about to snap under her feet, she threw out both arms for balance and raced for the far bank. Her boot soles skittered and slipped on the icy stone. Her heart banged against her chest.

Straining to hear the thud of Dan's boots over her thundering panic, Abby made it to the far side.

Almost.

She had less than three yards to go when the slab of ice crashed into the stone column. The weakened support crumpled on impact. Bricks and mortar tumbled into the black, rushing water. Inevitably, the arch supported by the column also began to fall. Like dominoes, the stones quarried and fitted carefully into place more than two thousand years ago splashed into the river.

Abby felt the wall beneath her boots give way and knew an instant of sheer, unadulterated terror. Then she was sailing through the air, propelled by a hundred and ninety pounds of determined male.

Dan's flying tackle carried her clear of the causeway and into the frozen riverbank. She hit with a whumph that knocked the breath from her lungs. The flashlight flew out of her hands. The supplies she'd stuffed into her pockets dug into her hips.

Dan came down on top of her. Shock held Abby immobile for seconds. Minutes. Hours, maybe, while his breath rasped in her ear and his body crushed hers. Finally, she dragged in enough air for a desperate gasp.

"Dan! I…can't…breathe."

Grunting, he shifted his weight to one side. Abby gulped in icy air and planted her hands palm-down in the dirt. Her muscles as wobbly as overcooked noodles, she squirmed around until they were chest to chest.

"You okay?" he growled.

"Yes."

Aside from a few bruised ribs and permanently pancaked breasts.

"How about you?"

"I'm all in one piece."

An agonized grinding of stone on stone whipped his head around. Abby lifted hers just enough to see another section of the arch give way. The pieces tumbled into the black waters, splintering the icy crust.

"Looks like we can't say the same for your bridge," Dan said in the stunned silence that followed.

"Looks like."

Silently mourning the loss, Abby flopped back onto the riverbank. Her shock wore off gradually, slowly. As it did, her agile mind clicked into gear and she instinctively started thinking in terms of damage assessment and repair capability.

If the villagers ever returned, they'd need some way to cross the river. Maybe Abby could convince her headquarters to send in a portable bridging unit with the Second Echelon Red Horse team scheduled to follow hers. The RH-2 would arrive with all kinds of heavy equipment. A bridge transporter didn't weigh as much as a front loader or bulldozer.

Her head buzzing with thoughts of deployable rafts, ribbon floats and modular bridging sections, it took her a moment to realize she was still partially pinned under one very solid major.

She brought her head around. Almost chin to chin with Dan, she couldn't miss the crooked tilt to his mouth. Or the glint that came into his eyes when they met hers.

"What?" she demanded, suddenly ridiculously aware of his hip gouging her pelvis.

"I can't recall many memorable Christmases in my life, but this is shaping up as one for the record books."

"*I'll* certainly remember it," Abby agreed with some feeling.

To her surprise, he lifted a hand and traced his thumb along her chin. The callused pad raised little shivers over every inch of her skin.

"Just to make sure…"

For the second time that night, he swooped in for a kiss. And for the second time in less than five minutes, the air whooshed right out of Abby's lungs.

Chapter Three

Dan rolled to his feet and reached down to help Abby to hers. She wobbled upright, trying to decide which had shaken her more—almost riding a crumbling bridge into a frigid river or the crush of Dan Maxwell's mouth against hers.

Given the way her lips still throbbed from his kiss, it was a no-brainer.

"Captain Trent!"

Father Dominic's frantic cry barely carried through the soupy fog and the swift rush of the river. Cupping her hands around her mouth, Abby shouted back.

"I'm here. We're both here."

"We made it across," Dan bellowed only inches from her ear.

Wincing, she slipped her radio from its shoulder clip. To the faint echo of Father Dominic's fervent "Thank the Lord!" she keyed the mike.

"Red Horse base, this is Red Horse One."

Her communications tech came on a few seconds later,

backed by a rousing chorus of "Angels We Have Heard on High."

"This is Red Horse base. Go ahead, One."

"Be advised Dervish Six and I have, uh, encountered a little difficulty."

Most of the units supporting operations in Iraq and Afghanistan had adopted nicknames appropriate to their locations. Dan's Special Ops squadron labeled themselves the "Whirling Dervishes." Hence Dan's call sign, Dervish Six. Appropriate, Abby thought wryly, given the man's propensity for stirring things up.

"What kind of difficulty?" her communications tech asked.

"We're stranded on the far side of the river."

"Come again?"

"We crossed the river via the old Roman bridge and can't get back."

"Why not?"

"You'll see when the fog clears," Abby drawled. "Tell Sergeant Davis he's in charge until I return to the site." She caught Dan's hand signal. "Hang on, Dervish Six wants to talk to you."

"Contact my unit," he instructed after she passed him the radio. "They'll need to fly in a chopper to extract us when the weather lifts."

"Roger that, sir."

Terminating the transmission, Dan turned his back on the river and eyed the dilapidated dwellings perched precariously above its banks. Like the houses and barns on the other side, these, too, bore the scars of war. Shattered windows looked out on the night with dark, empty eyes. Roofs had collapsed, some completely, some partially. Wooden doors hung crookedly on their hinges.

He scraped a hand over his chin. "Guess we should try to find the kid's sister."

"That's what we came for," Abby agreed.

Scooping up the flashlight, Dan aimed it at the ground and made a cautious trek up the cobbled lane. Abby followed, stretching her legs to walk in his exact footsteps. They both kept a wary eye out for trip wires and loose cobbles. Every few yards, she called out in English and the few Turkish phrases she'd picked up. She hoped the sound of a female voice would bring Constantine's sister out of hiding.

No such luck.

She and Dan poked through the houses, barns and sheds. They found scattered bits of clothing, crockery still on tables, and moldy vegetables in pierced tin containers—all evidence of the hurried departure of the residents—but no Maria. Thinking the girl might have glimpsed their uniforms and fled, they followed the twisting dirt road running along the riverbank as far as they dared.

After two hours of searching and shouting, Abby's throat was raw and her toes had turned to Popsicles inside her boots. She didn't argue when Dan suggested a halt to the search until daylight.

They chose the house nearest the bridge to set up camp. Most of its roof was still intact, but the frigid night poured in through shattered windows. Dan found blankets to drape over the windows. Abby, to her joy, discovered a stack of firewood beside the back door. Arms full, she hauled a load inside. Dan brought in more and piled together some kindling. Within moments, she'd plopped down in a rickety chair and was toasting her booted toes before a roaring blaze.

"We'd better set up some perimeter defenses before we get too comfortable," Dan warned.

"Right."

Sighing, Abby dragged her feet away from the fire. She reminded herself that she wasn't at home in Philadelphia. She was high in the Taurus Mountains, in an area savaged by rebels and government forces alike. The Turkish government had posted spotters at both ends of the pass that cut through the mountains, but there was always the chance the small bands of armed irregulars could slip past them. Best not to take any chances.

"We need to string some kind of alarm," Dan said when she'd dragged to her feet. "You poke around inside the house. I'll check the shed out back. See if you can find some string or twine."

He came up empty-handed. So did Abby, until she remembered the packets of Meals Ready to Eat she'd stuffed in pockets of her bulky field jacket.

"How about dental floss?"

One corner of his mouth kicked up. "That should work."

Hauling the MREs from her pocket, Abby dumped them on the table and ripped open a package of fiesta chicken. The vacuum-sealed container of chicken and Spanish rice tumbled out, along with a can of chemical heat to warm it. The package also included a minican of corn, a high-nutrition chocolate milkshake, crackers and a tube of jalapeño cheese spread.

Abby's eyes lit up. The cheese spread was one of the most popular items among her troops, worth two tubes of peanut butter and three of strawberry jam in trade. She'd make sure she took it back with her—assuming Dan didn't gobble it down for a late-night snack.

"Aha! Here's what we need."

She scooped up a small Ziploc bag packed with plastic utensils, Wet Wipes, a folded toothbrush with the toothpaste already injected and a small container of cinnamon-flavored floss.

Three MREs later, Abby had spread a veritable feast on the table and Dan was in possession of enough floss to rig alarms at strategic points on their perimeter. He and Abby stretched one bit of floss across the road, then popped the tops on two minicans of vegetables. Gulping the contents down cold, they threaded the floss through the pull-tabs. The cans bobbed and clanked merrily when Dan tested them with a boot.

"Crude, but effective," he announced.

By the time they'd strung the rest of the floss, Abby's toes were doing the Popsicle thing again. Once back inside the house, she dropped into the rickety chair and stretched her boots to the fire.

"Aaah."

"Feet cold?"

"Cold doesn't begin to describe it. I think I'm dead from the knees down."

The fire had warmed the room enough for Dan to shrug out of his heavy bomber jacket. Dragging over another chair, he hooked the jacket on the back and settled in.

"Let's get your boots off. I'll rub some circulation back into you."

He'd made the offer casually. There wasn't any reason for Abby's pulse to skitter at the thought of his hands on her. Or for her throat to go bone dry when he lifted her left foot into his lap and yanked at the laces.

The boot hit the floor with a thump. His strong hands took hold of her stockinged foot. Kneading and rubbing, they transferred their heat to the icicles that used to be her toes. When he went to work on her instep, Abby groaned and gave herself up to the pleasure.

Laughter rumbled in his chest. "Feels good, does it?"

"Let me put it this way. You've got a second career as a foot masseur waiting for you whenever you decide to leave the air force."

His rich chuckle filled the room. "That's not going to happen anytime soon."

She slumped in her chair, trying to ignore the close proximity of her heel to his crotch. "How many more years do you have to go before you can bail?"

"As many as they'll let me serve," he replied, kneading her arch. "What about you? What are you going to do when you finish your hitch with the reserves?"

"Go back to Philadelphia, I suppose. The company I work for is holding my position for me."

"You work for an architectural firm, right?"

"Not just a firm," she murmured, lost in the magic of his hands. "An institution. Peabody, Prescott and Benton, Incorporated. I think they designed half the state capitals and shopping malls in the Western Hemisphere."

"Which do you work on? State capitals or shopping malls?"

"Malls, mostly."

"Sounds like a waste of your talent."

The offhand remark took some of the edge from Abby's pleasure. She scooted upright in the chair and eased her foot from his hold. He let it go and reached down for the other.

"Have you thought about staying in the air force?" he asked, tugging at the bootlaces.

"Some."

Make that a lot. She'd been vacillating for months. She loved what she did. Most days she felt part of something important. But the homesickness that hit every military member on remote tours increased exponentially around the holidays. This past week, Abby had been struggling with the idea of spending more Christmases away from home, of missing her nieces' birthdays, her parents' anniversaries.

"My boss offered me a promotion and command of an RH-2," she admitted, dragging off her stocking cap to thread her fingers through loose strands of her hair. "That's a second-echelon, heavy equipment Red Horse unit."

"Yeah, I know. Are you going to take it?"

"I haven't decided. I'm not sure my civilian firm will hold my job indefinitely."

"So go regular and make the military a career. You're a natural leader, you know."

"No," she returned, surprised by her second compliment of the night, "I don't."

"C'mon. Your troops would walk through fire on their hands for you."

"Yeah, well, I'd do the same for any one of them."

The gruff response drew a smile from Dan. Fascinated by the way the skin at the corners of his eyes crinkled, Abby let her heel settle onto his thigh. His very hard, very muscular thigh.

His so-talented fingers massaged her toes and arch, then tugged down her sock cuff. When he went to work on her ankle, his touch generated a series of small electric shocks under her skin.

"I hear a job isn't all that's waiting for you back in Philadelphia," he said after a moment.

"Huh?"

"Rumor is there's a high-priced architect waiting, too."

A picture of Eric the last time she'd seen him flashed into Abby's mind. Handsome, sophisticated, more than a little annoyed that she'd actually followed through with her decision to join the reserves and was leaving Philadelphia for God knew how long.

"He said he'd wait," she admitted, "although I told him not to."

Dan's hands paused. He flicked her a quick glance, his eyes unreadable. He had the most arresting face, Abby thought. All those rugged planes and angles.

Then he slid his fingers under her pant cuff, and her attention made a startled leap from *his* face to *her* leg. Slowly, he kneaded her calf through the silky thermal long johns her mom had insisted would keep her warmer than the government-issued version. Abby stood the erotic massage as long as she could without giving in to the insane urge to strip off every bit of her clothing and give Dan access to parts north of his present location.

"Thanks," she got out. "I'm, uh, pretty well thawed now."

Ha! She was melting from the inside out.

She knew at that moment that whatever happened with her career, she wouldn't let Eric take their relationship to the next level, as he wanted to. She'd dated him on and off for almost six months. They shared the same professional calling and a good many personal interests. Yet his touch had *never* detonated small incendiary devices all over her body the way Dan Maxwell's did.

Curiosity about the man behind the major's leaves tugged at Abby. In the eight days they'd worked together, he'd been all business. She knew he was divorced. Also knew he was from California. That was about it.

"How about you?" she asked as he slumped more comfortably in his chair and stretched out his long legs toward the fire. "Do you have someone special waiting for you?"

"No."

O-kaay. That subject was obviously off-limits.

"I understand you call California home. Do your folks still live there?"

"My mother died when I was five. My father..."

He didn't move, but Abby sensed the shutters coming down. His expression hardened, and his muscles seemed to tighten under the easy slouch.

"Your father?" she prompted.

He slanted her a glance, as if trying to decide how much to tell her. Evidently she passed some sort of test.

"I haven't seen my father in going on ten years," he said with a shrug that was meant to come across as careless but didn't quite make it. "He's an alcoholic. Has been since shortly after my mom died."

Dear Lord!

Abby had grown up surrounded by love and laughter. She couldn't begin to imagine losing both parents at the same time, one to death and the other to drink.

"How awful for you. You must have been so lonely."

Lonely? That had been the least of Dan's burdens. Deliberately, he shut his mind to the memory of his father's crying jags. The days on end without food in the house. The childish hurt and confusion that slowly, inexorably turned to rage. He started to give Abby the same flip answer he always gave whenever anyone probed too deeply.

The grudging admission that came out instead surprised both of them.

"I was."

Where the hell had that come from? He'd never talked about his father or his childhood, even to his ex. Maybe because she'd never indicated any particular interest, Dan thought cynically. Thoroughly embarrassed by his descent into sloppy sentimentality, he pushed to his feet.

"It's going to be a long night. We might as well chow down, then I'll take the first watch."

She blinked at his abrupt transition from personal to professional. "Fine."

They feasted on fiesta chicken, lasagna and a variety of vegetables, snacks and condiments washed down with the chocolate shakes. Abby tried not to think of the mashed potatoes, dressing and cranberry sauce being dished up at the site.

"I saw a latrine out back," Dan said when they'd finished. "I'll take the flashlight and check it out."

Abby hid a grimace. Being assigned to a Red Horse unit often meant making do with a ditch or a hole in the sand. An outhouse wasn't much better. Thank goodness for those Wet Wipes!

Dan came back and gave the all clear. When Abby returned from her trip to the latrine, he was on the floor, shoulders to the wall, ankles crossed. He'd positioned his sidearm at his side. Abby passed him the radio before poking her head into the dwelling's one bedroom.

The residents had stripped the coverings from the bed and carted them away when they fled. A thin mattress still rested on the metal bed frame, but Abby's appearance caused a sudden flurry of activity. Several small creatures scurried across the mattress and disappeared into a hole they'd gnawed in the covering. She decided against joining them.

Returning to the front room, she put her shoulder blades to the wall and slithered down beside Dan. He lifted a brow.

"Mice," she explained succinctly.

A low rumble started in his chest. Next thing Abby knew, his whole body was shaking.

"What's so funny?"

"Think about it."

"What?"

Grinning from ear to ear, he launched into a singsong falsetto. "'Twas the night before Christmas, and all through the house, not a creature was stirring…"

"Not even a mouse," she finished, helpless with laughter.

Abby couldn't believe it. A few hours ago, she'd ached with homesickness. All she could think of were her mom's bright red dress, her dad's smoking jacket, her sister and brother-in-law and nieces gathered around the tree. Now laughter filled her heart.

Correction—Major Dan Maxwell filled her heart.

Without thinking, she lifted a hand and laid it against his cheek. His five o'clock shadow had come in with a vengeance. His skin was bristly under her palm and warm to her touch.

"Merry Christmas."

The amusement left his eyes. She saw herself reflected in their blue depths. Saw something else, as well. Something that made her breath catch.

"Back at you," he said softly.

She expected him to kiss her again. Okay, she *ached* for him to kiss her again. But it felt right when he didn't.

Felt even more right when he hooked an arm around her shoulders and snuggled her against his chest.

"Get some sleep. I'll wake you when it's time for your watch."

It wasn't Dan who jerked her from sleep some hours later, but Sergeant Davis. His voice came crackling through the radio, tense and urgent.

"Red Horse One, this is Red Horse base. Come in, please."

Abby's lids flew open. Confused and disoriented, she tried to blink the sleep from her eyes and the grogginess from her mind. She jolted up and stared blankly at the solid chest just inches from her nose.

"Red Horse One, come in, please."

"Here." Dan thrust the radio into her hand.

Abby keyed the mike, forcing her sluggish brain to function. "This is Red Horse One. Go ahead, base."

"We just got word. The spotters at the east end of the pass reported a small band of irregulars headed toward the village. They're moving up the pass on the west side of the river."

The same side she and Dan were stuck on. Her stomach lurching, Abby keyed the mike. "No indication whether these irregulars are friend or foe?"

"Negative. It was too dark for the spotters to ID them."

"How many?"

"Eight to ten."

Dan was listening in. "Ask what kind of arms they're carrying."

"Assault rifles and what looked like shoulder-held missiles," the sergeant returned grimly when Abby relayed the question. "Tell Dervish Six his unit is prepared to launch air cover, but the weather is still working against us."

No way Dan was going to call in an air strike. Not in these treacherous mountains, with zero visibility.

A brief consultation with Abby resulted in a new game plan. They decided to douse the fire and find a more secure spot to hole up until the weather cleared and Dan's unit could fly in a chopper.

"We're going to seek cover," Abby advised Sergeant Davis. "Maintain radio silence unless and until we contact you."

"Roger that."

As she scrambled to gather her gear, she realized the brief interlude of peace had passed. Christmas, she thought grimly, was over.

She and Dan left the house a few minutes later and went into the frigid night. The mist was as heavy as ever, slicking the cobbles and making walking an exercise in fierce concentration. She was so absorbed in keeping her footing that she almost missed the faint clatter of the cans they'd strung on dental floss.

Dan caught it, however. Whipping up his pistol, he spun toward the sound.

It came again, followed by a low, keening cry that ended on a sob. A young girl's cry.

"Constantine's sister," Abby breathed. "That has to be her."

A second later, a figure stumbled out of the mist. She held one hand outstretched in a desperate plea. The other cradled her huge, distended belly.

Chapter Four

When Dan spotted the girl's bulging stomach and pain-racked face, he had one thought.

Holy crap!

"I thought Constantine said his sister was *sick*," he growled at Abby, as though this was all her fault.

"He did. She is."

If you equated sick with very, very pregnant.

When they approached the girl, it was obvious their uniforms terrified her. She stumbled back, her eyes dark pools of fright as she took in Abby's field BDUs and Dan's bomber jacket.

"It's okay," Abby assured her. "We're friends, Maria. We came to find you."

The sound of her name stopped the girl's awkward retreat. Pressing both hands against her belly, she let loose with a torrent of frantic sentences.

"I'm sorry." Abby shook her head. "I don't understand."

Despite the icy mist, the girl's face was beaded with sweat. She was older than her brother by some years.

Abby guessed her age at sixteen or seventeen. A kerchief covered her dark hair and was tied under her chin. Her hand-tooled, sheepskin-lined boots looked warm enough, but her bulky coat wouldn't button over the mound of her stomach.

She launched into another passionate plea, only to break off in midsentence. Gasping, she crossed her arms over her belly and bent almost double. A low, tortured cry cut through the night.

"Oh, God!" Abby's heart ping-ponged around inside her chest. "I think she's in labor."

Dan swallowed the curse that wanted to rip free. Swearing wouldn't resolve the problem of a destroyed bridge, a heavily armed and as yet unidentified band headed their way, and a girl about to give birth. It would have made *him* feel better, though.

"Let's get her to shelter," he bit out instead.

The girl cringed when Dan approached but let him slip an arm around her waist. He half walked, half carried her back to the house they'd just vacated.

Abby hurried ahead. Dashing into the bedroom, she thumped the thin mattress to dislodge its four-legged occupants and dragged it into the front room, close to the fireplace. Dan lowered the girl onto the makeshift bed while Abby stirred the embers and added more logs.

"I saw a bucket out back," he said grimly. "I'll go down to the river and get some water."

Right. They always needed water in the movies. Hot water, for boiling the instruments.

Gulping, Abby looked around the hut. She spotted a few pieces of crockery, but no pots or pans. And nothing that remotely resembled instruments.

A sharp, keening cry from the girl dropped Abby to her

knees beside the mattress. Maria groped wildly for her hand and locked it in a bone-crunching grip. Wincing, Abby tried to sound calm and confident.

"It's okay. You'll be okay."

It seemed like hours before Dan returned with the water. He plunked the bucket down beside Abby, frowning as the girl bent her knees and thrashed them from side to side.

"How's she doing?"

"I don't have a clue. The closest I've come to a live birth is when I waited at the hospital for my two nieces to make an appearance." Gritting her teeth against the pain in her hand, Abby angled him a look that was two parts hope and one part desperation. "I don't suppose you know anything about childbirth?"

"You suppose right."

"Great."

"We've got the radio," Dan reminded her. "You can contact the medic on your team."

Senior Airman Haskell wasn't a real medic, but a combat engineer who'd received a crash course in emergency medical training. He could splint breaks, stitch cuts and administer morphine if necessary, but Abby seriously doubted his training had included a section on delivering babies.

On the other hand…

He could patch her through to Red Horse headquarters. HQ, in turn, could patch her through to a doc. Abby was reaching for the radio when Dan angled away from the girl and drew out his 9 mm Beretta. A quick click ejected the magazine. He checked the load, snapped it back in again and swung back around.

"You stay with the girl."

"Where are you going?"

"Downriver. I'll keep a watch for the irregulars."

"How will you see them in the dark?"

"There's only one dirt track leading through the mountains on this side of the river. I'll find a spot where I can see it. If they show and look like they mean trouble, I'll create a diversion to lead them away from the village."

Abby bit her lip. Coward that she was, she wanted to suggest they reverse roles. *He* could darn well stay while *she* performed sentry duty. If necessary, she could create a heck of a diversion.

But Maria still had her hand in a vise and Abby couldn't bail on her.

"Go," she muttered. "We'll manage here."

Somehow.

The next eleven hours were the longest of Abby's life. She spent them alternating between calls to headquarters, bathing Maria's sweat-filmed forehead and listening for the stutter of gunfire.

She didn't realize the damp, foggy night had given way to a damp, foggy dawn until slivers of gray showed at the edges of the blankets Dan had draped over the windows. Abby hooked one to the side to let in the light and returned to the girl's side. She dipped a cloth in the bucket, then wrung it out. Shadowed, worry-filled eyes pleaded with her as she dabbed at the runnels of sweat.

"I'm so sorry, Maria. I wish I could do something besides wipe your face and time the contractions."

They were coming about ten minutes apart now. The doc at headquarters said the baby might present soon. Or not. Nature had a way of taking her own sweet time in these matters. At this point, Abby was ready to give Mother Nature a hard, swift kick in the butt.

The girl muttered something in her own language and groped across the mattress. Hiding a grimace of pure pain, Abby twined her fingers with Maria's.

The minutes crawled by. The hazy light outside grew brighter. With the morning came a rather pressing need. Abby had to make a trip to the outhouse. Like, bad. But she hated to leave Maria without communicating the reason why. She was resorting to a rather ignominious pantomime when the radio crackled.

"Red Horse base to Red Horse One."

Tugging her now-numb hand free of Maria's grasp, she snatched up the radio. "Go ahead, base."

"We've just been advised the weather's cleared enough to launch. There's a Pave Hawk en route to your location as we speak."

Thank God! The Pave Hawk had to be coming from Dan's Special Ops unit. A highly modified version of the army Black Hawk transport helicopter, the HH-60G carried enough firepower to blast a hole through the surrounding mountains. It could also perform such humanitarian missions as civil search and rescue, disaster relief, international aid and emergency aeromedical evacuation.

"Please tell me there's a doc aboard," Abby begged.

"That's affirmative, One."

"What's their ETA?"

She held her breath, praying the chopper's estimated time of arrival would coincide with the baby's.

"We put them at forty minutes out."

That was thirty-nine too many for Abby's peace of mind, but she knew the Pave Hawk crew would push their aircraft to its max airspeed.

"We'll patch you through to the doc on board, One. Hang tight."

As if she could do anything else!

While she waited for the doctor's voice to come over the airwaves, Abby's mind raced. She didn't know how far Dan had traveled downriver. Nor did she have any means of contacting him to advise him the chopper was on the way.

She'd stay with the girl until the Pave Hawk put down, she decided. There was a chance Dan might hear its approach and return to the village. If not, Abby would get Maria safely on board and go after him.

At least she'd be able to take some backup with her. The Pave Hawk crew consisted of a pilot and co-pilot, a flight engineer, an aerial gunner and two pararescuemen, still known throughout the air force by their former designation of parajumpers, or PJs. The PJs she'd met during her months on active duty were a breed unto themselves. As tough as tempered steel, they could battle their way through jungles, over mountains and across deserts to rescue a brother in arms.

Ever after, Abby would swear she aged a year for every one of those forty minutes she knelt beside Maria. She tried to tell the girl help was on the way, but her hand gestures and arm flapping produced only a confused, wary expression.

Together, she and Maria sweated through several more contractions. They were coming fast and furious now. Between regular radio updates to the doctor and the preparations he advised her to take, Abby grunted and groaned and sweated along with Maria.

The chopper was less than five minutes out when the girl gasped and drew up her knees. With a hoarse cry, she spread her knees. Abby took one glance and knew they'd just run out of time.

"The baby's crowning," she advised the doctor as she positioned herself between Maria's legs. "I see the top of his head."

"Good. Support the head with your palm as it emerges. As soon as it's clear, check to make sure the umbilical cord isn't wrapped around the baby's neck."

"Roger."

Abby would have traded everything she owned at that moment for a pair of surgical gloves. She'd managed to boil some water in a dented tin cup. It stood at the ready, steam rising, along with the tube of antiseptic ointment and the stack of Wet Wipes she'd positioned close by.

Clenching her jaw, she poured the still-simmering liquid over her hands. Tears popped into her eyes. Abby blinked them away, swiped her hands with a towelette and made a special effort to dig the dirt from under her nails. After smearing on the ointment, she summoned a breezy smile.

"Okay, Maria. I'm ready when you are."

She knew the girl couldn't understand her. That was okay. They were beyond communicating by words.

A few moments later Maria's face contorted. She rose up on her elbows, emitted a fierce grunt and pushed. Hard.

The baby's head popped out. Slimy and slick and crowned with thick, black fuzz, it was the most amazing thing Abby had ever seen.

"I've got him."

Maria fell back on the mattress, panting. Abby supported the head with one hand while probing its neck with the other. She didn't encounter anything that felt like an umbilical cord, but then again, she'd *never* encountered anything that felt like an umbilical cord.

She was so caught up in the drama of the moment she barely registered the whump-whump-whump of the chopper setting down close by.

"Another push, Maria. Just one more."

The girl was still gathering her strength when the cavalry arrived. The door burst open and Abby threw a look of sheer, unadulterated relief over her shoulder.

Three men rushed in. Two toted assault rifles. The third carried a medical field kit and wore a jaunty red Santa Claus cap.

Abby gaped at the cap. She'd completely forgotten this was Christmas Day. She felt as though ten years had passed since Dan had kissed her under the mistletoe.

Dan! God, where was Dan?

With her thoughts zinging from the missing major to the tiny head still cradled in her palm, Abby edged over an inch or two.

"You want to take over here, Doc?"

"Looks like you're doing fine."

He flashed a reassuring smile at Maria and said a few words in her native language. Between hard, swift pants, she darted a doubtful glance at the Santa Claus hat. A moment later, she scrunched her face again and grunted.

"Okay," the doc said cheerfully. "Here we go."

Long minutes later, the fuzzy-haired infant lay tucked in Maria's arms. The doc—Lieutenant Colonel Howie Donaldson by name—snapped his medical kit closed.

"Mother and son are both doing fine," he assured Abby, "but we don't want to leave them here alone. We'll take them back to base with us until the girl can get word to her family."

Abby didn't tell him Maria's only family in the area was a very young brother. She'd advise Father Dominic of the girl's situation when they reached the base. The priest could take the young mother and her son under his wing.

Abby had already decided to contribute what she could to their health and welfare. She'd contact her folks back in Philadelphia, too. They donated generously to several charities and international aid organizations. Maybe they could direct some aid to this war-torn corner of the world.

The heavily encumbered PJs reached for the stretcher. When their assault rifles bumped against the handles, Abby offered to relieve them of part of their burden.

"I can carry your weapons."

She slung one rifle over a shoulder and tucked the other in the crook of her arm. The grateful pararescuemen hefted the stretcher bearing mother and child. Still wearing his jaunty red hat, Colonel Donaldson led the way outside. Abby took a last look around and followed the small entourage into the bright, cold morning.

The Pave Hawk had set down in a cleared patch along the riverbank, about fifty yards beyond the Roman bridge. When Abby got her first good look at the bridge in the bright light of day, she winced. One stone support column still stood, but the little that remained of the arch soared into nothingness.

Deliberately, Abby closed her mind to the damage. She didn't have time to regret the loss of the ancient structure. Her thoughts now centered on Dan, and only on Dan.

"We need to go after Major Maxwell as soon as we have Maria and the baby on board," she said to the closest PJ, pitching her voice over the whine of the chopper's engines.

"Roger that, Captain."

"Any update on the irregulars that were spotted heading upriver last night?"

"Nothing firm, ma'am. The word we got is that they were locals who melted into the mountains."

Abby sincerely hoped that was the case. She was pretty sure Dan hadn't been forced to resort to diversionary tactics. She hadn't heard so much as an echo of gunfire throughout the long, endless night.

The thought had no sooner popped into her head than a sharp crack split the air. This one did *not* sound anything like ice breaking.

Abby, the doc and the PJs all dropped into an instinctive crouch. Maria jerked onto her side, trying frantically to shield her child.

When an answering volley rifled on the cold, clear air, Abby didn't hesitate.

"Get Maria and the baby aboard!"

Dropping one assault weapon, she ripped the other from her shoulder and took off at a dead run. The PJ at the front end of the stretcher shouted for the doc to take over for him. Scooping up the rifle Abby had dropped, he raced after her.

He'd either run track in college or was in a lot better shape than she was. He caught up with her before she reached the ruins of the bridge.

"Sounds like small-arms fire," he said grimly.

She nodded, her heart pumping pure adrenaline. "It's coming from the far end of the village."

"Better let me take the lead, ma'am."

Since he had already outpaced her, Abby didn't have an opportunity to cast a vote. She charged after him…and almost crashed into his back when he skidded to an abrupt halt.

Just ahead, a figure had bolted out of a side street and was pounding down the lane toward them. The PJ whipped his weapon up. Abby reached around his bulk and knocked the barrel down.

"That's the major! Major Maxwell!"

She might not have recognized him if not for the bomber jacket. Mud coated his hair, his face, the lower half of his body. He must have spent the night burrowed into a ditch.

"Get back to the helo," he shouted, racing toward them. "The rebels are behind me, and they're not feeling particularly friendly."

Abby didn't need any further encouragement. Wheeling, she pounded back the way she'd just come. The two men caught up with her in a few strides and flanked her for the last twenty yards or so.

The Pave Hawk's pilot saw them coming and powered up. The engine's whine increased to a shriek. The slowly spinning rotor blades picked up speed. Her hair whipping wildly around her face, Abby ducked under the blades, tossed the assault rifle through the open side hatch and reached for the hands waiting to haul her in.

Once aboard, she scooted out of the way. Her breath came in sharp, stabbing pants as she crouched beside Maria's stretcher. The girl pushed herself up on one elbow and hunched over her child, once again trying to shield it. Her dark eyes frantic, she watched with Abby as Dan and the rest of the crew piled aboard.

While the flight engineer scrambled into the cockpit and strapped himself into his seat, the gunner swept the village through the sights of his .50 caliber machine gun.

The two PJs took up positions on either side of the open hatch, their assault rifles leveled. Dan pitched to his feet, wrapped a fist around a cargo strap and prepared to add his firepower to theirs.

The Pave Hawk rocked on its skids, gathering power. Before it could lift off, one of the rebels burst from the same side street Dan had. As he charged toward the chopper, Abby formed an instant impression of curly black hair, a young, desperate face, and a metal tube that could only be a shoulder-held rocket launcher.

The chopper lifted. The young rebel skidded to a halt. Dan, the gunner, and the two PJs took aim.

"Hayir!"

Maria's piercing shriek carried clearly over the engine's roar. The cry jerked Abby's head around and startled the baby into a high, thin wail. Maria screamed again, her frantic eyes locked on the ragtag rebel.

"Hayir! Hayir!"

Abby had picked up enough Turkish to understand the word for *no*. Unfortunately, she didn't have sufficient vocabulary to assure the hysterical girl that the Pave Hawk crew wasn't about to let the guy launch a missile.

He gave every indication of intending to do just that, though. Crouching, he brought the tube to his shoulder. The men aboard the Pave Hawk took aim.

Sobbing now with sheer terror, Maria grabbed Abby's arm and levered herself upright.

"Nedim!"

Waving wildly, she shrieked the same word over and over again.

"Nedim! Nedim! Nedim! Nedim!"

By some miracle, her piercing cries reached the young rebel over the whap-whap of the rotor blades and roar of the engine. A look of utter astonishment crossed his face. Slowly, he lowered the launcher.

Chapter Five

Aboard the chopper, a desperate Maria yanked on Abby's arm. As the aircraft lifted off, the girl stabbed a finger at the young rebel on the ground and poured out a torrent of incomprehensible pleas.

"Do you know him?" Abby shouted. "Is he a friend?"

"Nedim," Maria sobbed. "Nedim."

She accompanied her cries with unmistakable gestures signaling she wanted the chopper to set back down again. Dubious, Abby yanked on the pant leg of the man closest to her. That happened to be Dan.

"Maria knows the kid," she yelled.

"What?"

"The rebel. Maria knows him. She wants us to go back for him."

Dan shot a look at the tears streaming down the girl's face. Maria stretched out a hand in supplication. By now the chopper was in the air and banking hard.

After an endless second or two, Dan got on the intercom to the cockpit. Abby couldn't hear what he said to the flight crew, but they brought the chopper back around and into a hover. Slowly, it descended toward almost the same spot it had lifted off from just moments ago.

Fifty yards away, a look of incredulous joy replaced the astonishment on the young rebel's face. The launcher hit the dirt. So did his backpack and all his other accoutrements. Then he was running headlong for the Pave Hawk.

The men at the hatch kept their weapons trained on him every step of the way. Jumping onto a skid, he flung himself through the hatch.

"Maria!"

He scuttled across the floorboards on his hands and knees. Like the girl, he was sobbing unrestrainedly. It didn't take a rocket scientist to see both were crying tears of joy.

Once the chopper had lifted clear of the village and was zooming through the mountains toward the Special Ops main base, the pilot got on the radio to request a translator.

The flight engineer came back with headsets for Abby, Dan and the boy crouched beside the stretcher, his hand gripping Maria's. Up close, he looked a little younger than Abby had first thought. He couldn't be more than seventeen or eighteen.

Tapping the kid on the shoulder, Dan showed him how to put on the headset. Abby listened to the three-sided conversation as the pilot rapped questions at the interpreter, who in turn fed them to the young rebel. The young man confirmed his name was, in fact, Nedim, and that he was from Maria's village. He'd been marched away at gunpoint and forced to fight with the rebels.

He was also, the translator informed his small audience, the father of Maria's baby.

Oooh, boy! Abby thought. She'd bet Father Dominic would have something to say about that.

Less than an hour later, the Pave Hawk touched down at the sprawling Turkish military facility that housed Dan's Special Operations squadron. An ambulance waited to transport Maria and her son to the base hospital. The doctor climbed in with her. So did Nedim.

He hunched beside Maria in the ambulance, gripping her hand as though he'd never let it go again. His face filled with wonder every time he glanced at his son. Maria had her heart in her eyes but turned a pleading look on Abby before the ambulance doors closed.

"I'll see you at the hospital," she assured the young mother through the translator. "I'll come as soon as I get cleaned up."

She and Dan stood shoulder to shoulder as the ambulance drove off, threading its way through the aircraft crowding the flight line. The Turkish flag with its new moon and single star set in a red field showed prominently on the tails of many of the craft, but Abby spotted the flags of at least a half dozen other nations. UN forces used the Turkish air base as a staging area to support their growing involvement in the peacekeeping efforts in neighboring Iraq.

Surveying the jumble of transports, gunships and surveillance aircraft, Abby appreciated more than ever the need for the forward operating location she and her team had almost finished laying out. The site would relieve some of the overcrowding and move a detachment of Dan's Special Ops squadron closer to the action.

"You said you wanted to get cleaned up." His deep

voice rumbled close to Abby's ear, breaking into her thoughts. "My squadron is hard-quartered in a hotel just off base. You can shower there before we head back up to the site."

Joy leaped through her veins. "Are we talking a real shower? Hot water? Steam?"

"The works," he confirmed, grinning.

"Lead the way!"

After arranging a flight to ferry them back to the site later that afternoon, Dan did just that.

The hotel's exterior was strictly utilitarian, but its interior boasted the incredibly diverse architectural elements of a country that formed the bridge between Europe and the Far East. Abby followed Dan through the lobby, craning her neck to take in the brilliant Byzantine mosaics, splashing Mediterranean fountains and marble columns topped by fanciful capitals, imposts and architraves.

The guests at the hotel represented the same mix of East and West. Men in business suits mingled with associates in the more traditional baggy pants, collarless shirt and richly embroidered vests seen throughout Turkey. Abby spotted several other women in uniform, a number in smart dresses and several wearing the ornate headdress decorated with gold coins that indicated their marital status, wealth and standing in their clan. She and Dan raised a few brows as they made their way to the elevators. Dried mud still coated his hair and face. After helping deliver a baby, Abby didn't want to *think* about what coated hers.

"Oh, look!"

She stopped in her tracks, transfixed by the sight of a window displaying an array of stuffed toys. Although the

Christian Turks celebrated the feast of Christmas, the hotel shops owned by those of other faiths were open and doing a thriving business.

Delighted, Abby pointed to a large stuffed pony with a bright red bow tied around its neck. "I *have* to buy that for the baby."

"Let me guess." Laughter rumbled in Dan's chest. "A present from the Chargin' Charlies of Red Horse."

"You got it."

Since she didn't have any Turkish lira on her, he charged the stuffed animal to his room.

Abby, Dan and the pony took the elevator to the sixth floor, most of which was occupied by personnel from Dan's Special Ops unit. They passed a number of people in the corridor. Several did a double take when they recognized Major Maxwell under his layers of dirt. All wanted to know the scoop on the action up at the forward site.

"I'll give you a full report," Dan promised. "Later."

Grasping Abby's elbow, he steered her to the room at the end of the hall. She stepped inside and sighed. After eight days of living, sleeping and working out of tents, it was heaven to sink her boot soles into a thick Turkish carpet and look out through real glass windows.

"I'll give you first dibs on the shower," Dan offered magnanimously.

Abby wasn't about to argue. Depositing the pony on the sofa, she shed her layers on the way to the bathroom. Stocking cap, field jacket and BDU shirt all hit the floor. Her boots, pants and long johns came off inside the bathroom. Grimacing at the thought of putting them back on after her shower, she twisted the knob to full blast.

Within moments, steam billowed from the glass stall. A few moments more, and Abby had died and gone to heaven.

She hogged the shower until her conscience started to ping at her. Sure she'd never experience anything as glorious as that hot water again, Abby wrapped herself in an oversize Turkish towel and poked through the personal items on the shelf below the steamed-up mirror. To her delight, she discovered a spare toothbrush still in its plastic wrapping.

Abby appropriated it without a qualm. Scrubbed, shampooed and reveling in the taste of Crest, she gathered her scattered clothing and left the steamy bathroom.

"It's all yours."

Dan's glance made a quick trip from her wet hair to her bare feet and back up again. His mouth opened, snapped shut. That interesting little muscle at the side of his jaw began to twitch.

Abby noted the twitch with a raised brow. Her wet hair straggled down her back. She hadn't come close to anything resembling makeup in eight days. The thick towel covered her from her neck to her knees. Yet she suddenly felt naked and exposed.

And seductively, erotically female.

Her skin heated everywhere Dan's glance touched. Already flushed from her shower, she started to sizzle under the towel. She was seriously considering dropping it when Dan took one step toward her. Only one.

To her immense disappointment, he stopped and scraped a hand over his jaw. Little flakes of dried mud drifted to the carpet.

"Don't go away," he ordered, his voice husky. "I'll be right back."

Abby wasn't going anywhere. She couldn't have moved if she wanted to. Her breath seemed to have deserted her and every one of her muscles had coiled tight.

Gulping, she stood in the center of the room. Her glance shifted to the bed. To the tall, curtained wardrobe where Dan's spare uniforms hung. To the chair where she'd deposited the stuffed pony.

A slow smile tugged at her lips.

Dan set a new world record for showering, shaving and scraping twenty-plus hours of fuzz off his teeth.

He hadn't pulled in a full breath since Abby had strolled out of the bathroom wearing nothing but a smile and a Turkish towel. One glimpse of her bare shoulders and long, slender legs had pooled his entire blood supply below his waist. He'd gone into the shower hard and aching and almost doubled over with wanting her. He'd come out the same way. As he hitched a towel around his hips, he retained just enough sense to know what he had in mind was crazy—for a whole lot of reasons.

One, the air force tended to take a dim view of field-grade officers jumping junior officers' bones. He rationalized that problem away by the fact that Abby wasn't in his chain of command.

Two, they only had a couple of hours until they had to get back to the flight line. Less, if they wanted to swing by the hospital to see Maria and the baby. What Dan wanted to do with and to Captain Abigail Trent would take all night. Hell, all week!

Three, there was the matter of that high-priced architect back in Philadelphia. Abby said she'd told him not to wait, but the man would be a fool to do anything else.

Dan was beginning to suspect a woman like Abby Trent only came along once in a lifetime.

When he went into the bedroom, that suspicion turned to rock-hard certainty.

She was waiting for him, still wearing the towel, but she'd added to it. A bright red ribbon circled her neck. The bow fluffed just under her chin.

Laughing at his expression of comical delight, Abby strolled across the room. Her green eyes danced as she rose up on tiptoe and hooked her wrists behind his neck.

"Merry Christmas, Major."

His mouth curved. His arms went around her. His big hands cupped her bottom.

"Back at you, Captain."

When his mouth came down on hers, a fierce, urgent need slammed into Abby. There was nothing polite about it, nothing coy. She wanted his touch, his teeth, his tongue, with the same greedy hunger he wanted hers.

All too soon, even that wasn't enough. Her hands roamed his damp back. His did the same on hers. The towels disappeared, and the heat surged.

Abby was on fire when he scooped her into his arms and headed for the bed. Impatient when he made a detour to the wardrobe and rooted around in one of his uniform pockets. Amused when he fished out a condom.

"Remind me again," she said on a sputter of laughter. "What's the motto of Air Force Special Ops?"

His teeth flashed in a wicked grin. "Anytime, Anywhere, sweetheart. Anytime, Anywhere."

When they tumbled to the bed in a tangle of arms and legs and still-damp bodies, Dan fully intended to take his time with her. He'd fantasized about getting Abby Trent naked and under him too many times in the past week to rush this moment.

He'd reckoned without the smooth, slick satin of her skin, however. Not to mention her breathless little gasp when he took her nipple between his teeth. And when her eager palm closed around him, Dan abandoned any attempt at control.

Kneeing Abby's legs apart, he positioned himself between her thighs and thrust home. She welcomed him with a joyous gasp.

Dan's last thought, while he could still think at all, was that he would remember this Christmas for a long, long time.

When Dan and Abby arrived at the hospital, he still wore a silly grin and she carried the stuffed animal tucked under her arm. To his acute disappointment, she'd insisted on retying the red bow around the pony's neck.

Dan himself lugged the giant-size basket of infant clothing, blankets and disposable diapers the hotel concierge had hastily scrounged up for the baby. He was in a downright mellow and distinctly holiday mood until they reached the maternity ward.

The doctor who'd helped deliver her baby walked out through the swinging ward doors just as Dan and Abby prepared to walk in. The colonel's face was a study in frustration.

"There you are," he exclaimed when he spotted them. "I was just going to try to find you."

"Is there a problem?" Abby asked sharply.

"Yes."

"Is it the baby? Or Maria? Are they okay?"

"They're both fine," the colonel assured her. "But, well…"

He raked a hand through his hair. His Santa Claus hat, she noted distractedly, was stuffed half in and half out of his pants pocket. The fluffy white pom-pom at its tip looked incongruous against his black-and-green camouflage battle fatigues.

"This is a Turkish air force hospital," he explained. "We just use their facilities. I had to notify the hospital commander when I brought Maria and the baby in. He in turn was required to notify the civil authorities."

"And?"

"And they're wanting to know what name to put on the child's birth certificate. They're also wanting to know if Maria is married."

Abby's stomach did a sudden flip-flop. In keeping with Turkey's rich heritage, its people were a mix of East and West, European and Arab, Christian and Muslim. She didn't know what stigma might attach to an unmarried girl who gave birth in this country. She only hoped the consequences weren't as severe as in some Arab nations, where the women could be tried as adulterers and stoned to death.

"What did Maria tell the authorities?" she asked the doctor anxiously.

"Nothing yet. I stalled them by saying I didn't feel she was strong enough to talk to them."

Abby thought for a moment. She was darned if she was going to let some bureaucrat brand either Maria or her baby as outcasts. Or worse.

"Is Nedim with her?"

"Yes."

"What about a translator? Do you have one handy?"

"I can round one up."

"Good! We'll meet you inside."

Chin set, she pushed through the swinging doors. If Maria's wild shriek when she spotted Nedim was any indication, the girl was in love with him. His bemused expression when he'd climbed into the ambulance with her indicated the feeling was mutual. Abby figured Father Dominic could take it from there. First, though, she had to make sure the young couple wanted a Christmas wedding.

They did. They most definitely did.

Nedim looked too young to shoulder the responsibility of a family. According to the translator, however, he was nineteen, had inherited a patch of a farm from his grandfather and was willing to pay any dowry demanded by his bride or her father, when he returned. If he did not...

The grave, solemn young man squared his shoulders. He would provide for Maria, Constantine and the son that God had blessed them with.

When asked her druthers, Maria poured out a torrent of passionate assurances. She'd loved Nedim all her life. They'd grown up together. She'd turned to him when her father was taken and wept a thousand tears when Nedim, too, was marched off at gunpoint.

At which point she burst into sobs and added considerably to the tally. Her cries woke the baby tucked in the crook of her arm. He scrunched his face until it went beet red. His tiny fists beat the air. Opening his rosebud mouth, he let loose with a high, reedy wail.

"Wow," Dan said admiringly. "That's some set of lungs the kid's got."

Instantly alarmed, Maria and Nedim cooed and clucked to their child. When his wails continued unabated, Abby thrust the stuffed pony in Nedim's hands.

"Try this."

Popping his tongue to make the sound of a trot, the young rebel jounced the pony along the bedrail. The baby's fists stilled. His face unscrunched. His cloudy brown eyes weren't focused, but he responded to the noise and the moving blur with hiccupping silence.

"Well, whaddaya know," Abby said smugly. "Chargin' Charlie to the rescue again."

"We've got a chopper waiting to take us back to the site," Dan reminded her in a drawl. "If we're going to have a wedding here, we'd better get with it."

"Right. My radio won't transmit back to the site from here. We'll have to get your Special Ops command center to patch me through."

"No problem."

Within moments, Abby had Sergeant Davis on the link.

"Yo, Cap! Hear tell you've had quite a Christmas."

Heat flamed in Abby's cheeks until she realized he was referring to the bridge, the rebels and the baby. *Not* her recent tussle between the sheets.

"It's been interesting," she admitted. "I need you to drive down to the village and find Father Dominic. Like fast."

"Father D? He's right here. He came up to check on you and the maj and the girl."

"Great! Put him on the horn."

Father Dominic grasped the gravity of the situation at once, but it took the combined efforts of Abby, Maria and Nedim to convince him to conduct a wedding ceremony via satellite.

Abby and the translator acted as witnesses. Dan stood as Nedim's best man, or what they explained was the rough equivalent. Once Father Dominic blessed the couple, a relieved Doc Donaldson produced the birth certificate.

"All right! Father's name?"

Prompted by the interpreter, Nedim spelled his first and last names.

"Mother's name?"

"Maria," the girl whispered, blushing when she added her new family name.

"And the baby?"

The newlyweds put their heads together. After a whispered consultation that went on for some minutes, Nedim shrugged and Maria spoke a few, shy sentences.

"She says she wants to give the baby your name," the translator informed Abby.

"No kidding?"

An unexpected lump formed in her throat. She wouldn't hang a label like Abigail on the poor boy, but the shortened version would work just fine. Choking down the lump, she spelled it out for the doctor.

"That's A-b-i."

"Ab-i," Maria echoed softly, drawing a knuckle down her son's cheek.

"Ab-i," Nedim repeated, appearing pleased with the choice.

Dan joined in the chorus. His blue eyes held a special glint as he tipped her a salute.

"Nice goin', Ab-i."

Chapter Six

Abby and Dan arrived back at the site late Christmas afternoon. Despite the knuckle-cracking events of the past twenty-four hours, she felt revived and rejuvenated. The impromptu wedding, naming the baby and the full-course turkey dinner Dan insisted they down at the Special Ops mess hall before jumping aboard the chopper had put a decided spring in Abby's step.

Ha! Who was she kidding? As she ducked under the rotor blades and waved to the aircrew, she knew darned well she owed most of that bounce to that incredible session in Dan's hotel room. The question whizzing around in her mind now was how they would revert to their previous, all-business, let's-get-the-job-done personas now they were back on-site.

Dan, apparently, had no problem with the transition. Hefting the gear bag he'd hauled back with him, he headed for the tent he shared with the Red Horse crew.

"I'll dump this and meet you in the operations tent. We might need to revise the layout for the mobile-aircraft arresting systems based on the new deployment information I got back at base."

"First things first," Abby said crisply. "I asked Father Dominic to stand by until we returned to the site, remember? He's going to conduct a nondenominational service for the troops."

Abby knew the members of her sixteen-person team regarded the religious significance of the holiday in individual and very private ways. She wasn't about to impose her beliefs on any of them, but it was her duty as officer in charge to offer those who wanted it the opportunity to attend services on this of all days.

"I'll meet you in the ops tent *after* the service. Unless, of course, you'd like to join us," she tacked on politely.

Dan got the message. They were back on Abby's turf. She was responsible for the morale and welfare of her troops. He liked that she didn't hesitate to exercise her authority on their behalf. He liked even more the way the wind whipped color into her cheeks and ruffled the stray strands of her fiery hair. Clenching his fists against the memory of thrusting his hands through her wet, silky mane, Dan nodded.

"Good enough. Father Dominic first, the mobile-arresting systems second."

Buoyed by the easy victory, Abby took a moment to savor it. She hugged her arms against the cold and turned in a slow circle. The flat plain they'd surveyed and sited for the Special Ops forward operating element lay glinting under its thin coat of frost. The mountains surrounding it loomed stark and formidable against the sky.

Slowly, she completed the circle. Eyes narrowing, she tracked the course of the ice-crusted river that had carved the pass through the mountains untold millennia ago.

There, far below, were the scattered ruins of the village that straddled the river. And the ruins of the bridge.

With a wry smile, Abby eyed the one remaining stone column and the arch that now soared into empty air. The engineer in her ached to restore the ancient structure to its former permanence and beauty. The floating ribbon bridge she hoped to convince headquarters to send in with the second-echelon Red Horse team was functional, but it was also temporary.

Maybe one day, she thought. When she decided what the heck she was going to do with the rest of her life.

A piece of the puzzle dropped into place when she entered the mess tent and received a rousing welcome from her team. Most of them were there. Sergeant Davis. Sergeant Oakes. Senior Airman Joyce Carmichael. Everyone except the troop detailed to stand guard duty and the one manning the communications equipment.

A surge of emotion rushed through Abby. As she returned their greetings and filled them in on the details about Maria and the baby, she knew she was home.

Another piece of the puzzle dropped into place later that evening.

Exhaustion had pretty much wiped out Abby's euphoria over the incredible events of the day and the peace she'd derived from Father Dominic's simple, moving service. Her tail was definitely dragging when she made her way to the operations tent.

Dan was waiting for her, his laptop open and booted up. "Headquarters is testing a new mobile emergency arresting system as we speak," he said by way of greeting. "They gave me the specs on the new system and want to know if we can employ it at this site."

"That depends. Does it need to be installed on concrete pads, below grade or in semi-pits?"

"This one is trailer mounted, air-transportable to remote locations, and installed with earth anchors in an expeditionary configuration."

"Well, that makes things easier."

Her interest piqued, Abby peered over his shoulder. The schematic on the screen showed a retractable steel cable housed in a compact casing. According to the specs, the cable could stop anything up to and including a jumbo jet. Abby seriously doubted any jumbo jets would be touching down at this remote mountain site, but it was nice to know they could stop one if it did.

"I'll have to feed the specs into my site layout plan," she told Dan, "but I don't see any problem installing the new system here."

"Good. When you're done, I'll forward your assessment to my headquarters. They can coordinate with yours."

He popped the CD containing the specs out of his computer and passed it to Abby. Smiling, she tapped it against her closed fist. "Looks like Santa brought you Special Ops pilots a new toy for Christmas."

Dan tipped his chair back. He speared a glance at the communications tech hunched over the console on the far side of the tent and dropped his voice to a low growl.

"Santa already delivered one helluva present to this particular Special Ops pilot."

Abby's smile slipped. She'd had time to think about what had happened between them earlier. Not a lot of time, to be sure, but enough to realize that world-class sex did not a relationship make. Nor did different goals, separate careers and long-distance phone calls.

"Yes, well, we need to talk about this afternoon."

Dan hooked a brow at her reserved tone. Shutting down his laptop, he snagged his bomber jacket from the back of his chair. "You're right. We do. Let's take it outside."

Swallowing a sigh, Abby followed him into the frigid night. It was the only place they could find some privacy, but she'd bet her toes were beginning to believe she'd condemned them to a permanent state of icy numbness. Once she and Dan stood under the brilliant canopy of stars, though, she forgot her toes. She forgot everything but the strong, square line of his jaw and the way the skin at the corners of his eyes crinkled when he smiled down at her.

"About this afternoon…?" he prompted after several moments of silence.

"Right. This afternoon." She cleared her throat. "That hour in your hotel room. It was, uh, great."

It was better than great. It was the most spectacular hour of Abby's life. No sense letting the man's ego slip completely out of control, though.

Her deliberate tactics didn't work. Hooking his thumbs in his jacket pockets, Dan rocked back on his boot heels. His mouth kicked up in a smug, male grin.

"Yeah, it was."

"The thing is, we both got caught up in the rush of the moment."

"We got caught up in something," he agreed, his eyes glinting.

"It was this whole Christmas thing. You know, the holiday spirit, the mistletoe."

"Let's not forget the bridge collapsing under us," he put in. "That certainly added to the rush."

"And Maria and the baby. I'm glad you understand. That way you won't get nervous when I tell you I've decided to stay in the reserves."

The grin fell off his face. "What?"

"I'm going to tell my boss I want that promotion he offered me, along with command of a Red Horse Two unit."

"When did you decide that?"

"A little while ago."

Actually, the urge to stay in uniform had been creeping up on her for weeks. She'd just needed a push to recognize it.

He cocked his head, studying her through the screen of his lashes. "And your decision to stay in the reserves would make me nervous because…?"

"Because there's a chance my boss will put me in command of the second-echelon unit coming in here."

She sensed rather than saw a sudden quickening in his expression. His voice was level, though, when he acknowledged the possibility.

"Putting you in charge of the RH-2 would make sense. You know the area. You did all the prep work."

"It would also mean we'll both be on-site for several more weeks, maybe months. If so, we can't… We won't… That is, I don't…"

His eyes narrowed. "Spit it out, Abby. You don't what?"

"Okay, here's the deal. I don't want you to think what happened between us this afternoon in any way obligates you to a repeat performance at some unspecified date in the future."

A stark silence followed. Ten seconds. Twenty. Abby was wishing to heck he would say something, *anything,* when he blew out a ragged breath.

"Do you have any idea how hard it is for me to keep my hands in my pockets right now?"

Her heart skipped a couple beats. "No. Tell me."

"Let me put it this way. *If* we weren't at a remote site

with no privacy and *if* you didn't have to set an example for your troops and *if* I didn't respect the hell out of you as both an officer and an engineer…"

"Yes?"

"I'd be kissing you senseless right now."

"You would?"

"Yeah," he drawled, "I would."

"Well…"

Abby put her neat, precise engineer's mind to work on the problem.

"We'll finish the site prep in the next couple days," she reminded him. "*If* my boss approves my extension and *if* I get command of the RH-2, I'll have to fly back to base to put together my team and inspect the prepackaged, transportable construction kits. You, I'm guessing, will have to coordinate the follow-on deployment schedule for your unit."

"That's right."

"With any luck, we might just be able to arrange a little, ah, down time."

Dan's mouth curved. There was no "might" about it. Not in his mind.

"I'm sure we can work something out."

He had to touch her. Just a touch.

Abandoning his pockets, he drew the back of a knuckle across her cheek. Her skin was like cold, smooth marble. The reaction it generated in his gut was hot and raw and jagged. Dan had a feeling he'd be experiencing the same sensation on a regular basis for the next few weeks or months.

Or years.

A sudden blast of music burst from the mess tent. It was another rousing hip-hop rendition, this one of "Jingle Bells." Everyone in the tent joined in. The night was alive with song and bright, glittering stars and the woman who smiled up at him.

"Merry Christmas, Dan."

"Merry Christmas, Ab-i."

Epilogue

One year later

Abby shivered in her winter-white wool coat and tucked her hands in the fur muff that matched her jaunty, Cossack-style hat. The fleece-lined coat was warmer than the field jacket she wore when she pulled her reserve tours, but still no match for the fierce wind whipping down through the mountain pass.

She couldn't believe a whole year had passed since the last time she'd stood beside the ruins of the Roman bridge. Twelve crazy, whirlwind, fantastic months.

She'd extended her tour with the reserves and been given command of an RH-2. In that capacity, she'd directed the efforts of the team sent in to lay down the tents, kitchens, showers, latrines and electrical power generation for a seven-hundred-person encampment on the plain high above where she now stood. Her team had also set up portable aircraft hangars, airfield lighting systems, maintenance facilities and the new aircraft-arresting system Dan's unit put into service.

Their mission complete, Abby's RH-2 unit had rotated back to the States and stood down. After almost two years on continuous active duty, she'd returned to inactive reserve status. She now trained with her unit every month, engaged regularly in real-world exercises and was ready to pack up and deploy on sixteen-hour notice to any hot spot on the planet.

When not in uniform, she worked at her civilian job. Her *new* civilian job. She now consulted as a civilian engineer and technical advisor for the UNESCO World Heritage Organization. As such, she was actively involved in preserving the treasures of both the modern and ancient world. In the past six months, she'd consulted on such awesome projects as Angkor Wat in Cambodia and the walled city of Baku, in Azerbaijan. Soon, very soon, she would see work begin on this very bridge.

Happiness hummed through her at the thought. Life was good. She was holding down two jobs, both of which she loved. Being employed on a freelance basis gave her the flexibility to work around her reserve duties and to move her base of operations wherever she desired. She'd be relocating to Florida next month—just about the time newly promoted Lieutenant Colonel Dan Maxwell began a three-year tour of duty at Special Operations Command Headquarters at Hurlburt Field, in the Florida panhandle.

Smiling, Abby tugged her left hand from the warmth of the muff and admired the sparkling solitaire on her ring finger.

Life was *very* good.

"Hey! Ab-i!"

The shout whipped her head around. Dan stood in the shelter of the church, hefting her year-old namesake in the crook of his arm. With him were a glowing Maria, Nedim,

Constantine, Father Dominic and the villagers who'd returned to their homes once the large contingent of Americans had moved into the area.

Abby's parents were there, too. They'd flown over for the occasion, as had her sister, her brothers-in-law, and her two wide-eyed nieces. She couldn't very well have a Christmas wedding without her family in attendance.

With a last glance at the Roman bridge, she picked her way over the cobbles to the church where Father Dominic would conduct the wedding ceremony. Dan waited for her on the steps. Tall and incredibly handsome in his dress uniform, he smiled as the wind ruffled his dark hair and put blades of color in his lean cheeks.

Her heart singing, Abby laid her hand in his.

THE WINGMAN'S ANGEL

Catherine Mann

To my husband, Lieutenant Colonel Robert Mann, USAF.
Thank you for gifting me with my very
own happily ever after. I love you!

To Gracie Bailey, a treasured friend and fan
who truly embodies the holiday spirit of giving.

To my editor Melissa Jeglinski and my agent
Barbara Collins Rosenberg. Thank you for
making my holiday wish for a novella come true.
Merry Christmas and Happy Chanukah!

My apologies to the "Cool School" for any liberties I've
taken with their Arctic Survival Training Course.
Many thanks for lending your most awesome training ground
for my story—and for all you do to keep
our armed service members alive in
winter survival emergencies.

Chapter One

Mukluks planted on the flight deck, Lieutenant Colonel Joshua "Bud" Rosen, USAF, prepped to hurtle from the hovering helicopter onto the arctic tundra.

Over the years he'd been shot at by MiG-29s, pulled mind-blowing G-forces in his F-15E Strike Eagle, launched missiles on targets no bigger than a blip on his radar. But never had he faced anything more terror-inducing than this imminent mission. And he faced a jump of only five feet.

Of course, the knot in his gut had nothing to do with the snowcaps below and everything to do with his assigned partner.

Josh braced in the open door of the Army's Blackhawk helicopter, bitter winds howling. Chopper blades stirred a cloudy void waiting to swallow him, and his partner as well. Just the two of them. Alone. Not at all how he'd planned to spend the holiday season with her.

His hands fisted inside his gloves. Only twenty-four more hours left of the Air Force's five-day Arctic Survival Training—"The Cool School."

Before assuming his newly appointed position as second in command of the Alaska-based F-15E squadron, he needed to complete the extreme weather survival course. Just his luck, his teammate for the final land navigation exercise was none other than his soon-to-be ex-wife, Captain Alicia Renshaw-Rosen.

Freezing his ass off was the least of his worries.

His spouse of less than six months stood beside him in the gaping portal, ready to leap into this mock-up of a crash-survival scenario. Her feathery short blond hair stayed hidden beneath the fur-trimmed parka, only a small oval of weather-chapped skin visible, but enough to assure him her pert nose wasn't sporting its habitual smile-scrunch. Then she flipped her snow goggles down, shielding even more of her face from sight.

A five-foot-six dynamo, his pilot wife packed curves and confidence even layers of drab, green cold-weather gear couldn't disguise. Not that he would ever see her strip away her uniform again, and damn but that grieved him as much as the loss of her uninhibited laugh in his life.

How ironic that once they'd finally received a joint assignment to Alaska they'd split before unpacking even half their boxes.

"Go!" called the helicopter crew chief. "Go! Go!"

The repeated words snapped Josh back to the present. Finally, action. Screw musing.

He plunged into the alabaster void. Frigid winds locked around him, burned through layers of protective clothing, froze a path to his lungs.

"Ooof." Boots slamming to hard-packed snow, he hit the ground, rolled to his side to absorb the landing shock, a helluva lot less than if he'd actually punched out of his fighter with a parachute.

"Alicia?" he shouted over the growl of the hovering

Blackhawk. He shoved to his feet and crunched through the caked tundra.

"Here and in one piece." She scrambled up through the swirling powder. "Let's haul butt."

Side by side, they trudged at a molasses-speed run toward the tree line, clearing the area before the departing Blackhawk kicked up a fresh blizzard. Ten yards later he dropped to his knees beside Alicia, aircraft behind them. He covered his face while she mirrored his actions. The chop, chop, chop of the helicopter blades swelled, faster. Wind beat his back. A flurry of white blinded him. Howling winds and sheets of ice dominated his senses.

So why could he still hear Alicia breathing beside him?

Would it suck this bad all day, with him completely aware of her every breath? Talk about a never-ending afternoon.

Only one day past the winter solstice, the actual daylight hours would be short, about four hours of full sun plus the haze of dawn and dusk. But every minute stretched before him twice as long. Hell, the past days "camping" with her and their classmates had already stretched tension to a frozen thread.

Slowly, order was restored in the outside world at least. Snow settled. Quiet descended.

Standing, he took his bearings—tree line to his left, iced spruce and stark birches. Snowcapped mountains from the Alaska Range tipped the horizon. They faced a four-hour walk at most before dusk. Thank God the overnight portion of the newly implemented land navigation exercise had been scratched due to an incoming storm.

He extended a hand—which she ignored to rise on her own. Alicia swooped her bulky mitten-gloves over her parka to dust snow free. And *poof.* Just that fast an image of her magnificently and illogically naked in the drifts popped to mind. His very own voluptuous snow angel wore nothing but her short blond hair all whispery around her face, frost flakes glistening on her eyelashes and…elsewhere.

"C-crap," Alicia chattered. "It's c-cold out here."

Not where he was standing.

Batting along the fur ringing her hood, she knocked off persistent ice. She paused midswipe, angling her head his way.

"What's wrong?" She arched around to check behind her. "Did I drop something in the jump?"

Just all her clothes in his imagination. "You've got snow on your nose there."

"Oh. Thanks." She dabbed at her face. Staying dry was critical. Getting wet could equate to death out here.

Merry Christmas.

Happy Hanukkah.

Bah, humbug.

A grin twitched, cracking along his frozen face already dry and raw from days of exposure during training. Chuckles rumbled, drawing icy air into his lungs. He laughed, anyway. Long. Hard. Echoing through the pines. Why not? His personal life was so screwed up, there was nothing left to do but laugh.

Alicia unhooked her snowshoes from her gear and began fitting them to her mukluks. "Nice to know I amuse you."

"Well that's an egocentric thought. What makes you think I'm laughing at you?" He was too busy laughing at himself for panting after this woman until even sub-zero weather and an impending divorce couldn't cool him.

"Don't see anyone else around."

Like he needed reminding of that. Damn. He definitely wanted to bail out of more than an aircraft right now.

But this course was too important to half-ass. A military flyer's life consisted of constant refresher training, such as annual updates on his initial combat and water-survival classes. Compared to three weeks of eating bugs in the wilderness or being dumped alone in a shark-infested bay for a full day, this should be a piece of cake.

Keep it light. Easy. Pretend they hadn't ripped each other's hearts out.

Straightening, Alicia stomped her feet to test the fit of her snowshoes. "Let's not waste energy talking. We need to focus on finding the pickup point before those clouds overhead unload. I just want to sleep, eat, wake up. Get home in time to call my family and wish them merry Christmas."

"No problem. You'll be in your own bed by tomorrow night, the twenty-third. Plenty of time." Hanukkah had already passed for him, spent unpacking in his new office before heading back to his solitary bed at the BOQ—bachelor officer's quarters.

Reaching inside his parka, he tugged his compass from his survival vest. "We'll take a heading of one five zero."

Her brow scrunched in a frown. "But the pickup point is one nine zero."

He set his teeth. "Are you arguing with a navigator?"

"I thought you back seaters preferred to be called wizzos."

"Technicality." No matter what they called it, he enjoyed the hell out of his job as an F-15E wizzo—WSO, Weapons Systems Officer. Pilots rowed the boat while WSOs shot the ducks. And he knew his stuff. "If Chris Columbus had me with him, he would have known he wasn't in India."

"Goody for you. But the pickup point at the river is still one nine zero." His pilot wife's huffing breaths grew whiter, faster, fuller.

Ah, hell. So much for keeping things light and easy. She was getting fired up, which would fire him up with neither of them standing a chance of finding an outlet. "You know you're arguing just to argue."

"Could be." She flicked her goggles up to her forehead, pinning him with coffee-brown eyes. "But how about you explain your reasoning to me, anyway."

He wasn't used to people questioning him. Hell, he was a freaking genius after all. Literally. Just ask Mensa.

But Alicia always questioned him, something he actually respected most of the time. Today, the supply line ran short on patience. "The pickup point's on a river, right? If we navigate directly to one nine zero and step as much as one degree off, we'll miss the point. Problem is when we do hit the river, we won't know whether to turn left or right. But if we aim distinctly to the left of the pickup point, when we hit the river—"

"We'll know to turn right and follow the shore."

"Exactly." His irritation eased. Yeah, now he remembered why he didn't mind her questioning him. She always could follow his logic. She kept him on his toes, sharpened his thoughts, giving the world an edge he missed with others. "We'll walk a little farther my way, but we won't risk getting lost."

"Okay, Magellan, you've made your point." Bending, she tugged the bulky green pants over her mukluks, yanking the ankle zipper a final inch.

"Good." He stomped his snowshoes once, twice, testing the give of the ground. "Time to move out and we'll have you home in time for pumpkin pie."

He started toward the tree line, which would hopefully break the wind. When Alicia made those calls to her father, brother, sister, would she tell them about the breakup? He'd likely spend Christmas at the squadron, wading through stacks of paperwork in the silence. With tense crap shaking down in Cantou, he itched to be in his new office, anyway. Cantou might be a tiny-ass country over in Asia, but it harbored numerous terrorist-training camps.

Cantou's deposed dictator was still on the run, with powerful ties and a hunger for nukes. Recent CIA intelligence indicated the nutcase's minions were smuggling uranium out of the U.S. and Russia.

Thoughts of Cantou brought him too quickly back to memories of Alicia. A year and a half ago, they'd met flying missions in the Cantou Conflict, ousting that dictator. Alicia had strutted into the Officer's Club bar on her first day at Kunsan Air Base in Korea. That walk of hers managed to be cocky and sexy all at once, knocking him flat on his butt.

Watching her trudge ahead now, he wondered how she managed a strut even in snowshoes. It boggled the mind and the laws of physics.

A half hour later after endless ready-to-explode-his-head tension, he needed a distraction. Well, one other than thinking of her every other second while she ignored the hell out of him.

How freaking inconvenient that even when the love left, attraction still clung with tenacious claws that would put a polar bear to shame. "Damned boring, just walking, no talking."

He really hated being bored. Almost as much as he disliked being ignored by this woman when he couldn't stop snow-angel fantasies.

"Solve quadratic equations in your head," she answered without missing a step.

That might work. He'd done it often enough in grad school at sixteen, caught in the middle of keg parties with hot co-eds all too old for him.

By eighteen, he'd completed a master's degree, worked at NASA while earning a Ph.D. until he was old enough to enter Air Force flight training at twenty-one. NASA, navigator training and a below-the-zone promotion had brought plenty of women in his path. He'd saved the equations for work then.

Here he was, thirty-five years old and back to equations. Damn. "Excellent suggestion. Something like calculating the clamp pressure required from my teeth to rip off your panties should keep me occupied."

Ignore *that,* Renshaw.

She stopped. Turned with a grace that defied those damned snowshoes. Nailed him with a look frostier than the icicles spiking from the trees. "Thong or French cut? Cotton or satin?"

Oh, yeah. Now they were talking. "Obviously what you're wearing today." He swept aside a branch weighted low by snow, startling an artic hare from the underbrush. "Why would I care about anything else? If you're feeling shy about sharing first, allow me. I'm wearing Scooby-Doo boxers with a holiday theme since Scooby's sporting a Santa hat. Granted, they aren't very military-looking, but the regs only require that while in flight I wear a hundred-percent cotton."

"Thanks for enlightening me, but I'm so not interested in your Scooby snack right now."

Yeah, he pretty much got the message on that one loud and clear. Not for the first time he wondered about that dude in her past, the one she'd almost married except he'd died first. What secret had the poor bastard carried to his grave about understanding this woman?

"Ouch." Josh thumped his chest with his oversize arctic gloves. "You know how to wound a guy. But I recover fast.

Now, back to *your* underwear. I do believe I've solved the mystery."

"Oh, goody. And how did you manage that?"

"Elementary, my dear Renshaw. Since we just finished slipping the surly bonds of earth in an aerospace vehicle owned by the Department of Defense, I deduce, as per regulation, your undergarments are one-hundred-percent cotton."

Damn, it had been a long four days in the survival class with her, but at least they hadn't been alone together—until now. Stupid though it may be, he wanted some kind of reaction from her. "As far as what design? While you do have the butt for a thong, I'm going to guess necessity overcame fashion and you opted for something a little more practical."

Sighing, she hitched her hands on her hips. "You know, I really hate you sometimes. If only your brain and shoulders weren't so hot."

"You like my…brain?"

"Fine," she snapped. "You win. You want to talk? Let's discuss who gets what when we split up the household goods."

His humor faded faster than his breath puffing vapors into the sub-zero air. "One in four decisions made while cold will be incorrect, my love."

All the more reason he shouldn't be thinking about sex.

His traitorous Scooby snack throbbed, anyway. Good God, it was cold as hell. Just what he needed, a frozen erection.

"Don't call me that." Her chin trembled. From anger? Or something softer?

"Call you what?"

"My love."

"Why not? You can call me all sorts of things—Josh, Colonel, Bud, Rosen. Jerk. Take your pick. Meanwhile, I have…" He quirked his gaze up to the murky sky, ticking through numbers on his fingers. "Seventeen more days until our appointment with the attorney to start the process whereby we officially begin making you no longer 'my love.'"

After streaming a long cloudy exhale ahead of her, she ignored him. No surprise. He deserved her disdain. He was being an ass and he knew it.

He should shut up, except damn it all, he was working to survive on a lot of levels today. Must be the whole holiday season dragging him down. Since a gunman's siege at his college right in the middle of December semester exams, he dreaded this time of year. He'd hoped to make happier memories with Alicia in front of a fireplace with a bottle of merlot, some mistletoe and no clothes.

But he'd grossly underestimated the amount of effort required by marriage, and all the damn logic in the world hadn't helped him figure out this woman. "Maybe we could both take leave and fly down to Mexico for a quickie. Divorce, I mean."

"I know what you mean." Her voice might be quiet, but she snapped with tension louder than the crack of fallen branches underfoot. "And you are so not funny right now."

"Yes, I am."

"Comedy and arrogance. Just what every girl looks for in a guy."

"Arrogant?" He plastered an over-innocent look on his face, chapped skin pulling tight at the effort, but it was a helluva lot easier to joke than vent his real frustrations. "How so?"

Her snowshoes slapped the ground, wafting a powdery patch. "Don't be a smart-ass."

"But I am a smart-ass." He checked his compass, adjusted their steps. "My IQ's just a fact, a fluke of birth, nothing I can take any particular pride in."

And that IQ told him he'd mastered funny, a talent he'd developed to help him fit in when he entered college at thirteen. He didn't intend to go through life as an ostracized whiz-kid freak. He'd needed something to help him assimilate into the college community until he hit his growth spurt, which, thank you, sweet God, finally happened at seventeen to the tune of six feet tall.

Of course, he'd quickly learned that humor was harder than landing a perfect score on the SAT, which made it more of a challenge. And damn, but he loved a challenge.

Alicia was his biggest challenge ever, more so than studying the rim-shot humor patterns of the Three Stooges' comedic routines. Problem was, he was losing this challenge.

Losing her. Not that she'd ever really been his, with her walls so damned high.

Right from the first time he'd seen her in the Kunsan O'Club, he'd been freaking mesmerized by her uninhibited laugh and stand-back confidence. She'd worn civilian clothes instead of her flight suit. How somebody could carry off an orange silk shirt with purple jeans and black thigh boots anytime other than Halloween, he didn't know. But then Captain Alicia "Vogue" Renshaw was all about the unexpected.

For a man who pretty much had life wired through sheer intellect, her unpredictability brought him to his knees.

He'd pulled together his best laugh lines, talked to her for a half hour before asking her out. He remembered his words distinctly. *Would you like to get a drink? I'm buying.* Not all that original, but she'd said yes.

Then she'd invited five other guys to come along. After all, Rose-Bud was offering to pick up the tab.

Even now, a smile tugged at him. He should have been pissed. The night had ended up costing him three hundred bucks, but he'd been laughing too hard to be mad. She out-thought him, and he liked that for a change.

Or he used to, anyway. Not so much anymore. "What do you want, Alicia? Do you even know?"

The question fell out before he could think, which said too much about his frustration level.

Silence answered him for at least eight trudging steps under the cover of silent trees, her arms swinging along her sides. "I want to finish this course. I want to start my job here. Simple stuff. Nothing complicated. So quit placing me under a microscope. I'm not an equation for you to figure out. I'm just…me." Her snowshoes smacked the ground with increasing force and sound. "And most of all, I am not your love. Not anymore, if I ever was."

He *had* loved her, damn it, before too much distance and arguing had killed it for both of them. She could just bite him if she thought otherwise.

Not that he intended to mention the point and thus offer up the rest of his heart for target practice. "Thanks for clarifying. Consider the microscope officially packed away. We'll walk. No talking other than directions. Speaking of which, veer left at the Y-looking birch tree up there."

So now this crappy day would be silent. Fair enough. Couldn't get much worse, anyway.

Snowflakes whispered from the murky sky.

Chapter Two

Snow pummeled Alicia.

Who'd have thought flakes could be so heavy? But after three hours of combating the early-arriving blizzard, she found every flake weighed a ton against her dwindling energy.

Nothing to do but march, focus on survival. And ignore the niggling notion that this training mission was going way wrong.

Josh plowed ahead of her, his broad shoulders cutting the gale winds to half force. She longed to argue that they should take turns leading, but if he walked behind her she couldn't have heard his navigational calls over the shrieking storm. The niggle inside scratched harder.

Damn it, they were not going to die out here. Josh wouldn't die. She refused to let that happen. Death had already hammered at her world too often.

Much as she wanted to rage at fate for sending crummy weather ahead of time, authentic survival situations didn't promise ideal weather conditions, either. At least discussion of cotton thongs versus Scooby-Doo Santa boxers had ended.

How could Josh be so perfect and such an arrogant jerk

at the same time? And now she would be spending one final night with him after all.

They couldn't reach the pickup point before dark since they were barely making pace. Radio connections had been staticky, but clear enough. Find cover. Hole up until morning.

She'd wanted to dig out a snow cave, but Josh insisted he remembered a marking from a chart indicating an abandoned mine within walking distance. Give it an hour and then they would try her way.

Fifty-two minutes and counting, Magellan. What she wouldn't give for a mug of eggnog to drink in front of a fire—with a garland-trimmed fireplace, please.

Sheets of snow and ice parted around him while she shuffled behind, too numb to be cold. His big body continued its brutal pace. Unrelenting. Unconquerable. And damn it all, she admired the determination and brains he packed under a thick head of jet-black hair and body ripped with muscles.

Right now, she wanted to complete this course outside of Fairbanks with her sanity intact and start her new job in StanEval—Standard Evaluation—giving check rides to other pilots. She looked forward to the challenge and even the routine after life at high-speed flying cover over Afghanistan, Iraq and Cantou. By the time she and Josh transferred to Elmendorf AFB in Anchorage, she'd been stretched to the max professionally and personally.

A military brat, she understood the pressures of moving. Before her mother died, her parents had rattled the windows with their shouts over where to hang pictures.

Of course their fights had always ended with her father smiling, then her mother tearing through her purse to unearth five dollars for Alicia to walk her brother and sister to the corner shop for a soda and candy bar. *And take your time, honey.*

Teeth clattering, Alicia lifted her leaden leg, shivered. One foot in front of the other. March, soldier. She was pretty much feeling like a frozen wooden Nutcracker soldier this holiday season.

Hers and Josh's final fight hadn't concluded as well as her parents'. She was running scared, a pathetic fact from a combat recipient of a Silver Star and Distinguished Flying Cross.

Still, she couldn't be what Josh wanted. She'd thought if she ignored the past it would ignore her. If not, she could bluff when memories from eight years ago dogged her.

She'd known she shouldn't marry Josh, or anyone for that matter, not with her unresolved feelings about Ben. But she'd been so in love with this incredibly smart, sexy man tromping ahead of her, and he'd insisted they were right for each other. His confidence was infectious. She'd relented and now they were both paying the price.

Josh stopped at a small clearing filled with mounds. The front of her snowshoe landed on the back of his. She wobbled, fell forward, grappled to brace herself with gloved hands the size of Ping-Pong paddles.

She slammed against the broad expanse of Josh's back. His arm shot around behind him to steady her.

Too late.

Swaying, she twisted to untangle herself from him before... They both landed in a heap against the hardpacked snow. This was supposed to be sexy, right— twined arms and limbs? He'd even angled to take the brunt of the fall for her.

But she had a face full of snow tingling her skin. Cold air lanced her lungs with every gasp. Lopsided snowshoes slammed against the backs of her thighs.

Definitely not sexy. Even if she wasn't pretzel-twisted, the extreme temps required too much gear for her to feel the enticing muscles banded across his chest. His washboard stomach, which she may have drooled over more than once in the past, stayed hidden somewhere beneath a parka, survival vest, snow pants, a flight suit, thermal underwear—not to mention Scooby-Doo boxers.

His hand knocked aside his snow goggles. "Are you okay?"

Emerald-green eyes burned like lasers at her with an unblinking, narrowed stare. Snowflakes drifted around wonderland-style, wind and drifts blocking the rest of the world until it was just her. Josh. And the intensity of his stare focused only on her, his mouth three inches away.

"Totally fine." O-kay. Now she understood the allure of a snow-swept embrace. Thank goodness her survival essentials included toothpaste, because in another couple of seconds she might well angle for a lip lock with her hunky hubby.

"Why'd you stop walking?" she asked, her minty breaths cloudier than could be attributed to simple speech. "I thought you were getting into this whole Lewis-and-Clark gig."

"Fifty-nine minutes." His full, sensuous lower lip enticed her as he spoke.

"What?" ChapStick. She'd applied it, right? Only for practical purposes, not because she anticipated a make-out session.

"I found the abandoned mine with one minute to spare." His cocky smile spread all the way to glint in his green eyes.

A dozen downy parkas couldn't keep her from wanting him, all the more frustrating because she knew that her desire would never be satisfied.

Talk about an icy splash of reality.

"The mine?" She wriggled to roll off him. "Where?"

"Over there." He pointed with an elbow toward an arch in the snow, the sliver of an opening showing above piles of snow.

How he'd spotted it, she would never know. But that was Josh, always beating the odds. Except when it came to them.

Her bulky snowshoes clunked against his. Her butt slid to the side while her legs remained tangled, her torso draped over his. Not too many clothes after all, because that surely was a washboard stomach under her cheek. Crap.

She shoved off him, kicking her legs free. "Lead the way, Rose-Bud."

All right. Low blow with the nickname he hated to re-establish boundaries. Guys around the squadron swore Josh's call sign Bud stood for buddy, everybody's pal.

God, she would miss his smile. Tears froze in the corners of her eyes. Wind howling past her ears, she shoved to her feet, teetered for two precarious seconds before regaining her footing, nice for a change around Joshua Rosen.

Dusting himself off, he surveyed the area around the thin crack of an entranceway showing above mounds of snow. "Looks clear. No animal tracks other than a few rabbit paths, maybe a lynx set over there. No footsteps from other people, which can be good and bad. Anything sleeping inside there would have had to come in before the storm. Shouldn't take long for us to dig through."

"I'll start gathering tinder to start a fire inside. We'll need to melt drinking water soon." Her mouth parched at the thought of sharing a sip with him mouth to mouth as they'd shared champagne after their wedding.

All that snow around and they couldn't risk taking so much as a taste until it melted. Eating snow lowered the core body temperature and risked further dehydration. "We could also rig traps. Maybe we'll luck into an arctic hare to eat."

The snare wire inside their survival vests would take care of supper.

Nodding, he unhooked his snowshoes and used one to trench aside the drifts in front of the opening. All right, they were working together without arguing. Maybe the night wouldn't be unbearably tense if they kept things professional, just two Air Force officers. Piece of cake.

Hah. Not.

Alicia crouched to block the wind from her hands—and conveniently block Josh from sight until she steadied her heart rate. She tugged her mittens off with her teeth one at a time to reveal her fitted flight gloves underneath. The green stretch fabric and leather cut some cold, but she couldn't count on that for long.

Lightning fast, she scraped birch bark, jammed it inside her parka. Rustling sounded inside the branches overhead, startling her, reminding her of hidden threats beyond just the cold. Birds broke free, white-tailed ptarmigans, almost invisible to the eye against the snow with their winter plumage. So beautiful, like one of the ornaments she'd planned to place on her Christmas tree.

She shook free from frivolous thoughts and stuffed pine needles into her parka on top of the bark. *Ouch.*

If they didn't luck into some heavy-duty wood inside, they could come back out. Wrist-size tree trunks snapped easily when frozen. They'd have a good fire to warm them. All night in a cave—alone.

Her traitorous eyes glanced over her shoulder. Josh still shoveled, boots braced. Broad shoulders dipped and rose.

Gulp.

Alicia jammed her stiff fingers into the Polartec mittens again. She straightened to find Josh stepping away from a crawl-hole opening to a dark tunnel. He tugged free the flashlight they'd been issued with their gear, then reached for his survival knife.

"That should be enough to let us in without admitting all the wind and blowing snow." He unsheathed the knife, jagged edges glinting and reflecting moonlit sparkles off icicles. "Let's pray no one else is snoozing inside."

Bears. Unease prickled over her, for Josh more than herself, because she knew all equality of service aside, he would throw himself between her and any threat in a heartbeat. This wasn't like in their airplane where they were both strapped into the cockpit with their designated roles.

She slipped her knife from the leather holster as well, following Josh as he ducked to enter. Crisp fresh wind gave way to air heavy with musty mold.

The murky cave greeted them. Dank. Dark.

Empty. At least near the front, anyway.

Tension dissolved from her kinked muscles. Exhaustion too long ignored roared to life faster than the campfire she would soon build. Not in a garland-and-bow-bedecked hearth, but she wasn't feeling all that picky anymore.

Josh pivoted, strobing the flashlight beam ahead. "Looks clear. We can explore once we have a fire to make a torch."

They would need to stay on guard, but at least they wouldn't freeze to death. Away from the wind, her body began warming to life with painful tingles. "Fire?" She swept off her goggles. "No problem. I've already got the tinder."

"You make a good partner, Renshaw."

His words echoed and bounced around her, mocking her with how she'd failed at just that. "Thank you, but it's my job."

"Yeah, right. I'll scrounge around outside for something to eat, some ice to melt, before the storm gets any worse."

And he was gone, swallowed by the sheets of snow rippling and twisting like linens on a line. The cave doubled in size without his shoulders and booming voice. So much for professional distance to carry her through this night alone.

She dropped her mittens to the slick black ground. She unzipped her parka and released the bark and needles into a pile near the mouth of the cavern to vent the smoke. From a pill bottle, she extracted a Vaseline-soaked cotton ball and dropped it on top of the kindling.

Kneeling, she struck her survival knife against the magnesium stick, launching sparks. She swooped again and again until the cotton ball poofed with flames. Kindling crackled, warmed. Acrid smoke singed the air and her lungs. Once the fire roared, she clicked off the flashlight to save the battery.

The entrance sealed closed. She startled, knife drawn, then relaxed.

Josh filled the entryway again, logs in his arms. "I set traps. We'll shoot hoops to decide who cooks. Loser skins Thumper."

How could she not smile at the reference to their old hoops ritual? All the same, she could have done without the reminder of Josh's better qualities. Smart. Funny. Hot. Air sense in the plane that left people of all ranks bowing in worship. And oh yeah, hot.

Her traitorous gaze skipped over to him as he dumped the wood. Hard, angular features gave him a raw appeal, softened just short of scary by long dark eyelashes. A scar along his jawline provided a touch of humanity to his god-like perfection.

Perhaps it was his humanity that scared her most of all. "Left or right side?"

"Pardon?" He squatted down in front of the fire, stripping off his mittens.

"Left or right side of the rock bed? After we eat."

Josh glanced up at her, eyes clear with understanding of her unstated boundaries. He flipped back his hood. "Right side, by the light, so I can read myself to sleep."

He obviously wanted an easygoing tone, too, like with the shooting-hoops comment. Still, tension lines radiating from the corners of his eyes sprinkled guilt all over her. She couldn't squelch the desire to smooth her fingers over them.

Danger zone. Back off notions of touching.

She opted to be up front. Dodging the obvious wasn't helping, anyway. "Kinda tense, huh? Being here together. Things will be better once we're both settled at work. We won't see each other so much. Ops officer duties will have you hopping, being called out to the flight line every time there's an emergency. I'll be busy giving check rides and filling out form eights. Even when we do see each other, we'll both be too exhausted to notice."

Liar.

"Sure. Sounds great." He brought a longer log down over his knee. The frozen brittle wood snapped in half, the crack echoing. Crouching, he dropped one piece, then the second onto the fledgling fire.

Sparks showered up, blazing higher to throw dancing shadows along Josh's beard-stubbled face. He so didn't deserve the pain she'd brought to his life.

She inched closer to him, woodsy smoke teasing her nose on its curling path outside. "You can have the apartment if you want. I'll look for somewhere else to live. I know you'll be busy keeping everyone current and spun up in case things flare in Cantou again."

He grunted, still staring down into the fire.

"Josh? We have to learn to be civil. This isn't the only time we'll be working together."

"Fine." His face snapped up. "Glad you're ready to talk. Let's start with why the hell we ever got married."

Whoa! Scream on the brakes. Blood rushed to her head as if she were pulling G-forces. She was thinking more along the lines of "You get the blender and I'll take the food processor."

She opted for the simple answer. "Your biological clock was ticking."

He snorted. "A guy's clock doesn't run down."

"Whatever." He'd wanted babies and she'd wanted to give them to him. So why hadn't she been able to just go for it?

With a long stick, he prodded the fire, stoking. "So why did you marry me?"

"My biological clock was ticking." Partial truth.

His incredulous look shouted a louder answer than any he could have shot her way. Okay, so she'd delayed having children. Again. And again, even though originally they'd agreed to start a family right away, both of them impatient.

Then their final explosive argument while unpacking in their new apartment had ended everything. She'd turned the spare bedroom into an office. He'd been planning more along the lines of a nursery.

She couldn't stop thinking how damned scared she was to take that final commitment step, because someday he would demand answers to questions she saw crowding his eyes about her past. She hadn't told him, but she suspected he knew at least a part of the story thanks to her blabber-mouth younger sister.

Josh pitched a final branch into the fire. With deliberate, predatory intent, he leaned forward. She should move away, but couldn't find the will. No surprise around Josh.

He stroked aside her hood, exposing her face to the grazing knuckles of his caress. "It's a damned shame we couldn't get our clocks in synch, because you know there's nothing I would have enjoyed more than giving you a baby for Christmas."

Alicia held herself still under his touch, unable to pull away, unable to move forward. Her heart twisted with longing. She'd had such hopes for their first holiday season as husband and wife. Her gift for him remained wrapped, hidden, an antique sextant for her navigator husband.

The heat of his fingers scorched her chilled face, stirring the hunger that simmered inside her anytime he touched her. She couldn't ignore it, but she refused to act on that hunger. "You really need to stop with the sexual innuendos. It's going to be uncomfortable enough sleeping next to each other tonight."

He stared back at her, inscrutable thoughts scrolling across his eyes. Would he push?

Finally, he just smiled, letting her off the hook for now. "I'd much rather sleep beside you than a bear."

"Thanks, I think."

His hand fell away. "But you're right. This sucks, being stuck out here together. I'm sorry it had to be this way."

She didn't want him to be nice, especially not now when they faced a final night together. She'd already cheated him of so much. He deserved better.

From the start, she'd known he was only getting half a person after what happened eight years ago. She'd hoped that maybe if she loved him enough, went through the motions of normalcy, everything would work. He would never know that she couldn't give him a hundred percent of herself.

She'd been wrong.

Alicia rocked back on her heels, suddenly certain she could not curl up next to him and hold firm to her resolve. "Maybe we shouldn't sleep at the same time after all. Once we finish eating, we could take turns sitting guard to keep the fire going. You should sleep first since you walked the lead."

With some luck, they could take turns sleeping until morning, never awake at the same time for long. And somehow forget that they were stranded together during one of the longest nights of the Alaskan winter.

Ten hours later on the longest night of his life, Josh held a branch-rigged torch overhead to add to the flashlight rays. Still, the beams barely pierced a dark deeper than outside. While Alicia slept, he wanted to scout around the cave. He needed to work off restless energy after his four-hour power nap.

They'd eaten, drunk melted ice, all silently. The talk of babies for the holidays had axed right through any hope of joking away the evening.

So her biological clock was ticking, which meant she just didn't want *his* babies. That delivered a kick in the seat of the pants harder than an afterburner.

He focused on the task at hand, surveying their surroundings, scouring for anything that might help their survival situation, like animal furs or food. So far, he'd only found an empty rabbit's nest and a few rats.

And a surprising lack of anything else.

Other wildlife should have taken up residence in this shelter. Yet he couldn't find so much as a footprint. The cave floor looked as immaculate as his mother's fresh-mopped kitchen.

No one was here now, but his instincts blared that someone had been recently. And that someone didn't want anyone else to know.

"Hello?"

He jerked to look over his shoulder, torch swooshing around to light an empty corridor.

"Josh? It's just me." Alicia's voice bounced around a corner a second before her flashlight beam ricocheted off the wall.

He turned before she could draw closer. "Careful about sneaking up on me."

"Sorry."

Soft regret carried on her single word, the sentiment obviously for so many more things between them. Her sleep-husky tones tempted him to hold her, shake her, kiss her, insist they give things another chance. But did he really want to keep trying to repair their broken relationship?

Not if she wasn't willing to be straight up with him.

He'd had a bellyful of people holding back from him. Hell, it wasn't like his brain made him a mind reader. Yet even while he mainstreamed enough to fit in, people always kept up walls with him as if his intelligence allowed him an understanding of their inner secrets.

If he could do that, then he wouldn't have his crap dumped at the BOQ. "Go back to sleep. It'll be an exhausting trek with the extra snowfall. You've got maybe four hours left before we start out." He raised his torch to illuminate her.

Big mistake.

She stood silhouetted by the halo of light, her hood flopped back to reveal blond hair, spiky, tousled, as if mussed from his hands during sex. Her unzipped parka flapped open to her sides, revealing soft curves encased in her flight suit.

Heat surged south with unerring navigation.

Hitching the torch ahead, he charged past toward the last corridor left unexplored. Four steps in, his instincts blared an undeniable warning. He eyed the irregular hacks in the cave walls, fresh indentions that had nothing to do with nature and everything to do with human intervention. The mine wasn't abandoned anymore.

White suits dangled from pegs in the wall beside a tarp-draped mound no bigger than the new dining room table he and Alicia had bought the day before their split.

"Josh? Is something wrong?" Alicia asked from a step behind him and, hell, but he hadn't even heard her approach this time.

"I'm just hoping I'm not seeing what I think I'm seeing." And now he intended to keep Alicia plastered to his side until he knew for certain. "Stick close."

Illumination swelled in the small rock chamber as they walked deeper inside. He strode past the canvas-covered bulk to the white suit bags dangling like ghostly apparitions from a Dickens tale.

Holy crap.

Alicia's gasp behind him echoed his realization. "Protective clothing and breathing apparatus. God, Josh, these are better quality than the chemical gear we're issued and new. What the hell's going on here?"

He swept aside the tarp to reveal boxlike machinery with levered doors and gauges. And thanks to a stint at the nuclear-weapons officer course at Sandia Labs at Kirtland AFB in New Mexico, he knew exactly what he was seeing. None of it good.

"Apparently someone has set up a small-time mining operation here. This machine—" he gestured to the device on the left "—measures mass of the rock. The one on the right measures radioactivity. Combine those two machines and they perform radiometric sorting, which separates preferred uranium from rock and lesser uranium."

"Whoa. Uranium? Hold on. This mine's supposed to be shut down." She hooked her hands on her hips, spinning a slow circle. "Wouldn't someone have noticed all the activity from hacking out so much rock?"

"Usually with uranium to rock mass, you have to haul away a helluva lot of rock." He knelt on one knee in front of the black metal stretch of machinery, flicked a dial gauge. "Unless I miss my guess, they've struck a vein of pure uranite, probably a highly concentrated form. Uranite can be up to eighty-five percent concentrated, which makes small parcels. A mom and pop operation could pull this off without their activity being detected."

"And this uranite has been sitting in a training base backyard?"

"People see what they expect to see. Up to five seconds ago, I thought the only place to find this particular ore was in Blind River, Canada."

"I may not be a genius, but even I know Canada's mighty darn close to Alaska."

"They're probably taking out maybe a grocery-bag-size amount per day, then using a small plane or helicopter."

Alicia stared at the suits. "I'm guessing a helicopter since we didn't see tracks outside other than the rabbits'." She filled in the blanks as quickly as he thought them. "Helicopter blades would blow away footprints upon take off."

"Good guess." Damn, why couldn't they figure out marriage this easily? "Granted, it's raw uranium and has to be enriched. But it's enough uranium to build a bomb the size used in World War II."

"So with that grocery bag, either paper or plastic, we could be totally screwed."

He fingered the Geiger counter attached to one of the suits. "That's not even taking into account skipping the enrichment process and building a dirty bomb."

His skin tingled at just the thought of radium exposure even as the Geiger counter in his hand told him they'd been exposed to less than an X ray.

Alicia backed away from the suits. "Rose-Bud, as enlightening as this discussion is, I think it's time we took it outside."

Fair enough. Radiation may not be a major concern, but the people who inhabited those ghostly suits could do some serious real-life haunting.

Josh doused the torch, the flashlight more than adequate for hauling ass out. He clasped her hand and tugged her along behind him, grip tight. He wasn't risking losing her in the maze of tunnels. "We'll call from the radio once we're outside and can pick up a frequency. Hopefully the weather's cleared enough to send a chopper."

"What an excuse to get out of finishing the class."

"It'll make the logbooks for sure."

She stumbled behind him.

"You okay?" he called over his shoulder.

"Just tripped over something in the dark. I'm fine."

Tripped? Trip. Trip wire. Ah, hell.

A sixth-sense premonition burned over him a half second before rumbling echoed behind them. A collapse? No. More of a squeak. Rolling. Opening. Like a gate or door.

Woof.

A bark. Another. Growls grew louder behind the walls, not the storm howling at all. Guard dogs or wolves? Either way, a death pack. Josh's hand convulsed around Alicia's.

"Shit," he bit out. "Run!"

Chapter Three

Alicia gripped Josh's hand.

She held tight, not from fear of the snarling reverberations chasing them through the cave. But out of a gut-sure sense that her husband would do something recklessly macho if he thought she was in danger.

Holding firm, she sprinted, her feet slipping along the slick rocks and frozen mud. The flashlight beam bounced ahead.

Josh's heat, sweat and intensity seared through their form-fitting flight gloves as they ran. Around a corner. Left or right? Josh shoved right.

Ten steps later, the mouth of the cave came into view.

"Gloves," she shouted. "Grab them."

Her hand sailed down to scoop up her discarded arctic mittens. No time to snag the snowshoes. Thank God they had their goggles dangling around their necks.

Alicia scrambled on her belly through the narrow opening. Her boots sunk into the snow. Snow flurried and she yanked up her hood.

"Trees," Josh huffed. "Back into the forest. Climb up. We'll call for rescue from there."

The trees were farther from their pickup point. But the snarling beasts were closer.

She trudged through the drifts in a high-stepping run that screamed death. They needed to go faster, but the deep snow turned their sprinting into slow motion.

Ominous barking swelled from inside the cave. Then *pow,* the deadly symphony cleared the cave and exploded full force across the open tundra.

The trees grew closer. But were they close enough? She vise-gripped Josh. Ran. Prayed. Worked to dispel the image of hounds tearing at her husband.

She could feel the steamy caress of hot breath as her hood flopped behind her. Was it her husband breathing beside her? Or were the beasts that near? She didn't dare look.

Snowfall thinned from tree cover. She picked up speed, plunging deeper into the icy forest. She searched for a pine or birch strong enough to hold them.

There.

Five more steps. Josh knelt, hooking his hands together in a step.

She opened her mouth to protest and send him up the tree first to make the call while she…what? Scrambled up as best she could.

"No time to argue," Josh shouted. "Go. That's an order, Captain."

Her soldier soul couldn't ignore the command even as her wife heart screamed in protest.

"Yes, sir." Stuffing her survival mittens inside her flight suit, she placed her boot in his cupped hands. She bounced once, twice for leverage, and up…

She grabbed for a low-hanging branch. She gripped, her flight gloves slippery around the icy branch. Please God, no missing that would cause Josh to stay on the ground longer. A firm hand landed against her butt. Supported. Shoved upward. She flailed her other arm, smacking a branch.

It held. Yes.

White birds flapped from the branches in protest. Dangling, swaying, she hooked her elbow around. She swung one leg up, then the other.

Josh.

She sprawled onto her belly on the thick branch, wrapped her legs and one arm around before reaching down. The barking grew intolerably closer. Josh grabbed a droopy pine limb, levered himself up with a boot. His gloved hand slapped into hers.

The first snarling wolf skidded to a stop at the base of the tree, a mangy gray creature with fangs bared. Flashing teeth latched around Josh's leg. Her heart lurched as the other wolves closed in.

The sound of ripping fabric mingled with snarls. She stared down into Josh's face, icy branch slick against her parka. Determination stung through her. He kicked, thunking his boot against the wolf's head, once, twice.

Her hold strengthened. No letting go. The beast would have to pull them both down.

Pine needles, clumps of snow, lethal icicles rained from the shaken branches. A wolf yelped and fell. An icicle poked from its side while the animal thrashed in death throes.

Alicia slipped to the side. She stifled a shriek.

Josh's eyes narrowed. She read his intent too well. He planned to let go. He would fall to his death to protect her.

"No damn way, Joshua Rosen!" she shouted through gritted teeth. "Don't you dare let go out of some misguided macho-ass idea of saving me."

Her arms strained, one burning from the exertion of holding on to the tree. The other stretched to the limit from her hand locking with Joshua's. "If you fall, then I'm going down with you. There's not a chance in hell I can sit up here while those wolves tear at you. So you hang on tight because I look forward to chewing you out once you get—"

"Roger. Understood." A smile pushed dimples into his face, so at odds with the moment as he hung there somewhere between the branch and a pack of hungry wolves with white teeth and at least five pairs of crystalline eyes flashing up.

"Not letting go." Josh inched closer. "So quit wasting…energy talking and just pull."

Up.

His booted foot swung free from the fanged jaws. Somehow his feet found purchase along the icy trunk. He hooked an arm around a limb, hefted himself over and settled, straddling a swaying branch.

Chest pumping quick bursts of vapor, Josh inched closer to the trunk. Finally, he sagged back against the frosted bark. The howling dogs continued to snarl and jump at the trunk, but their growls didn't sound so loud to her ears now that Josh was safe.

He turned his head to look sideways up at her on a bough six or more inches above and over. White clouds from his mouth wafted around her. "Thank you."

"Thank you for the leg-up first." Relief coursed through her, cooling the adrenaline-induced sweat on her body. Minutes whispered by uncounted while she allowed herself to soak in the vitality of Joshua. Alive. Nothing else mattered at the moment.

"Are you okay?" His gaze raked her.

"Me? I'm not the one who had a wolf hanging off my leg by his teeth. Are you all right?"

"I'm fine. The snow pants kept him from actually biting me. Now, how are you, damn it?"

"Just winded." Scared, relieved, scared all over again. "Screw this saving ourselves crap. Arctic Survival School has concluded for us now. We need to report in about what we found in the cave. God, I can't believe anyone would be brash enough to mine uranium right in the backyard of a training area. Scares the hell out of me to think where they might be shipping it. Josh?" Why wasn't he talking? "Don't you agree?"

Cloudy breaths with no words continued to fill the night.

"Are you ready to call in a rescue?"

"Look down."

Fishing her flashlight out of her pocket and scared all over again because she couldn't even remember putting it there, she arced the light down. Had she really climbed that high? How in the world had she reached to pull him up? The reality of how close they'd come to dying prickled over her, leaving her a little dizzy until the tundra below jiggled.

Alicia jerked her gaze up again. "I'd really rather not. It's a helluva long way down, and it's not like I have vertigo or anything, I mean, jeez, I'm a pilot, right? But I really prefer to have a parachute strapped to my back anytime I'm up high." Oh, God, already she was growing loopy from the cold and they still had at least a couple of hours until dawn. "What was that about looking down, anyway?" Suck it up, Renshaw.

Rosen?

Ah, hell. Whatever her name was.

Securing her grip on the pine, she looked down again. A trio of wolves remained in sight, one nuzzling the limp carcass of the impaled beast. Blood stained the white perfection of fur and snow.

She swallowed hard, scanned the other animals busy prowling, circling the base of the tree. All but one. A lone wolf stared up with the survival radio clamped firmly in its jaws, bits of torn snow pants hanging from his teeth.

No wonder Josh had wanted her to look down.

"Ah, hell." She sagged back against the sturdy trunk that still swayed under the force of the stormy winds.

Arctic Survival School was definitely over. Time to put their teaching to the test for real.

"De-e-eck the halls with boughs of holly…"

Alicia's warbly carol drifted around the tree, working better than a mega-jolt of caffeine to keep Josh awake.

His wife couldn't sing for crap. Her voice—a questionable contralto—carried on the tearing night wind. He figured any safety benefits to shushing her were outweighed by the need to keep her awake.

Keep him awake as well.

Luckily the storm that had sent them into the cave in the first place was likely keeping the bad guys away for now. He and Alicia sat with backs against the trunk, legs stretched out on the limb to evenly distribute weight.

The branches seemed sturdy enough. But too easily he could envision the effortless snap of breaking off frozen wood for the fire earlier outside the cave.

Only another hour till sunrise and he could scatter the wolves, climb down. Too risky in the dark, though, where the wolves could lurk behind a tree under the cover of darkness.

Brief flashes of the stars overhead helped him gain his bearings again after their off-course run. How he could see the North Star so clearly through the storm clouds, he didn't know. And he didn't intend to question.

A miracle? Maybe. All love of science aside, he would take help any way he could tonight. He would do anything to keep Alicia alive. No way in hell would he let her be the victim of a holiday siege.

Like before.

He'd only been fifteen years old, that growth spurt no-damned-where in sight. With the gunman waving his AK-47 and extra ammo around, Josh couldn't do a thing but sit at his desk with a half-completed final exam for Advanced Incompressible Aerodynamics in front of him.

After twelve hours of tense negotiations, the masked gunman had opened fire. Josh had thrown himself across the aisle, toward his classmate who had a houseful of kids at home. His chin still ached from cracking on the floor.

Seven students had died before the gunman turned his weapon on himself. Still Josh had sprawled over the silent woman who'd been dead before she hit the ground. Memories focused in on only the blood dripping off desks and splattered on the wall, crimson against white like the dead wolf in the snow below.

The next day, he'd marched into the ROTC office to discuss joining up once he was old enough. His goal had shifted. Working for NASA after graduation had become his intermediary job until flight training.

Red as a holiday color carried a whole different meaning for him.

"Fa-la-la-la-la," Alicia rounded off the holiday classic, "La-la-la-laaa."

"Bravo." He clapped his gloved hands together in the bitter cold. Even his damned nose hairs were frozen together. "You should take your show on the road."

"Sure hope Carnegie Hall leaves a message on my voice mail. Oh, or what about a USO tour? My sister could haul me around in her cargo plane to perform for the troops. Ah, but there's just that matter of my job. Got my own plane to fly. Too bad we can't harness those hounds like reindeer and pilot us out on Santa's sleigh. And oh, man, am I getting loopy."

"You're doing great. Just hang on and keep singing if you need to."

"You pick the next s-s-song." Her teeth chattered. "What kind of holiday tunes did you sing growing up?"

Amazing how they'd fought about everything except their differing faiths. "Nah, you go ahead with your next riff."

With memories still clogging his head like an oncoming sinus infection, he didn't want to be funny. He glanced down his stretched legs to his squadron scarf tied around a leg of his survival pants to cinch where the wolf had torn the fabric—jarring loose his radio. Frustration kicked through him again.

"Alicia? More serenades?"

"I've pretty much caroled through the whole Renshaw canon of Christmas tunes."

He scrambled for a new topic that would launch her into a lengthy explanation. They really didn't know much about each other's holiday traditions since they'd been apart last December for different deployments. "What did your family do for the holidays?"

"Regular stuff, the tree, church, Santa, presents. Lots of fruitcake and peppermint hot chocolate. Ah, man, what I wouldn't give for hot chocolate." Her voice went dreamy. "Sometimes we celebrated on a different day than the twenty-fifth…like the year Dad shipped out before Desert Storm cranked into gear."

"Sort of like how Hanukkah dates float from year to year."

"Never thought about it that way, but yeah. It was all

about being together for us anyhow because we never knew for sure when Dad would fly out again."

She shifted on her branch, rustling pine needles to the ground in a shower that brought a yip from below. "This one year movers lost a box of my mother's Christmas decorations."

"I imagine she'd collected things from all over."

"Sure, but those weren't the ones lost. The missing box had the decorations we'd made in school. There was a star with my picture in the middle. And some from when we painted ceramic Twelve Days of Christmas. Hank Jr. and I whipped through eleven days in ten minutes. Darcy worked on her lords-a-leaping for an hour, then realized she'd forgotten to paint the back."

"Ah, man, that bites." An only child, he had different memories. Not bad, just lonely sometimes, which had more to do with being so many grades ahead of everyone else. Probably part of the reason he wanted lots of kids.

He wondered, not for the first freaking time, if she'd wanted kids with that other guy who'd left such a mark on her life she wouldn't even talk about him to her husband.

So why didn't he just ask? Easy answer. Because it was one thing to think she still loved the poor dead bastard and another altogether to hear her say it.

"Actually, Mom told Darcy to leave the half-painted ornament just like it was. She wanted us to remember that we are a work in progress and to keep improving." Her sigh wrapped around the tree, around him. "So that year, she put up all the pretty ornaments. It was a gorgeous tree, no question. But when Mama went to an Officer's Wives Club Christmas tea one night, Daddy brought us construction paper and glue and glitter and popcorn string. We worked for two hours straight to junk up Mama's tree."

"I bet she loved it." His head thunked back against the trunk.

"She really did. It was a perfect Christmas with snow. A couple of weeks later, she died from a fluky aneurysm."

Ice chilled inside him colder than outside. He'd known her mother died, just not when. Which proved how little talking of any importance he and Alicia had done over the past year and a half.

How ironic that the view in front of him—trees, snow, a star streaking through the darkness—resembled a picture-perfect scene worthy of any Christmas card, and yet it carried such deadly undertones. Just as that year had for her, only she'd been unaware of the lurking tragedy, something they shared in common after all.

He reached around the tree trunk to rest a hand on her arm. She probably couldn't feel the gesture through the layers of winter gear, but he couldn't keep his distance.

"The first Christmas without her was hard. I knew there was no way I could make things better for Dad, but I really wanted little Hank and Darcy to grow up with holiday memories, too. Maybe not as cool as the ones Mom would have made with us, but they would have their stories to tell."

"What did you do?"

"I had Dad take all three of us to a big Christmas mall. We shopped for hours trying to pick out a crèche. Except I'd like the Mary in one, but the lambs were goofy. Darcy wanted a certain angel, but thought the Wise Men looked creepy. Then I remembered Mom crying over that perfect tree because she wanted her hodgepodge one back. So, we just played mix and match. We bought our favorite piece from each set to create a whole new set that was uniquely our own."

He could see her, so young herself but taking charge while recognizing the beauty of their individual tastes. How could this woman tempt him in the middle of a blizzard when he couldn't even see one inch of her luscious body?

Josh cleared his throat, if not his thoughts, that were tumbling faster than a plane in a barrel roll. "So that explains your clothes."

"Huh?"

"No matched sets."

"Oh. No." Her laugh floated round, packing more of a punch than her sigh. "Actually, I just don't have any fashion flair since there wasn't anyone around to teach me. Hey, scratch that last part. It sounds un-PC and totally ungrateful to my dad. But he wore his uniform all the time and didn't have a clue about clothes. A couple of the other squadron wives tried to help, but, uh, you may have noticed I'm a bit prickly in the pride department."

"No? Really?"

"Smart-ass," she answered, but her tone was lighter, and damned if those two words didn't sound a little affectionate. "I knew they meant well. Maybe I didn't want to shop without Mom. Who knows? But those pity looks really bugged me. So next time we went somewhere, I deliberately mismatched. I found I liked it better than 'normal,' anyway. Now, after wearing a uniform all day, playing with colors is fun."

Fun. That described Alicia well. Dating her had been a wild ride, full of the unexpected. Like the time she'd called and insisted he put on his mess dress uniform before she arrived. She'd been wearing a hot-pink formal gown with ridiculous ruffles. Since he'd never had a senior prom, she'd planned to treat him to the whole experience…a few years late.

At the first sign of resistance from him, she'd threatened to make him wear a tux with a fuchsia cummerbund and bow tie to match her dress.

He'd relented—and had an uninhibited blast.

Ah, shit. He didn't want to remember falling in love with her. He needed distance from Alicia, a damned tough proposition considering they were stuck in a tree. "So back to your cotton panties. What color are you wearing under all those uniform layers right now?"

God, her husband could be such an ass sometimes. And right after being so sweet listening to her sappy childhood stories and distracting her from her numb toes.

Nothing to do but ignore him and his obnoxious question, try to forget the steady comfort of his hand on her arm while she'd talked about her mother.

Wind whistled through the trees even though the storm had eased. Thank heaven they weren't out in the open and only had to wait a few hours until daylight. Still, her hands shook from the cold. She ached all the way to her bones from sitting still so long.

She tapped her thumb against her pinkie in a quick check to make sure her fingers still worked. Which made her worry about Josh. While she wouldn't see her siblings for Christmas since they were all stationed at different Air Force bases, at least she had siblings to call, unlike Josh.

Sympathy tweaked harder than the bite of bark pressing through her protective clothing. "What holiday memories do you have?"

"More traditional ones, I guess. My mother collected menorahs, some really fancy like your mother's perfect tree and others that would probably fit in with your more eclectic tastes."

"Which one was your favorite?" The classic beauty or the eclectic surprise? And now, wasn't that fishing for a flipping reinforcement that maybe she'd been at least partially right for him during their short-lived, messed-up marriage?

"This one my nonni has that looks like a moose."

A moose?

Eclectic, sure, but not quite the complementary analogy she'd been seeking. Still, his quirky answer warmed her frostbitten feet that just happened to be sporting quirky reindeer-patterned toe socks under all the other layers of socks. "A moose? How so? I'm having trouble picturing it."

"With candles on each antler."

"Ah. Okay, now I can envision it." Why had they never taken the time for this before when she could have fully enjoyed it, when she wasn't a frozen ice sculpture? Drawing her knees up to her chest, she tucked her face down, arms inside. The bough held. "Sounds like something a boy would enjoy. What else?"

"I had a dreidel to play with, but, man, did I ever want to play with Nonni's old one up on the mantel. Mother said no, but Nonni said I could if I helped her make potato latkes."

"You in an apron? Now, there's an image."

"Hey—" his deep bass growled from the other side of the pine "—I make a mighty damned good potato latke."

"I'll trade you some for my grandma's fruitcake recipe." She tried for lighthearted, except she knew better. They would never swap squat again, and the knowledge wedged itself in her throat like dried-out leftovers. "It's about time to climb down, isn't it?"

"Soon," he agreed, his voice sobering. "We need to make tracks the minute daylight breaks. We have to put space between us and whoever sicced these Cujo spawn on us. If we stay in the woods, covering our tracks should be easier. Of course, that also makes it tough as hell for anyone to rescue us."

"Well, don't those options all suck."

"Pretty much. Someone will have stayed at the pickup point. We'll just keep trying to make our way there."

"How far off do you think we ran?"

He stayed silent. Not good.

All right, then. One problem at a time. She pointed down at Fluffy still sharpening his fangs on their radio. "Do you have any ideas on how to make the big guy there abandon his favorite new chew toy?"

"I've been praying for another killer icicle for the past hour. Doesn't seem to be working."

Her low laugh spiraled out into the horizon glowing orange and purple with a cresting sun. Not how she'd planned to spend the dark hours with him, and oddly somehow as intimate as sleeping in his arms.

And now their last night together had ended. "Any ideas on how to get them to scatter?"

"I've been thinking about it. We could use the gyro-jet flare gun on them, but that could also signal whoever set them loose in the first place."

"Flare gun, last resort."

"Yeah, which takes me to plan B. How about break off one of those branches to your left. The less snow and more pine needles the better."

She heard him rustling on his branch. Clumps of snow thudded, rousing Fluffy and Cujo to glare up with ice-blue eyes. "Uh, okay, but do you mind if I ask what you have planned?"

"Flaming branches."

"Should work and won't be nearly as visible as launching a flare. But how do you plan to kindle a spark up here in the tree? And without burning us out?"

His arm extended with a Bic lighter in his fist.

Shock stunned her silent. But only for a second. "You had this all the time even though we're in an official training course?"

"Duh. What are you? New?"

So he was back to being an ass, sensitivity long gone, probably only generated to keep her occupied, anyway. "You snuck a lighter into survival school? Omigod. I can't believe you did that. What other contraband have you stuffed in your pockets?"

"Hey, back off. I checked the rules and nowhere did it say I couldn't bring one."

"Well the rules don't say I can't have a pup tent, but you don't see me shoving one up my parka."

"Somebody's mighty cranky without her morning coffee."

At least he wasn't talking about her underwear anymore. "Damn it, Rose-Bud—"

"Do you want out of this tree or not?"

"Light the damned branch." Lack of coffee? More like frustration from hanging out with the tender, funny Josh all night until even smart-ass Josh couldn't erase the warm glow swelling inside her.

"Yes, ma'am."

Rustling sounded behind her, followed by the flick, flick, flick as he worked the lighter. Alicia scanned the endless horizon, hazy purples and blues banding the skyline like one of her mismatched outfits that somehow went together. So many cold miles they had left to walk, and they were undoubtedly more than one degree off their original plan. If they even hit the river in one piece, would they turn right or left?

Making it home in time for Christmas calls was now the least of her worries.

Chapter Four

Josh took a navigational heading off the sinking sun, wondering where the hell they would end this day. Home? Pickup point?

Alone in the elements again?

There'd been no sign of anyone—good or bad. Their flaming-branches trick had worked like a charm. Other than the fact that they couldn't recover the radio, since Cujo made off with it before they could even reconsider using the flare gun on him.

Now it was just the two of them, met only by a herd of musk ox in the distance, the occasional snowshoe hare. At least they hadn't run across any bears. A bear could down a moose with one swoop.

Alicia walked beside him now since they were both so damned cold and brain-numbed he was afraid he might lose her if she walked behind. Progress had been slow due to covering their tracks and frequent stops to warm up with a fire. Thank goodness his trusty Bic was holding out. Still they would have to take shelter soon.

Intellectually he understood that soldiers died in training.

Training hard kept combat casualties substantially lower. But he'd never expected to be a statistic.

Damn it, he wouldn't let the cold defeat him with negativism.

If they could just make it to the river. He was certain they were heading that way at least. They were more likely to stumble on help the closer they were to water.

People did live out here. The place wasn't totally abandoned. With some luck—or another miracle—maybe they would stumble onto a cabin, or at the very least a rustic Quonset hut, erected by the military or abandoned by some ice fisherman.

And if they found one?

Wait. Scratch that. Not *if*. When.

He must be colder than he thought if he was allowing doubts to creep in. Strange. He never worried about Alicia in the air. That wife of his had grit, focus and invincibility to spare in the clouds. But right now, he was scared as hell of being stuck out here watching her die.

"Talk to me," he demanded.

"Talk," she huffed, "to yourself, Rose-Bud."

Apparently she had some grit left in reserve. "Still need that caffeine?"

She stomped ahead. Pissed?

"You're mad?"

"What would I have to be mad about?" she snipped.

Uh-oh.

Alicia high-stepped around a drift. She walked along their zigzag path close to trees where branches blocked the bulk of the snowfall. God, she was hanging tough when he'd expected her to collapse long ago. His own muscles shouted in protest, but he was starting to realize Alicia was a wingman who held her own on the ground, too.

Why couldn't they apply that synchronicity to their home life as well as the workplace?

"You know what really torques me off, Rose-Bud?"

"Haven't a clue." But no doubt he was about to learn. He liked that about her, her take-no-shit attitude. He liked a lot of things about her, such as her grit.

That grit also made it hard as hell to resolve anything. If he wanted to try. Which he didn't anymore.

Did he?

She ducked around a tree, her foot landing on a fresh patch of snowfall. "You let me work my butt off starting that fire in the cave and all the time you had a lighter."

Scooping up a branch, he knelt to sweep away her tracks. "Wouldn't want you to break rules."

A snowball thunked him on the head.

Well, he'd claimed to like her unexpectedness. Just about as much as he liked surprising her right back.

Slowly, he rose, finding Alicia waiting with another arm arced back, snowball missile aimed and ready. "Watch it, my love. You start surprising me too much and I'm going to get turned on."

He waited for the explosion.

Instead, she laughed, surprising him again.

"Good God, Josh. It's fifty below. I can barely feel my toes. How in the world can you feel your…uh…well… you know."

Yeah, he sure did know, and damned inconvenient timing it was. Shouldn't his body be focused on survival? Instead, it was screaming for him to procreate before he died.

Back to her question and off thoughts of procreating. "I trusted you could start a fire in the cave, so I figured it was best to conserve the lighter fuel for an emergency."

Her arm sagged to her side. The second snowball splatted to the ground, icy missile and anger diffused. "Thank you."

"For what?"

"For trusting me to pull my own weight."

Her sincerity knocked him off balance as much as her unexpected anger. He couldn't afford to have his concentration shaken, especially not now. Time to regain distance. "No problem. And, hey, that's a mighty fine butt you were working off anyhow."

Her laugh echoed again, hoarser this time. "Good thing you're my husband or I could write you up on sexual harassment charges for a statement like that, Colonel."

Except he was only her husband for a short time longer, which made her joke fall flatter than the abandoned snowball.

A holiday miracle sometime soon sure would be nice. But he'd given up counting on miraculous rescues when he was fifteen years old watching people bleed out all around him.

These days, he knew if there was any saving to be done, he could only count on himself.

She was in trouble.

Alicia battled to stay awake. Walk. One foot in front of the other. She would hold her own. She absolutely would not slow Josh down, but she felt pretty much like an ice sculpture from an Alaskan snow festival they'd once discussed attending.

They'd stopped twice already to build a quick fire and drink. Thank heaven for his Bic lighter, faster than her flint, but probably running low on butane.

Pretty much like her energy supply.

He'd offered to drag her along, dogsled style. She'd told him to eat his shorts. She wasn't quitting. Surely they would stumble on something soon. Meanwhile, think happy thoughts.

Flying always made her happy, in control of her craft and her fate. Kicking ass and taking names. Saving lives and making a difference while following a calling to serve that hummed through her veins in a legacy passed down from generations of Renshaw warriors. The drive to serve called to her aviator sister and brother as well.

Her fingers twitched convulsively as if around the stick in her F-15E Strike Eagle. Exhaustion lured her mind back to that life-changing mission, the day she'd earned her Silver Star.

Asleep on her feet, she dreamed of the first time she'd flown with Josh…

Sweat flowed freely in the F-15E. The two-seater cockpit was overheated from stress, raising damp spots on her flight gloves. Alicia kept her hold loose, light, her thumb poised over the control buttons. She would stay calm—even though more perspiration plastered her hair to her head under her helmet as clouds whipped past her windscreen.

She drew measured hits off her oxygen mask, microphone embedded to pick up her every word, even their breaths. Her WSO's exhalations echoed through the headset Darth Vader-style in an alternating rhythm with her own.

They'd been on their way to attack an ammunition depot when the call for emergency close air support came midflight. Enemy fire had downed a CH-47 Chinook helicopter full of Army Rangers. They needed close air support ASAP until a rescue force arrived.

Her first real combat engagement.

She'd been deployed for Afghanistan and Iraq, but mostly Southern Watch patrolling missions. Never had she waded into the hairy action or needed evasive maneuvers on those sorties.

Which explained why they'd paired her—a young captain—with a combat-seasoned weapons system officer for her early missions in Cantou.

Major Joshua Rosen sat strapped in the WSO's seat behind her—the fella who'd hit on her in the O'Club bar. Nothing inappropriate, just genuine interest from Major Tall, Dark and Hunky who happened to have a kick-butt sense of humor.

She'd dissuaded far pushier in the past. Yet still, something told her this magnetic man wouldn't be as easy to keep at a distance as the others.

None of which she could afford to think about now.

Easing the stick forward, she pointed the nose down, rolled in and out of the clouds. Asian jungle sprawled ahead of her, puffs of smoke rising from the trees. Little sound invaded the cockpit, just the minor whispering of air. The roar of engines filtered away behind them. The plane hauled full out, bringing them down, near.

Radar wouldn't do crap for them now. Bad guys looked pretty much the same as good guys on the screen. Visuals combined with talk-on from the ground would guide them.

Close air support was scary stuff. Any mistake could make the difference between taking out the threat—or their own people. Bud Rosen in back would be helping her scan visually with the aid of binoculars when necessary.

Her focus wired in on the stick in her hand, the voices in her headset, the five multifunction display screens in front of her.

Her headset crackled with calls from the ground. Gunfire and explosions popped and crashed through the airwaves. "Hound twenty-one, we need these guys taken out. We can't hold 'em off much longer. I need some fire on the top of the east to west ridge, north of the downed helicopter."

"Roger." Josh's response clipped through. "I think I've got it visual. Are you talking about the guys two hundred meters west of the rock cropping?"

"That's affirmative, Hound twenty-one."

More clipped instructions and questions batted back and forth through her headset as the commander on the ground talked them onto the target. Her control panel blazed like red-and-green Christmas lights.

"Where are the friendlies?" Josh asked.

"We're a hundred and fifty meters west of the target, just north of the downed chopper."

Alicia's fist clenched the stick, her eyes glued to the steering commands on the holographic images on her HUD—heads-up display. A hint of a mistake on her part and they would drop the munitions on their own troops.

No more time for questions. The call went up. Put down laser-guided five-hundred-pound GBU-12s—guided bomb units.

Circling the plane over the target, she continued her steady stream of situational awareness updates to Bud. With his head now down in the infrared scope in the back picking out targets, he needed her to keep him updated on the bigger picture. Damn, she hoped the info and her voice were steady.

Rosen put his forward-looking infrared camera on the target, squirting the laser once, locking in the range finder to compute a bombing solution. "Give me a right three-sixty. Come back to a heading of zero four zero. Bomb pickle ten seconds after roll out."

Countdown.

Everything else faded, the vibration of engines, blur of sky and trees. Only the target and Bud Rosen's voice, his breathing, remained. She drew on the confidence of this invincible aviator who never once questioned her ability even though there were times on the ground when she seriously doubted her own judgment.

When had their breathing synched up?

Rosen's bass pulsed in her headset. "Laser on. Here comes impact... Weapon impact complete. Looks like a shack."

A direct hit. She bit back her sigh of relief. They weren't through by a long shot.

"All right, Vogue. Bring us back around and line her up again."

Three more go-rounds left. She hoped his confidence in her would hold because she sure as hell appreciated the safety net. "Roger, Bud, coming around...."

"Hey, come around." Josh's voice echoed in her head, dragging her back to the bitterly cold present.

The snow-speckled horizon flickered in front of her face with a large gloved hand waving in front of her.

"Are you with me, Alicia?"

She blinked, the swirling haze so much like the clouds in her windscreen for a confusing second. Odd that she should have that memory now. She could make it on her own without Josh's strength, but she'd always appreciated it, continued to be grateful for it now. "Sure. I'm fine. Totally okay."

"You don't look okay."

"*Okay*'s a relative term here." She planted her feet to combat the urge to sway in the wind like the towering pines.

"This sucks, big time. I'm freezing my butt off. I'm hungry. I'm exhausted. But I can keep going."

"Your skin's waxy." He tugged off an overmitten with his teeth, reaching to touch her face, the rasp of his flight glove a phantom caress to her numb cheek. "You look like hell."

"And your manners stink, Rose-Bud."

Even his light chuckle gusted a hefty white swell. Temps were dropping fast. She needed to hang tough for him.

"Well, I imagine we both probably stink by now and just don't know because the stink is frozen. Regardless, you're still pasty. We need to stop. You will not lose so much as a toe on my watch."

Uh-oh. Overprotective alert. A safety net was all well and good, but not at the cost of his own life. Death, loss of dreams, loss of trust in happy endings had haunted her holiday season once too often. His, too.

When Josh had told her about the siege at his college, she'd wanted so much to tell him more about her past, but the words wouldn't pry free. Then or now. "My toes are fine. I'm wiggling them inside my boots as we speak and I really don't have the energy to waste arguing. So no, don't bother asking me what my socks and underwear look like."

"Fair enough. As long as you're sure. You're absolutely certain your feet are okay?" He jerked her to a stop, not much effort required on that one. As he leaned forward, his parka hood nearly met hers, sealing off the snowy world. "No faking for my benefit?"

"Damn it, Josh, I am not faking." She stomped her numb feet. "Do you hear me? Why in the world would I fake anything?"

"You tell me."

The silent heat of his words combined with the somber laser of his eyes stilled her. Trees rustled overhead in the silence. Snowflakes trickled through the tree cover to dot their forest-green extreme-weather gear.

He couldn't actually be accusing her of… Oh, God, he was. He was insinuating she faked during sex.

And damn him, he was right. "What did you just say?"

Josh stifled the urge to let loose a string of curses, all directed at himself for being a dumb ass and spilling the one thing he'd vowed never to say to her. He'd been tempted to mention it—in the beginning when his ego stung like hell. But he'd kept his yap zipped, certain that with time he could work through whatever was holding her back.

Time had run out. He pivoted away. "Nothing. I didn't say one damned thing."

"Oh, no, hotshot." She grabbed his shoulder, thumping until he turned to face her again. "I heard you."

"Then why are you asking me?"

"I want you to be clear."

"I didn't say shit," he snapped, his words like one of those frozen boughs after enough hellish weather and life for one day. Week. Year. "Just three words to make sure your toes aren't about to fall off."

"Not buying that for even a second, Rosen." She thrust her mittened hand against his chest in what he imagined was a pointed-finger jab. "Your eyes said a lot more than three words and none of it had a thing to do with my toes."

As if he wanted to think about her toes right now. Cute pink toes that were probably as waxy as her face. "So your toes are fine. Then let's keep moving."

He levered away and charged ahead. The last thing they needed was a sex discussion where he confirmed that yes, he knew she faked the big finish.

She enjoyed the hell out of foreplay. He wasn't so dense he missed that. But near the end of the actual act, that woman could talk herself out of an orgasm faster than the emergency barrier could stop a plane on a short runway.

Not that she was actually speaking out loud during those moments. Yet he could hear the gears turning in her head until the door clanged shut on any hope of a screaming finish. Sure, she continued to go through the motions. Acrobatic motions, incredibly sensual motions.

But only half there.

Every time he'd thought about confronting her on the subject—gently, of course, he wasn't a totally clueless male— her defensive expression afterward left him with no doubts. If he brought up the topic, this prideful woman would bolt.

So he'd tried his best, read anything on the subject he could find, and worked on strengthening his relationship with a wife he couldn't come close to understanding. He'd had hopes for their leave time together in their new home, romancing her in front of the fireplace with spiced wine and presents.

Only to have her bolt before they could unpack the wineglasses or untie the first bow.

Okay, so *he'd* walked. Technicality. But she'd made it clear she wanted him gone.

His senses heightened back in the moment. No footsteps crunched behind him. His feet slowed, halted. Not a man who believed much in retreating, still he appreciated the wisdom in battle prep and choosing his ground wisely. This was not it.

Staring ahead while too aware of her behind him, he forced low, controlled words through his teeth. "Now is not the time or place. Walk, damn it."

"Why did you marry me if you thought the sex sucked?"

Ah, hell. The very reason he did not want to discuss this with her. Logic wouldn't win him squat. "I did not say that."

"Your eyes implied it."

God, it killed him inside to hear the hurt under her defensiveness. So what if they froze? Damned well looked like that might happen, anyway.

Besides, logic also told him one's mental state contributed to survival, which offered the excuse he needed to delay walking farther just yet.

He strode back to her, gripped her shoulders and tugged her under the protective cover of a tree. She really did need a break even if she was too prideful to admit it. "That isn't what I meant. Being with you is…was…incredible."

Her defiant eyes met his, her face trimmed with the white fur around her hood, which almost managed to hide the tremble of her chin that had nothing to do with chattering teeth. "Apparently not if you felt something was lacking."

His fists clenched in her jacket. "Damn it, you're not lacking, but you *are* trying to pick a fight."

"I'm not the one who brought up faking, Colonel Freudian Slip."

How could he explain that being with Alicia when she was half there was better than being with anyone else completely in the moment? What a hellish line to walk, reassuring her about a relationship that was already over, opening them both back up to the slashing pain.

But he'd never been one to take the easy way out, and he'd once loved her enough to marry her. He owed her something, owed them both some peace.

"Okay, I admit that at first I expected things to be—" damn, but he was entering a minefield "—different between us."

"You thought because I'm unconventional on the outside that you were getting somebody more uninhibited?" She slumped back against the tree trunk, arms folded defensively over her chest. "Poor baby. What a shocker for you."

"Never mind." Screw this. He thrust away from the tree. "I'm bailing out of this conversation."

"Like hell you are." She hooked both her hands around his arm.

"Let's get this straight right now." He pivoted, smacking one hand over her head and meeting her nose to pink nose. "I was not disappointed. The attraction was there, no damn doubt about that. And that attraction was…is…so freaking intense I'm hard from just standing here with you, thinking about being inside you. The draw between us is that strong. Rare, even. Worth working for. I was certain that given time, we would have something—" heat flamed through him in spite of the arctic winds "—unsurpassable."

She sagged back, some of the fight seeping out of her in palpable waves. Her lips parted, begging to be kissed. "I am attracted to you, so much. I want you to know that."

"I know." And damn, damn, damn, but that knowledge blazed through him until he wanted her all over again. Here, now, against this tree until her cries of completion reverberated through the forest.

Why the hell did she keep closing herself off from him? The thought that it might be because she still loved some man long in the grave made Josh want to pound the tree. Blast something out of the sky.

He'd thought often enough if she would only be honest with him, he could have handled his gripping frustration better. He'd even reached deep to tell her about the holiday siege at his college in hopes she would open up. No dice.

And now here they were all open and chatty, and he didn't feel one damned bit better. "Don't the magazines all say a percentage of sex is in the woman's head? I figured the problem had more to do with how much we were apart. You needed more, hell, I don't know. Time. Time to be comfortable with me."

To forget about the other guy.

She stared down at her booted feet, not so much avoiding but seeming to absorb his words without having to meet his eyes. "Why didn't you say something before?"

"And willingly have this discussion? Shit. I'm screwed no matter what I say here."

Finally, she looked up, so much pain and remorse in her eyes, he had to restrain himself from gathering her against him—the fastest way he could think of to send her running.

And damned if maybe he might want to hear the rest of this conversation after all.

"It isn't you, Josh. It's me. I guess I'm one of those percentages of women who just don't—"

"You could." And, man, he wanted a second chance to prove that to her.

"God, you are so arrogant. Where is it written that whoever has the most orgasms wins? Do you really believe climaxing equates with love? If so, I'm not so sure I like what that says about you." Her pain swelled, mixing with typical Alicia fire and bravado. "What? You don't have an answer for that, genius?"

His momentary flash of hope at a second chance fizzled, replaced by a dawning sense of how much deeper their problems went than miscommunication in bed. Because still she wasn't being straight up with him.

He started to wonder if maybe he was hoping for too much from life. He could toss all the wisecracks out there and somehow there would still be a wall between him and the rest of the world.

Josh canted closer, his mouth hovering just over hers. "Maybe it's you who thinks coming equals love, otherwise why fake it? Why not be honest with me?" The answer unfolded too easily in his head, stomping that ember of hope dead even as her chin tipped to bring her lips nearer. "You thought I'd walk. And I'm not so sure I like what that says about what you think of me."

Her hand clamped around the back of his head. She yanked him down.

Josh jolted in surprise. He should have seen it coming, if for no other reason than it made zero sense. Alicia was all about the unexpected, after all.

She arched against him, her mouth open, hot and needy under his just as he remembered from so many times before with her. The hot pulse of lust surged through him, lust and something else he didn't want in his life anymore. Her tongue met and tangled with his, stroking insistently with a moist heat that warmed him from the inside out. Little whimpers tore from her throat, vibrating against him and assuring him nobody was faking anything at the moment.

Plastering herself to him, Alicia locked her arms around his neck, her body flattened to his until he could almost swear their layers of clothes melted away. He pressed her against the tree, no clue where this was going but unable to scrounge the will to stop after weeks without the feel of her against him.

A fresh gust of wind battered his back, but he barely felt it. Rustling branches overhead sounded too much like rustling sheets for his comfort level.

Splat.

Except sheets didn't dump snow on his head. The cold thud brought a needed splash of reality. His fogged brain cleared enough for him to sense the desperation and frenzy in her.

Josh eased away. "We need to stop and find cover for the night."

Alicia's hold stayed strong. "No. Later," she mumbled, tracing his bottom lip with her tongue. "Soon. Not now."

He backed away from the tree. From her. From the temptation to say screw it all and keep kissing her instead of talking, because he knew well the woman enjoyed the hell out of kissing him. "Come on. We are done with this topic of conversation. And anything else, for that matter. I'm going to find somewhere to camp and you'd damn well better follow."

He swiped aside a branch and forced his feet forward.

"You don't like what I'm thinking about you? Well you *did* walk, Joshua Rosen." Her accusation full of pain chased him on the wind. "You're walking now."

Huh? He stopped without turning. "Are you saying you didn't want me to move out of the apartment?" When she didn't answer, he glanced back over his shoulder. "Well?"

Panic flared in her eyes along with poorly shielded hurt. "Um, you know, I think you were right earlier. This isn't the time to discuss anything important. The one-in-four-decisions-sucking rule, remember? Besides, the longer we stand around, the longer we're cold."

He started to snap right back, then hesitated. He'd seen his wife face enemy fire without flinching, yet now her voice trembled from fear over…what? Not the cold, but something else that apparently he'd been too wrapped up in his own bruised ego to notice before. If he ever expected to move on with his life, he needed to bank his anger and settle things with her one way or another. He couldn't live in this limbo any longer.

Turning, he planted his boots and stood his ground. "I asked you a question. Were you just pissed and not serious when you told me to get the hell out and don't come back?"

Tears pooled and crystallized in the corners of her eyes. Tears—holy hell—from Alicia?

"I'm sorry, Josh. And I really do mean that. I thought that…" She paused, struggling for words. "That what we had would be enough. That I could get past— That I could be—"

Tipping her face to the sky, she blinked fast.

He stepped closer. "Alicia—"

"Stop." She held up a shaky hand as if to place fresh barriers between them. As if there weren't enough already. "This isn't going to get us anywhere."

"Were you or were you not serious?"

"I meant every word."

"Do you still mean them?"

She hesitated a second too long. "Yes. Of course."

Not buying it. "Maybe we should—"

"No," she insisted, both hands up, palms facing out to stop him this time. "I know you. You resent not being able to decipher something. Figuring me out has become a challenge to you. That's all."

Apparently she understood him pretty well. "I'll admit to that. But it's not the whole picture."

"Regardless, how about I clear up the mystery for you? This isn't something you can fix. The problem is mine and it's not fixable," she insisted with a strength that suddenly seemed brittle.

"Why are you so damned sure? Maybe I might have an answer for you, but we'll never know for sure since you're holding out on me, and I don't mean in bed."

She stilled. "I don't know what you mean."

"I think you do. Even if we end up in divorce court, we meant something to each other. I do not want to spend the rest of my life wondering where the hell I screwed up."

"How many times do I have to repeat myself?" Her voice cracked. "It wasn't you. You need all the facts? Fine. Eight years ago, I was dating a man. Ben. We were thinking about getting married. But I imagine my blabbermouth sister has already told you that much."

He didn't bother acknowledging the obvious.

"What my sister didn't know was that over Christmas break, I turned down his surprise gift of a two-carat solitaire engagement ring."

Turned down?

He definitely hadn't seen this twist coming. "So why does this guy still have such a hold over you?"

"His possessiveness had become smothering." She forced the facts out on labored wafts of air, but with shoulders braced. "He didn't take it well. But I was prepared for that and it didn't worry me. After all, I was only a semester away from being a commissioned officer. A warrior. I could protect myself. Or so I thought."

The answer he'd been waiting for roared to life inside him ahead of the rest of her words. He knew what would come next. And no. Hell, no! He wanted to back up this conversation, somehow roll back time eight years to wipe out what he was now certain had happened to his wife.

Bilious rage burned up his throat, only to be frozen into a choking chunk of frustration.

Alicia met his gaze dead-on, warrior strong even when wounded, her face as wind-raw as her words. "When I told him it was over, he attacked me."

Chapter Five

Alicia held herself still and tall, so brittle inside she feared the building winds might shatter her. Even more than the storm winds, she feared Josh's reaction.

Her gaze raked from the hard lines of his stoic face to his fisted gloves, all the way down to his mukluks planted in the snow, while she waited for him to absorb the words she'd never told anyone. Snow pouring from the sky collected on his shoulders while he waited for her to finish.

Whoever said confiding heartache lessened the burden had been a big, fat fraud. She didn't feel one bit better. In fact, the burden so overpowered her right now, she longed to sink into a drift or climb up one of those towering trees again and hide.

Not behavior worthy of her uniform.

She didn't want to remember that night from eight years ago, much less talk about it. But somehow Josh slipped past her defenses, pushed her buttons, pushed her until the words had spilled free.

Apparently she hadn't kept him in the dark after all. A mortifying thought. She wasn't totally inexperienced. She knew enough to realize Josh was good in bed. Really good. Generous and sexy.

She just wished she could fully benefit, that they both could.

He deserved an explanation. But why did it have to be now? Although something about this stark, ends-of-the-earth landscape echoed the rawness inside her.

Josh's silence left her fidgeting until finally she blurted, "He didn't assault me sexually, if that's what you're thinking. You can relax."

"Relax?" He shook his head slowly, still not moving otherwise. "I don't think so."

What was he thinking? She forced words up her throat, each one scraping like icy shards. "He was...beyond upset. But somehow I still didn't see the first punch coming—"

A rustling sounded from behind her, and how she welcomed the distraction as a chance to gather her thoughts. Her instincts kicked in, and survival thoughts took over.

Josh's head jerked up. He shoved past and ahead of her, predictably protecting. Rather than argue, she decided to watch his back. The man needed it whether he realized it or not.

She dipped her hand inside her parka to pull her flare gun from her survival vest. Steps stealthy, they dodged larger drifts, minimizing the crunching of snow as much as possible.

Her heart pounded in her ears, pumped in her chest so hard surely her jacket must be pulsing. Branches swayed and crackled ahead.

"Down," Josh ordered in a whisper.

She dropped to her stomach beside him. Birch boughs swept wide. She tensed, hand gripping the gun. The ground trembled under her.

Caribou raced into sight.

Catherine Mann

She exhaled a gust of relief. The small herd loped past, kicking up a cloud of dusty snow behind them. Tension seeped from her. Rolling to her side, she steadied her heart and studied her husband.

Oops, not the best way to steady her heart, but still she couldn't help but stare at him to reassure herself he was whole and not seconds away from meeting some illegal miner's rifle. "Josh? Are you okay?"

"Look." He pointed to the gaping tunnel formed by broken branches.

Dragging her eyes from him, she looked ahead, squinting. Slowly, the fragmented landscape came into focus to showcase a small clearing.

And shelter.

A rusty metal Quonset hut filled the area, apparently abandoned. Leaving her with no other excuses to avoid the rest of her discussion with her husband.

Josh rechecked his newly fashioned lock on the door inside the Quonset hut. Not exactly the Hilton in Hawaii, but more welcome.

He wedged a piece of wood against the door, which was pounded by battering winds and sheeting ice that picked up force and speed with each passing minute. He'd managed the best he could with security and was fast running out of tasks to keep his mind off Alicia behind him preparing to wash. Taking off her ice-caked clothing and draping it over fishing wire strung across the lone room.

Focus on survival, not the sound of rustling clothes and water trickling into a metal basin.

Padding along the wood floor in his bare feet, he surveyed the twenty-by-ten-foot metal shelter, which looked more like half a rusty metal cylinder dropped onto the ground. But it blocked the howling snowstorm kicking back up full force. The single door also made guarding their backs from intruders a helluva lot easier, not that anyone would be coming their way until the renewed blizzard passed.

The woodstove already snapped with a fire, cranking the temp inside up to a balmy fifty degrees while melting a second basin tub of ice. The open grate allowed the flames to cast a low haze of light through the room, along with dwindling sun through the thick Plexiglas window in the door. They would be able to conserve their flashlight batteries.

Luckily law enforcement and other government agencies kept such buildings stocked with rudimentary survival supplies, a routine part of the state budget. Rarely were the places looted. There wasn't much to take, anyway, just a small box of dehydrated foods, a couple of aluminum washtubs, a woodstove welded to the floor with stacks of wood beside.

And four sleeping-bag bedrolls.

He'd think about the bed part later.

The fishing line swayed under the weight of the drying winter gear, his parka and snow pants as well as hers, creating a makeshift curtain to conceal Alicia while she washed.

Except it didn't block all of her from view.

Her feet shuffled in a semicircle—in toe socks patterned with reindeer sporting neon noses. The festive garb seemed out of synch with the stark setting and yet so…her. Somehow that view of her tempted him as much as if the curtain vanished.

Exhaustion swamped him. He must be near dead on his feet, otherwise he wouldn't be standing around gawking at her socks.

Nothing left to do but strip down, too. Survival first. Clothes damp from snow and sweat were killers out here. He peeled off his flight suit, socks, thermal shirt and pants. Washed, shaved. Dumped in more buckets of ice to melt. And still Alicia hadn't come out.

What was taking her so long? Damn, but he hated not knowing what to say to her. He scooped his hands through the lukewarm water, splashing up on his face and over his head until he saturated his close-cropped hair and admitted to himself he'd delayed thinking as long as he could.

Finally, he let his mind settle on what she'd told him. She didn't still love the other guy after all. The bastard had hurt her. How much, Josh couldn't even let himself think about yet or he would go crazy from inaction.

Why the hell hadn't he considered it before? The reason for her reticence made perfect sense. He wanted to pound his head against the wall for his own idiocy.

He watched her reindeer socks shuffle until he couldn't wait any longer to do something for her.

"Are you all right back there?" he asked, for now and the past.

"Yeah." Her voice drifted over the line, husky from so long in the stark elements. Please God, not from crying. "Just trying to balance everything until I finish up."

Too easily memories of helping her bathe in the past came to mind. They'd lucked into a joint TDY, staying in a bed-and-breakfast with an incredible spa tub. She'd been so slick and hot and all over him. He hadn't misread her desire, damn it.

The line of dripping green survival gear rippled from her movement, her feet padding to the end. His gut knotted. She stepped into view. He forced his eyes to stay locked on her pale face, the dim light of the fire throwing a candlelight glow all around her.

A sheepish smile played with her lips as she pointed to her matching bra and panties that he would not, would *not* look at.

"Red-plaid underwear. Flannel," she declared. Her toes wiggled in her Rudolph socks, a safer place to keep his gaze. "Mystery solved. Nothing near as sexy as a thong."

He disagreed.

So much for keeping his eyes on her face. Holiday plaid stretched across her generous breasts, dog tags dangling. The sports-bra style covered much while leaving nothing to the imagination. He didn't need to look further. Her every curve, the dip of her waist, slight flare of her hips stayed imprinted in his photographic memory. His hands remembered well the contrasting feel of her soft breasts and toned muscles.

And damn it, but he was starting to become aroused. Starting? Hell, he was already there, and no way to hide it.

Way to be sensitive, dumb ass.

Wincing, he turned away to stoke the fire, the one in the woodstove, since the one in his boxers was roaring just fine. "Damn, hon, I'm sorry. You're just so—"

"Josh, please don't go getting all weirded out on me about this." Her feet whispered across the floor, closer, until the heat of her seared his back without their skin even touching. "I'm the same person I was four weeks ago when you walked through our bedroom naked with pretty much the same action going on then as now."

"Roger. No getting weirded out." He turned, an inch of crackling air between them. "And I'm not. I just don't know how you need me to react."

"I need you to be honest."

He wanted to note that honesty from her might have been helpful over the past months, but that didn't seem wise. He stuffed down residual anger at her, himself, and most of all at the bastard who'd hurt her. "We have to talk about what you told me."

"I know we do, and we will. Soon. I promise. It's just not easy." The confident brace of her bare shoulders faltered. "I've never told anyone before."

No one? In eight years?

His momentary flash of victory over being the one she'd told faded as he realized how high walls eight years in the making would be. Unease dripped over him like the water plopping from their clothes onto the cracked wood floor.

He stared down, no answers scrolled on the planks. But he did discover a distraction to buy time until he could figure out what to do next. "Let me see your feet."

"Huh?" Confusion puckered her brow even as she grinned. "You're one sick puppy, Rose-Bud."

"I need to check your feet for frostbite."

"Oh, how are yours?"

He lifted his bare feet one at a time. "Doing well. I may have some skin peel off, but I'm not going to lose any toes."

In front of the woodstove, he unfurled the sleeping bags and unzipped them. He draped one for padding and insulation on the floor. He zipped two together to make a double bed—she would just have to live with that because sharing body heat was practical. Then he draped the final open bag over top, musty but clean.

And too inviting. He stepped back. "Now, sit."

"Yes, sir." Shooting him a half salute, she dropped onto the dark green beddings and rolled off her socks.

He crouched on his haunches in front of her. Sitting with her on their bedroll seemed to be crossing a boundary best left in place until after they talked more. He lifted her left foot, grazing his thumbs along the tender instep to check circulation.

Goose bumps prickled over her very bare skin.

His gaze jerked up to hers. She was watching him. Intently. Aware. Her breasts rose faster. Only shrieking wind and groaning metal rivets filled the silence between them.

He returned his focus to her feet, safer territory. Sort of. He rifled through his survival vest in search of the salve for blisters. He shuffled aside the magnifying glass, two pressure bandages, an eye patch, fishing hooks, until he found Band-Aids and the tube of disinfectant.

After tending one foot, he lowered it and lifted the other, careful to keep his touch firm this time. "I'm sorry you won't get to call your family on Christmas Eve morning."

"That's pretty much the least of our worries right now."

Okay, that caught his attention. Until he realized she meant whoever set up that mini-mining operation and not the fact that he could barely keep his hands off her. "We're okay for the next few hours at least until the storm lets up again. I added an extra wedge in the door while you were bathing. The flare guns are loaded. That's the most we can do for now."

She forked her fingers through sweaty locks swirled into loose curls around her face. "What a way to spend the holidays. Maybe I should start singing again or something. There were these two people in my sister's squadron who got stuck in the desert for Christmas Eve. They put together a whole survivalist celebration with a scrub-brush tree and cactus-slice cider."

Her story told him more than perhaps she intended. She wanted easy. Normal. Not weirded out. He could do normal, funny. For her, he would do damned near anything. "Is that a hint for me to hump my butt back outside and start gathering up pinecones to rig decorations?"

"Hey, we could string them over the stove with snare wire, like a garland."

He laughed. She didn't. His humor faded. "You are joking, right?"

She blinked back at him. Already his skin chilled over just the thought of tromping outside again. Had she gone unhinged from the stress? But shit, if she wanted pinecones then he'd get them. He started to push up from the floor.

A wicked smile split her face. "Gotcha."

His laugh burst free, tangled with hers. "Yeah, you sure did."

In more ways than one. Laughter faded.

He needed distance to make it through the night. He tugged out two packs of dried apples and tossed one to her. "It's about the closest I can come to apple cider."

"It's great. Thanks."

Silently they tore open the packets and reconstituted them with melted ice. He ate, trying not to watch her fingers scoop out the sweet fruit and suck the syrup off her fingers.

Ah, hell.

What was it about this woman that grabbed hold of him and wouldn't let go? A woman who didn't need a damned thing from him and would only be open about her feelings when pressed to the wall. A woman with pain in her past he didn't have a clue how to heal.

Failure didn't sit well with him. "What was it you were having trouble with behind the screen?"

"Oh, um, I wanted to wash my hair." She set aside her empty fruit packet. "Ridiculous vanity, but I still feel gross. Probably silly to risk catching a cold."

Well, hell. There was something he could do for her after all. He may not be able to address her deeper wounds, but he could damn well wash her hair. And right now he needed action. He needed to feel like a man taking care of his wife.

A sexist thought? Probably. Especially considering his warrior wife could protect herself. But hey, he'd keep the words to himself. "Why not go for it? There's enough melted ice. It's warm in here. Storm's going to last through the night. You'll be well dry by morning."

She chewed her bottom lip but didn't say no.

Two long strides took him to the clothesline. He ducked behind to retrieve the extra metal washtub and place it in front of her. "You can lean over this. I'll pour the water from the other one over your head. No big deal."

Suddenly, an image of washing her back in that European hot tub splashed across his mind—a mighty damned big deal. But after months of her keeping such a crucial piece of herself away from him, he needed this sign from her. He may not ever have her love again, but he needed her trust.

She was only trusting him to wash her hair. No big deal, right? She wasn't giving him her heart again.

Just lean over that tub and let him pour some water over her head. It wasn't like they had anything else to do while snowbound in a rusted-out Quonset hut. Nope. Nothing else to do—except get naked together or talk.

Washing her hair sounded like a fine idea.

Alicia folded her hands in her lap to conceal the fact that they shook more than before her first solo flight in pilot training. "You really want to wash my hair?"

She watched him heft the water-filled tub from the stove, muscles rippling across his back, bulging along his legs. How unfair he had such a great butt that even Scooby-Doo boxers looked macho.

Josh crouched beside the two washtubs, beside her. "Consider it my Christmas present to you since we're stuck out here. And hey, a little secret between you and me." He winked, his best Josh-charm smile in place. "I really stunk at arts and crafts when I was a kid. I failed Paper Chain Making 101, so it's a fair bet any pinecone garland I string would suck."

He ripped a sheet mixed with the bedroll into towel-size strips, his flexing chest broad with dog tags nestled between toned pecs, bare, inviting. "I think we're better off if I give you the rustic salon treatment."

Even through his jokes and keeping things light for her, she could see his need for her trust. He was talking about a lot more than a hair wash right now and they both knew it. As much as she believed she had a right to her secrets, she also should have been honest with him. Or cut him loose.

She'd married this man while holding herself away. Their marriage might not be salvageable, but she still owed him something in honor of the love they had once shared.

The shaking in her hands spread to her insides until she feared she rattled as much as the Quonset hut against the roaring winds. But she wasn't a coward. She would start with the hair first, secrets later.

"Thank you. Since I can't have the pinecone trimmings, I'll graciously accept the hair wash."

Shifting her legs under her, she sat on her feet and leaned her head over the tub on the floor by the one full of clean water. Her dog tags clanked against the metal. Smoke from the fire drafted surprisingly well up the pipe until only the sweet scent of burning wood remained, almost sweet enough to cover the musty smell of bedding and damp clothes.

She gripped the sides of the basin, trying not to feel silly and oh so vulnerable with the back of her neck bare as if for an executioner. Her spine arched right there for him to see, curved in such a submissive pose.

Come on, Josh. Talk. Or do something other than tempt her with the warm whisper of his breath across her shoulders. The fire snapped and popped like the nerves inside her.

He cupped his hands in the water and trickled it over her head. Lukewarm, but still she shivered.

"Do you want me to heat it more?"

And wait longer? Or explain why now she suddenly didn't mind having grungy hair because the mere thought of being so exposed to him left her feeling weak and hungry? "No. Thanks. Go ahead and finish."

His hands continued to scoop until her hair was saturated. He reached for the bar of soap and lathered it in his hands. Not a salon-quality shampoo, but she would settle for clean.

Soon, please.

He palmed the crown of her head, slowly working over her hair to spread the suds. Strong fingers from an even stronger man massaged gentle circles along her scalp. Lethargy spread through her exhausted body. Against her steely will, her head lolled forward.

As long as she was doing the vulnerable gig, she might as well go for broke and finish spilling her story. At least this way she didn't have to look him in the face when she talked. "When I told him, Ben, that it was over, he seemed so surprised."

Josh's fingers slowed, then picked up pace again while he stayed silent.

"He just sat there behind the steering wheel, staring stunned out the windshield over the city. I thought all the signs were there that the relationship needed to end, but he seemed clueless."

And what were her instincts telling her now? That she wanted to climb all over Josh and lose herself in his arms. In him. She yearned to forget everything and roll with him on the sleeping bag, bathed in the warmth and light of a crackling fire and his equally hot touch. But even if she trusted him, she wasn't so certain she trusted herself.

Stay strong. Hold it together.

Even if that meant being alone? Losing the incredible feel of Josh's hands, so conversely comforting and stimulating.

Her hands clinging tighter to the metal rim, she rested her forehead against her knuckles. "Then he started crying and begging me not to leave him. I actually felt sorry for him—until I realized he was playing me. When the tears didn't work, he got angry." An understatement. Her jaw ached at the memory. "He hit me. I still don't understand how he gained control over the situation so quickly. I guess he caught me by surprise. And then I was dazed. My head hit the dash pretty hard."

His fingers twitched against her skull. Veins stood out along the tops of his feet. His hands fell away and she almost cried out at the loss. Then she heard the swirl of water, caught a flash as he scooped through.

Water trickled over her head and into the basin, parting murky suds. If only the past could be that easy to clean away, but she knew otherwise. "Eventually, he realized what he'd done."

After more blows than she could count or even fully remember. She couldn't begin to explain her mad scramble trying to get the hell out of the car. Every one of her nails breaking as she scraped her hand across the door, her vision clouded from a swollen eye, snarls of her hair, tears born of terror.

She couldn't bring herself to go into that much detail, but surely Josh would understand how those horrible details imprinted themselves in the mind after his college trauma with the gunman.

A strange new thought flickered. Why had she never thought of Josh understanding because of his past? Likely because he seemed so damned invincible she couldn't imagine him feeling so weak. "Ben panicked. I think. I'm not really sure what was going through his head. He started the car."

She blinked back tears that wanted to slip into those streams of water Josh kept pouring over her with soothing regularity. "He drove for maybe a mile or two before the car went off the road. We rolled down an embankment. He died and somehow I survived."

The water stopped. Josh cupped the back of her neck with one hand. She didn't bother protesting, just let the comforting heat of his touch seep into her. "At the hospital, they all assumed my bruises—" the broken ribs "—were from the accident. I didn't see the need to tell anyone otherwise. It would have only hurt his family even more when they were already grieving."

She swiped the cloth off the floor, pressing it to her eyes, then up over her wet hair until she ran out of delay tactics. She looked up at Josh, his face calm even while veins bulged along his arms as well as his feet now. A pulse popped in his temple.

He shoved the washtubs aside with overly controlled movements. "You still didn't tell anyone? Just for you, to let it out?"

"And risk having it get back to his family? Or mine?" The towel fell to her lap along with her hands. "You know how overprotective my father is. When he heard that both Darcy and I wanted to go in the military, he blew a gasket. One of the few times he ever lost his temper with us. I stood him down straight off, but baby-girl Darcy had a harder time winning. The last thing I needed was more reason for him to think I couldn't protect myself. No. It was better just to let it go."

One brow shot up so high he didn't need to say a word.

"Or at least try to let it go." She twisted the damp towel around her hands. "I know it's been eight years, and yes, I still have boundary issues. I have some serious trust issues as well way beyond whether or not to let go during sex."

He hunkered beside her, letting her talk, giving her space. But did he have to be so broad and big and looming in doing it?

She combed her fingers through her hair, more for something to do than from any real need to tame her short locks. A few months after Ben's death, she'd chopped off her long hair that had impeded her view on that horrible night. One of a million little ways she'd struggled to resurrect her confidence.

"My head can tell me all day long that he was just a creep, but I trusted that creep for nearly two years. And when a person you trust betrays you in such a fundamental way… It breaks something inside that I'm not sure I can ever fix. So yeah, you were right when we argued back at the apartment about me not giving my all to the marriage. I haven't been a hundred percent yours in ways that had nothing to do with sex."

There. She'd admitted it. God, why couldn't he just put his arms around her and tell her everything would be fine? Her body still hummed with the awareness from the way he'd seduced her with a simple hair wash.

And she suffered no delusions. She'd been thoroughly seduced by his touch. But where did they go from here? "Will you just sit down," she snapped, then felt like a total witch. "Please. Don't you want to talk? Or ask me questions? Or yell at me for not telling you sooner?"

He lowered beside her, his long legs stretching to the end of the bedroll. "Do *you* want to talk more?"

About as much as she wanted an icicle in her eye. "Do you?"

"Right now isn't about me. It's about you. And actually, I think you've had enough of talking for one night."

Her stomach twisted tight with nerves … and an undeniable anticipation that transcended good judgment. "Oh. So do you, uh, wanna go to bed?"

Chapter Six

Go to bed? Hell, yeah, he wanted to go to bed with Alicia. More than he needed air he longed to toss a few more logs on the fire, recline them both along the padded length of the stacked sleeping bags and celebrate that they were still alive. They wouldn't even have to worry about birth control thanks to her Norplant.

He always burned to bury himself inside her, an ever-present desire Josh didn't see waning anytime soon. If ever. Especially not with her on a blanket wearing nothing but a red plaid bra-and-panties set, looking like the best gift ever waiting to be unwrapped. Her slicked-back hair reminded him too well of the feel of her seeping into him while he massaged soap into her scalp.

But right now, more than sex, he needed to hold her and he suspected she needed the same. So he watched for some sign that she wouldn't bolt if he gathered her pride-filled body against him and offered her the comfort he knew she would never let down her guard enough to request. Sex could wait.

Sex?

Making love, he amended, because hell, yes, he loved her.

Even as pissed as he was right now over her keeping such an important part of her past from him, he couldn't deny the obvious any longer. He still loved his wife.

How damned inconvenient that he should figure it out at a time when things between them seemed bleaker than ever, with her words still hammering around inside him, pounding echoes of emotions that were anything but gentle. Anger. Rage. All at a dead man, which left no outlet.

He shoved aside his own selfish urge to stomp out his frustrations and focused on Alicia. "Bed it is. We both need sleep."

"Sleep. Right."

Tension dissipated from her lowering shoulders so visibly he almost laughed. Then he saw a flicker of disappointment in her eyes.

She wanted to do more than sleep? Whether it would be making love or sex for her, his body still shouted a great big throbbing *go for it!*

Not wise. She deserved the cosseting, holding, sympathy no one had known to give her eight years ago.

He tossed two extra logs on the fire. Flicking aside the edge of the double sleeping bag, he slipped inside onto his back, arm cranked under his head, and closed his eyes.

"You're not fooling me with that laid-back attitude, Joshua Rosen."

God, he loved her spunk that kicked right through after a day that would have leveled most people from the get-go.

"Good." He kept his eyes closed. "Then you'll know it's better not to mess with me right now. Climb in and go to sleep before you turn into a Popsicle."

More like a Dreamsicle, with all that creamy skin he didn't have to see to envision, and, yeah, he wanted to lick every inch of her.

Covers rustled and shuffled with the intrusion of another body—*her* body and heat. Fifty degrees felt like a furnace now.

She shifted, settled, then rolled right up against his side. Well, damn. There she went surprising him again. Sure, she was only doing the practical thing, but practical wasn't always easy as he could tell too well from her rigid muscles.

He slipped his arm out from under his head, working not to elbow her in the minimal-maneuver room. He wrapped his arm around her shoulders, drew her closer. Her sigh warmed over his chest as she melted against his side in cuddle mode.

Day by day, he forgot how small she was, the force of her personality, her confidence and expertise in the plane surpassing anything to do with height and frame. Right now, she felt very mortal against him, at the mercy of the elements outside and some faceless threat likely on their tail.

The clean scent of soap and the warm softness of her skin saturated his senses. He might not be able to fight the demons in her past, but he would damned well stand down any and every one in her present. He didn't even bother trying to ignore the primal need to protect. He just let it all seep into him while his body succumbed to exhaustion, sleep demanding he surrender his hold on logic and let dreams take command….

God, he respected this woman's no-surrender attitude in the air. Just what he needed in combat from a front-seater in his F-15.

Sky streaked past his windscreen, jungle below blooming with secondary explosions. He didn't doubt for a minute he could nail those narrow-margin bomb targets and hold off the enemy until rescue came for the pinned-down Rangers. As long as his pilot didn't blink.

He'd expected to walk her through the rough stuff on her first mission in Cantou, play the senior officer role. But she was holding up her end of the team spirit with twenty Rangers on the ground counting on them.

He'd been paired with her because of his experience in the cockpit. Her two-star daddy kept his eye on his kids— even when they didn't need it. And Vogue definitely didn't need slack. Her even breaths echoed in his helmet at a steady pace with his own.

She had plenty of stick time and skill, but the true test didn't come until that first hairy combat mission. This one more than qualified and she was hanging tough, leaving him free to concentrate on his job.

Laser squirt. Target set. He launched his last GBU. Shack.

The victory was short lived since now their bombs had been depleted. "We're Winchester bombs," he announced, clipping updates to the commander on the ground. "All we've got left is about four passes of a twenty mike-mike." A twenty-millimeter mounted for a strafing run— a low level run with the pilot shooting the Gatling gun cannon at targets. Definitely hairy flying, especially while shooting.

Time to put Vogue's feet to the fire.

His headset crackled with the response from the ground. "Roger that," the Ranger commander answered, machine guns rat-tat-tatting in the distance. "We're taking a lot of fire from the north-south tree line. Three hundred meters west of our position."

"Copy. Help on the way. Descending now." In concert with his call, Vogue dipped the nose of the F-15, catapulting them into the same fire that had downed the helicopter full of Rangers.

Bullets spit from their F-15 toward the ground. An enemy vehicle exploded. They were so damned close he could see a vehicle door fly to the side and slap the ground.

The plane slowed, swooped, turned inward into the spiral to reverse the negative G-forces into a more manageable positive level. Josh felt his G-suit compression pants inflate along his legs, pushing blood back up to his head so he wouldn't lose consciousness.

His fingers flew over his control panel, eyes scanning the sky, all the while he snapped updates through the headset, filtered information from the ground to Alicia—Vogue. Not Alicia. Damn, where was his head?

The pressure of G-forces increased. He fought against the fog, worked the blood back up to his head. Vogue's voice popped requests and questions between labored breaths. Slowly the figures in mottled cammo morphed, transforming into jeans-clad students at desks.

In the middle of the jungle?

That didn't make sense. They'd saved those Rangers and been awarded a Silver Star for the mission. Except when had dreams ever made sense or allowed their victims control?

Josh grappled for consciousness even while the nightmare sucked him deeper into a past with guns blazing in a time when no amount of confidence or training could save anyone. Except he took Alicia with him, and now there was plenty of blood everywhere.

Bullets tore into the ground. Faster, in circles. Faster still. Cycloning mud and blood up. Spiraling toward Alicia. And there wasn't a damned thing he could do to save her.

Her husky tones and heavy breaths filled his mind. "Josh? Where are you? Come on back to me...."

"Josh?" Alicia nudged her sleeping husband's bare shoulder. Gently. Definitely gently. She knew enough about combat nightmares to be wary of startling somebody in the grips of one. His mumbled radio calls and flight lingo left her in no doubt. He was deep in battle mode. "Where are you? Come on back to me. We're here. In Alaska. Safe."

For now.

She stroked over his shoulder, down his arm to either ease him awake or soothe him into more peaceful dreams. How long had they been asleep? Was it Christmas Eve yet? No light filtered through the lone window. Low embers glowed from the fire, the murky dark shrouding the metal hut with intimacy.

Alicia continued to caress his shoulder and mutter shushing noises. Muscles bulged under her touch, launching a tingling shower through her while she was still too sleep-woozy to resist. Oh, boy.

She'd really expected them to have sex after his sensual hair wash. She'd actually hoped he would wash away the memories with his body against hers. His arousal had been more than obvious. She'd been more than a little turned on herself, and yet he'd shut her down. Fast. So what if he was being practical?

She didn't want him to feel *practical* around her.

Alicia jabbed his ankle with her toe. Josh bolted upright. She jerked back, flinched. His eyes snapped open. Blinking, his chest heaving, he scrubbed his hands over his face.

Guilt tweaked her. She was being selfish. He was right to keep his distance if just talking to her brought nightmares.

Sheesh. Like they needed any more complications in their relationship.

She forked her fingers through her dried-crazy hair and decided it probably didn't look any wilder than when she tousled it with gel. And why was she worrying about her appearance, anyway?

Duh.

Because of Josh, whose close-cropped black hair looked just fine. Great, for that matter—right over a brow still furrowed. "Are you okay?"

"Yeah, I just hate the way dreams are so damned illogical." He scratched his chest absently. Did he have to keep drawing attention to those hunky pecs if he didn't intend to let her touch them? "It's like the cosmos is playing a big trick on me when I don't have my brain engaged to override it. Which is a lame thing to think since it's my brain doing the dreaming. I just need to clear my head."

He flipped back the sleeping bag and stood, leaving a cold draft beside her. Inside her as well. She watched while he stoked the fire to life, adding more wood from the two large stacks beside the cast-iron stove. Flames flickered higher, bronzing his already tanned skin in an amber glow.

Heat blossomed from the grate over her.

She needed to know how he felt about what she'd told him, even if it hurt. "Is what I said earlier freaking you out?"

He jerked to face her. "No. Absolutely not. Well, not the way you're implying, anyway."

"In what way, then?"

She could all but see the wheels turning in his head as he struggled for words to corral thoughts bigger than simple language allowed. "And could you please, please come back into the sleeping bag before you freeze your cute butt off."

Shadows flicked over the smile playing at his mouth. "There you go, surprising me again."

But he didn't argue, instead slipping those long, corded legs into the cottony warmth beside her. Gulp. "Uh, Josh? In what way have I freaked you out?"

"I've always trusted that you could hold your own in the air, but this isn't about flying. And before you go getting your back up, I really mean that. I'm okay with your fighting in combat. That's work, and you're trained."

"Then what do you mean?"

"This other thing going on…it's not about work." He stared into the open grate, flames licking higher, sparking from the logs. "I'm a man, damn it. Your husband. Call it Cro-Magnon, but it's tough for me to accept there's no way I can right this wrong done to you. Hell, give me somebody to punch or a target to take out. I'm having trouble not being able to fight back. That's why I joined the Air Force after the crap that happened in college. I needed to defend." He shook his head. "I know, I know. It doesn't make any sense. This should be about you, anyhow, not about me."

She admired the way he'd found to make something positive out of something so awful. If only she could have managed the same.

"What you're saying makes total sense. And I've pulled you into this, so it's definitely about you, too." She hugged her knees to her chest, resting her chin on them. "It was strange afterward. I wanted him to come back to life so I could file charges with the police. I wanted to take that bastard to court and make him pay, have a role in putting him away so he never hurt anyone again. By protecting others from him, it would somehow make up for not being able to protect myself. So yeah, I understand."

She'd just never expected him to understand, not her invincible husband. Something warm unfurled inside her, relaxed and spread as he became a bit more human in her eyes.

Very human. And hunky. With the sleeping bag pooled around his waist, there was still plenty of naked Josh left for her eyes to feast on faster than a holiday dinner.

She tried to remember the reasons they'd split, why she shouldn't reach and explore the rough texture of dark hair sprinkled across his muscular pecs. She really tried not to think of splaying her fingers along the ridges of his flat belly.

Tried. Unsuccessfully.

Her mind reeled with images of doing each of those things and much more in the past. Yet all those undeniably erotic memories didn't come close to arousing her as much as simply gazing at him now, boundaries lowered. No secrets between them.

A little voice niggled in the back of her head, reminding her that she'd only shared her secrets with him when pressed to the wall and surely that said things about their relationship she didn't want to think about. Not now.

With the storm raging outside, the world on hold but threats still looming, she wanted to take this moment. Explore this deepening sensation.

Explore her husband.

Restraints snapped in her mind and she winged a silent cheer that they didn't have to worry about birth control thanks to her Norplant. Her hand floated up, gliding to a perfect landing on Josh's chest. A spark tingled through her fingertips, up her arm, singed deep in her stomach, and at just one touch. How much more could she have?

He clamped her wrist. But he didn't move her away. "Alicia," he growled. "This isn't smart."

"Maybe for once I'm smarter than you are. Or wiser at least. Wisdom is more important than smarts, don't you think?"

She flipped her hand to twine her fingers with his. Gliding forward, she trapped their linked hands between them, her breasts flattening against the warm, hard wall of his chest. Her body writhed of its own volition in a sinuous arch against him, bringing her lips closer.

"I think you want me, too," she whispered against his mouth before her other hand slid to his lap and found… Oh, yeah. Her smile caressed him. "I *know* you want me."

"That's never been in question."

"Then what is it?"

"Your timing. I'm not clear on your reasoning."

Great. She wanted Josh and he wanted logic.

Still, with the throbbing evidence of his arousal under her hand, she couldn't help but be touched by the fact that he was holding back for her. "I wish I could give you some fabulously brilliant Einstein-esque explanation, but I can't. I only know that this life-and-death-struggle business has pushed aside boundaries for me. Will they be in place again once we return to the real world? I hope not. But what if we don't get the chance to find out? What if now is all we have? I want now, Josh. I want you."

His already impressive arousal twitched in her hand, which she took as a definite endorsement to continue. She stroked upward to his chest until her palm landed on his heart again, perhaps just as strong an indicator of his intent as his erection.

"And how can you be sure this is right for you?" he asked, his heart slugging against her fingers.

"Maybe there's something liberating about know-ing you don't have certain—" awkward moment alert! "—physical expectations from me. It seems like now I can just enjoy what I enjoy, the process, and not worry about the rest. While I know this isn't the most festive of settings, something about the season just makes me hopeful that maybe we can work things out. Could we try to believe that for now?"

His heart continued to thud an affirmative against her fingers. If only his brain and mouth would join in.

Alicia watched the war in his bottle-green eyes, until… She saw that glint, the glimmer of a man challenged. *Yes.* She canted forward.

He raised a hand between them. "We need to set some ground rules."

Good God, the man was going to talk her to death. What in the world was up with that? A guy wanting to talk while the woman wanted to jump in the sack before she had time to think. "Why can't we be impulsive? You're messing with the mood here."

He trailed a lone finger along the length of her nose, down to tap the upturned tip. "The mood's going to take care of itself just fine in a few minutes."

"Really?" She wanted to believe that. So much.

"Yes. But not if we go about this the same way we have before."

"I'm not following you."

"Before, you kept secrets. I may be a few IQ points ahead of the rest of the curve, but I'm not a mind reader. I need you to tell me what you want."

Big-time awkward alert. "But you're experienced."

He didn't deny it, the jerk. "The most important thing a guy can learn from experience is that every woman is different. And by the way, I don't want to talk about any other woman except you."

Okay, not a total jerk. "Fair enough. I'm not interested in hearing about them, either."

"Good. Now, on to my ground rules before either of us ends up on our back." His emerald eyes flashed with a sensual intent that seared her from the inside out. "No secrets. Tell me what you want. Exactly. In detail."

Gulp. "What about you?"

"I can guarantee that the sound of your voice telling me what your body craves will be damned near enough to send me over the edge."

Her heart rate stuttered. "Maybe I'm not sure what I want." She forced herself not to look away—or fidget—or do any of those telling vulnerable impulses itching at her. "I know you don't want to talk about past experience or who else we've been with, but there hasn't been that much for me. Just him, and one other before, uh, briefly."

She risked a glance up and caught the quick flash of surprise an instant before he smoothed his angular features.

"Well, jeez, Josh. You don't have to look so shocked."

"Whoa. Time out." He formed his hands into a T. "It's not like you have some wild reputation, but everyone knows you've dated, and you exude…physical confidence."

"A defense mechanism to keep creeps from seeing me as some virtuous challenge."

His hands fell to cup her shoulders, calloused fingers rasping a gently abrasive arousal against her oversensitized flesh. "So you're not sure what works for you."

"That pretty much sums it up." Although the musky scent of him mixing with the subtle smoky air was working well for starters.

"All right. We can amend that first ground rule."

They could? Which meant he intended to go through with this. Relief shivered through her. They would really sleep together again. If she could ever shut him up. Why wouldn't the man just get to it, already? Didn't he know the anticipation all but had her shaking?

Or maybe he did know just that.

His fingers started a light massage along her neck much like the tantalizing hair wash earlier. "Tell me when I'm doing something right and don't hold back from nudging me in another direction if I'm a little off."

His hands slid forward until his palms rested just above her breasts, while his fingers continued caressing the base of her neck.

She swayed in a fog that had nothing to do with smoke from the fire. "Uh, won't that be kind of weird? Me barking orders at you?"

"I like it when you get bossy, Captain." His hands inched lower, not low enough to ease the ache in her tightening breasts. "And I can guarantee you won't be barking, but I'm mighty damned hopeful you'll be shouting."

She wanted to shout at him right now to strip away her bra and touch her. Still, drops of insecurity threatened to douse the fire within her that so desperately wanted to spread. Lower. Soon. "What if I don't? Shout, I mean."

"That brings me to the most important ground rule of all." His hands stilled and he stared into her eyes, into her soul. "Honesty. If we don't hit it just right this time, then okay, we'll try again. And again." His husky promise rumbled between them and over her skin as sensuously as a caress. "You said you enjoy the process, right?"

With a lone, sure finger, he flicked aside her bra strap from one shoulder, then the other. Only a slight swipe from him would peel away her bra altogether and expose her to his touch, his mouth. She yearned. And still he waited.

He wanted to hear from her. Fair enough. If he could stretch the need so taut inside her with a few simple strokes and this new honesty between them, she wasn't sure how much more of his "process" she could take before she imploded.

But she wanted to find out.

Alicia arched up to bring her face closer, which conveniently brought her breasts right into the perfect cradle of his palms.

Her lips a whisper away from his, she nipped his bottom lip. "How about process this, Colonel."

Chapter Seven

Processing things came easy to Josh. Most of the time. Not so much now.

Alicia bemused him, frustrated him, dazzled him at different times. Any one of which he could handle. But all at once? He hadn't been this disoriented since his first inverted spin in navigator training.

More than ever he needed balance to handle the situation, handle her, without mistakes. Yet finding level ground now wasn't as simple as taking a few deep breaths and checking an instrument panel. Today, he was flying totally by instinct, instinct being the only weapon he had left in his arsenal when dealing with this woman.

His mouth dropped to the curve of her breast. He wished he had a more romantic setting than some dank rusted-out hut and smoky woodstove firelight, but they weren't guaranteed forever.

Josh drew deeper on her through damp fabric. Alicia's breathy sigh proved as encouraging as any words. He peeled the plaid sports bra up and off, tossing their dog tags into a tangle. He broke contact with her skin for only a second—

forever for him—before returning to kiss up her neck while his hands moved lower.

He cupped the warm weight of her breasts, plucking, tugging gently at her nipples while his tongue delved deeper and explored until a moan vibrated her chest against his. He wanted to taste more of her, now, sooner. But he held back, lowering his mouth to take her lips instead, tasting apples and warm, moist Alicia.

Her fingers trekked down his sides, slipping into the waistband of his boxers.

"Slow down. We have all night." And he intended to make full use of every minute of that long night, longer than normal thanks to the storm and lengthy Alaskan winter solstice.

She smiled against his mouth. "I'm thinking I'll enjoy the second process more if we finish the first process fast."

Ever-efficient Alicia. He shook his head.

"No?"

"Definitely no." His hands slid from her breasts around to her back, and she groaned her regret before teasing her nipples along his chest. His vision fogged. He inhaled a steadying breath. "Plenty of time."

Swinging a lithe leg over, she straddled his lap, the heat of her burning clear through cotton underwear. "You told me to let you know what I want."

She kissed him, long, deep, moist, and somehow the rest of their underwear went flying away without either of them breaking apart. His hands roved her back while he invested serious energy in exploring the perfect curve of her ear with his mouth.

"Josh?"

"Yeah, my love?"

"Since you wanted me to talk," she interjected in a

breathy ramble, "and just in case you're wondering, that's just right. Perfect. More would be…"

"A good thing?"

"A very good thing."

"For both of us, since there's nothing I enjoy more than touching you." Making out with Alicia by firelight certainly posed no hardship for him.

She sighed into his mouth, her pleasure sparking through him. "And Josh? I just thought of something else I like. A lot."

"What's that?" He'd be all over it in a heartbeat. Hadn't he always been first in the class?

"Touching you."

The woman was a natural seductress. "Then feel free to indulge to your heart's content."

Her hands stroked him with a thoroughness that left him gritting his teeth against the need to take her. As much as he longed to lay her back on the giving softness of the sleeping bags, he also wanted to hold on to this moment longer. Nothing could equal the sensation of her hands, the sound of her whimpery sighs.

Damned straight he should go slow, but his hands glided lower, anyway, just to her hips. He could touch, grip, caress a little more of her without losing it. Right? Her gasp hitched somewhere in her throat, her breasts branding him as surely as the woman had branded herself in his mind.

While he nibbled along the line of her shoulder, he watched the firelight playing over her body, even better than his fantasy plan of romancing her by their new fireplace with merlot because he appreciated her more now. Their struggle of the past days taught him too well how intolerable it would be to live in a world that didn't include the vibrant presence of Alicia.

She rolled her hips against the length of him, hot and moist Alicia embracing him with a hint of the satin he would find deep inside her. Her head fell back, eyelids sliding to half mast. Watching her eyes go smoky proved headier than merlot.

"Tell me," he demanded. "Talk to me. Do you want more of this—" he brought them closer, increasing the frustrating incredible friction "—or this?" His hands returned to her breasts.

"Both, as long as you're looking at me. Most of all I melt over the way you look at me. The way your eyes turn a different shade of green when you're seeing me, just me. I didn't notice it at first. I just thought," she babbled in a litany of near indiscernible encouragement, "that…they were always this color. But then I started watching you too and I realized they were different for the rest of the world, more kelly-green."

"And what about when I'm looking at you?"

"They're darker, emerald. Hot." She leaned to kiss him, her molten brown eyes staying open. "Warming me all over."

"Keep talking," he growled.

"I remember," she purred against his mouth, phrases and kisses alternating, "the first time you kissed me."

"Oh, yeah?"

"The day our rotation in Cantou officially ended."

"And we weren't working together directly anymore." His initial pursuit of her in the bar had been stalled once they were paired together for war missions. But he'd known it was only a matter of time until their rotation ended. Then he would make his move, because every day he spent with her made him more determined that she would be his.

"You were heading back to England and I was returning to North Carolina." Her hands traveled over his shoulders into his hair while she talked, kissed, rocked, a master at multitasking and driving him crazy. "You met me at my plane and right there in front of God and the whole squadron you asked…"

"Want to go get a drink sometime?" he said, repeating his words from more than a year ago, the past and present merging in a mating dance even more important now with the stakes all or nothing in this their last chance. "Preferably just the two of us this time. Although, if you want to ask the whole damned squadron along for drinks, too, I can deal with that, because when you walk in a room it's not like I even see anyone else."

She stilled, her eyes wide, her heart hammering against him. "You remember."

"I remember. And you answered…"

"It's a date. I'll meet you in the Azores." Islands halfway across the Atlantic, the midway point between them at that time, and somehow those thousands of miles seemed easier to cross than the emotional distance between them lately. "I didn't think there was a chance it could work. But then you kissed me."

He stroked her tousled hair from her face. "Right there in front of God and the whole squadron."

"And then I knew it had to work."

Her words sent his heart hammering as hard as hers.

He had to touch her, more of her, all of her. His hand skimmed down, parting her, stroking lightly. He couldn't think about much of anything except the scent of her damp, satiny heat against him, her moans and sighs and yes, more pleadings.

A passionate flush spread along her skin, an unmistakable sign of how close she was to completion. A good thing since he was about to lose it and he hadn't even been inside her yet.

Better not think about being inside her.

Even with the need to finish thundering through him, he kept himself in check, in the moment, so damned grateful for the chance to touch her again he vowed not to squander even a second. Anything with Alicia was better than everything with anyone else. And this was more than just anything.

He tried to scrounge words to keep her talking to distract her from thinking too much. Words were tough to find. Maybe he should have spent more time distracting her out of bed, too, so she wouldn't have pushed him out of her life.

She was anything but pushing away now. The flush along her body darkened and he stroked her higher and higher until...

Her whole body tensed, bowed, the velvet heat clamping and massaging her release along his fingers. The sheer honesty of it all threatened to hurtle him over the edge with her.

In this moment, at least, she was completely his.

The afterglow swallowed Alicia completely. She sagged against Josh, grateful he still had the ability to hold her up because her sated, mellow muscles weren't working all that well at the moment.

How could she be so glad and scared at once? And why did she have to think? She wanted to enjoy her hot, naked husband.

Alicia traced bunched muscles along his back. "I can feel you smiling against my neck."

"Is that a bad thing?" His steamy breath caressed her.

A much-needed laugh broke free. "Not really, I guess. I'll give you thirty more seconds for your macho-male testosterone victory dance."

He raised his head and chuckled into her mouth with his kiss. "I'm just happy for you."

"I'm happy for me, too. And we're about to be really happy for you as well."

"Oh, we are?"

His laugh and smile untwined fears and tension working to coil inside her again. Light and simple was good. Before, sex with them had been so intense. She enjoyed his sense of humor and yet they'd never brought it into the bedroom with them, an odd oversight.

He'd told her to let him know what she needed. Well, she needed fun. Light. Uncomplicated. And him. On his back. Most of all, she wanted to give to him as much as he'd given her.

Alicia shoved him backward onto the sleeping bags, walking playful fingers down his chest. His eyes widened in surprise and, my, how she enjoyed surprising this man. She understood great sex couldn't sustain a marriage, but she wanted to tell herself if they could fix this, somehow that could fix everything else.

She took him in her hand, took him inside her, and yes, this process was every bit as wonderful as she remembered. More so since she could simply glide in the moment as she glided against him. No thoughts of the past or future or worries about what he would expect from her, just the present and them.

"Talk to me," she commanded in impish retaliation.

"Talk?" he growled through clenched teeth. "In a few more minutes I'll recite the whole preamble to the Constitution for you, but at the moment you've pretty much shut down my brain."

The sleepy seduction of his definitely dark green eyes sent a shower of heat tingling over her skin. Tension knotted inside her again, surprising her, because wait, hadn't she already…

And then she couldn't think anymore. Her head fell back, her eyes tight as she focused on the firm grip of his hands on her hips, the synching of their rapid breaths. Increasing need climbed along with the rising passion. Together. This was more than just a process.

She didn't know what to call it, just wanted to devour the moment.

"Open your eyes," he demanded. "See me see you."

Eyelids heavy, she forced herself to look down, and was it ever worth the effort. Deep green stared back up at her, only her, until tension pulled tighter within her. His hands trekked up to cup her breasts, to her shoulders, up farther until his fingers threaded into her hair. He massaged a firm caress that brought back the sensual unraveling of the hair wash earlier, water and Josh pouring over her.

The burning tingle along her skin increased. Her gasps paced with Josh's, matched rhythm, just like in the plane, until a shout rolled deep inside her, out to mingle with Josh's hoarse groan of completion. Echoes cycled around them like a spiraling aircraft.

Alicia collapsed forward onto Josh's chest, his arms already around her. Aftershocks rocked through her, physical and emotional. And as much as she wanted to bask in the moment, fear flickered. For a woman accustomed to taking charge of her life, the thought of giving her heart fully left her shaking all over again.

Until this moment, it hadn't occurred to her how little experience she had in equal give-and-take relationships of any kind. Her mother had died so early, leaving Alicia to step into more of a parental role with her siblings. And of course her dating history pretty much sucked.

What she felt for Josh went far beyond anything she'd felt for Ben. She knew she could trust this incredibly funny, stubborn, honorable man beneath her. She just wasn't certain she could trust herself. And with her heart lying there at his feet, she realized more than being hurt, she feared hurting him.

Two hours later, Josh buried his face in Alicia's neck while angling on his elbows to keep his weight off her. After round three of loving Alicia, he willed his slugging heart to slow to a halfway normal pace. He wasn't smiling against the soft curve of her shoulder now.

Already, he could feel her retreating from him. Making love to her each time with no holds barred had been every bit as incredible as he'd expected. Just the thought of her unraveling in his arms had him throbbing to life inside her. But their pocket of time here was ticking to an end. They would have to dress soon and evaluate what to do next.

He turned his face against the sweet scent of her skin toward the hazy glow rippling across the Plexiglas. Northern lights streaking across the night sky cast banners of purple and pink through the dark in their own holiday light display. Sunrise wasn't far off. "Merry Christmas Eve."

She kissed his shoulder. "I'm sorry you had to spend Hanukkah alone."

He didn't want to think about their last fight or the breakup. They'd had every reason to be happy, finally living in the same city, and still they'd screwed up. "We could always float the date, like you used to do as a kid so your whole family could celebrate together. We could make this the holiday season for both of us. We've had your star to follow by. And it seems my Bic lighter has an endless supply of fuel."

"You know how I love quirky and mismatched, so it definitely works for me. Hey, maybe we should create a pamphlet for military folks since they spend the holidays in so many odd places. Something like a thousand and one ways to celebrate the holidays in a tent—or Quonset hut."

He nodded absently, humor tougher to scrounge than normal.

She tapped his forehead. "What are you thinking? I'm not a mind reader, either, you know."

Honesty. He'd demanded it of her and she deserved the same from him. He rolled off her onto his back. "I'm wondering what we'll do when we return to base."

And they would make it home, damn it.

She sat up, sleeping bag clasped to her chest. "I don't know how we went so wrong. You're the answer man. I only know that no one can touch me, frustrate me, hurt me…move me as much as you. I suspect that much, at least, is mutual."

He stroked the backs of his fingers along her jaw. "That sums it up."

"We're so different. You with your logic, me with my quirky ways and mismatched clothes."

He needed reason and plans in his life. She was all about the unexpected, flying by gut and instinct while he plotted the odds and targets.

Josh sat up beside her, dropped a quick kiss on her mouth before standing. "We should get dressed. The storm's easing and we'll need to start moving again. My guess is that this Quonset is near the river. We shouldn't have far to go."

He stepped back into his boxers and unhooked his flight suit from the clothesline. His snow pants and parka swayed like ghostly apparitions, reminding him of those chem-gear suits hanging in the cave. More than their own lives depended on them returning to base in one piece.

Leaning back against the wall, he rolled on his socks. Sounds of Alicia dressing tormented the hell out of him. He could wade through quantum physics without hesitation, but he didn't have a clue how to ease the awkwardness between them. Whatever happened to reveling in the afterglow of great sex?

Incredible sex.

Alicia padded to a stop beside him, her reindeer toe socks making a perfect Alicia-contrast to the military precision of her flight suit. "We should have dated longer."

The cross-Atlantic relationship had frustrated the hell out of both of them while they spiked long distance bills to rival the national debt. Sure they had leave time, but scheduling it to coincide was nearly impossible. Getting married was the only way to guarantee a joint assignment. And even that had taken six months to shake down before they'd both made it to Alaska—two people so much in love, married and virtual strangers even after eighteen months.

Add the stress of a move and high-pressure military jobs and was it any wonder they'd crashed and burned on the relationship front? So logical he should have seen it coming, but he hadn't stopped hoping for a different outcome all the way to the ground.

He tugged the zipper up on her flight suit until his knuckles rested against her delicate collarbone. The buzz in his head predicted failure if he didn't get his act together. "Yes, we should have. But we didn't have that luxury."

She reached to clasp his hand in hers. "Have we already done too much damage to our relationship?"

To our love? The rest of her sentence stayed unspoken but was clear as the spirals of light playing through the window. The echo of her softly spoken words rattled around inside his head along with the buzz in his brain.

"I don't know."

The drone increased. Built. Until he realized it wasn't in his head at all.

A vehicle was approaching the Quonset hut.

Chapter Eight

Josh yanked Alicia by the arm, jerking her away from the small window inset in the door. He shut down emotions until his brain focused only on processing information. "Someone's out there. Snowmobiles, I think. Sounds like two."

She scooped her mukluks as he dragged her toward the woodstove. "Let's hope it's a rescue."

Sure, he hoped. His gut told him otherwise. He jammed his feet into his boots. "We'll know soon enough."

Military rescue forces would call out first. Of course someone from the mining operation might try calling out with a bluff, but he was damned good at detecting bluffs. Either way, he wouldn't let the past replay again into some kind of twisted holiday massacre, most definitely not with Alicia playing any part.

Where to go? He considered standing to the side of the door and simply ambushing whoever came through. Answers could come afterward.

He started a step in that direction—then stopped. Frowning, he studied their tin-can shelter. Serious intruders would shoot first, enter later, and the thin metal of the rusting Quonset hut would barely slow a bullet, much less stop it.

"Between the stacks of wood, lie flat," he ordered. Not much of a hiding place, but it would provide protection with the stove beside them as well.

He couldn't allow himself to look at Alicia with her blond hair still tousled from making love. Crouching, he scooped his survival vest and tossed Alicia's to her, as well. He tucked behind the stacked logs with her, shrugged into his vest, drew his flare gun.

Headlights swooped across the Plexiglas window, no stealthy approach. A good sign.

Low voices permeated through, but nothing overly loud or specific to discern - which meant bad news. This wasn't a military rescue or they would have announced themselves. Still, he could only see two figures. Could there be more lurking?

Alicia held up two fingers in the dimly lit corner, a question puckering her brow. "Only two guys on the snowmobiles?" she whispered.

"Seems so." With some luck, these were only a couple of hunters.

Hunting on Christmas Eve? Yeah, right.

Part of him wanted to blast the two men lurking outside now, but his military training overrode baser instincts. As much as he wanted to protect Alicia at all costs, he still needed to establish the men had hostile intent. They could be lost and wandering, something he doubted but couldn't risk.

Damn, how much longer were those two bozos going to weasel around outside? They had to know from the smoke that someone was inside. His grip tightened on the flare gun. Alicia's body heat radiated beside him. Primal protectiveness still churned from their earlier discussion about the bastard in her past. And now it all roared stronger. Louder.

He wouldn't end this day with even one hair on her head injured.

More muffled voices echoed along with a sound he recognized well—the click and rattle of a machine gun being raised. Ah, hell.

He grabbed the back of Alicia's neck and pushed.

"Stay down," he hissed. He flattened onto his belly beside her.

Bullets riddled the shelter. Pinging. Popping through the walls. Ricocheting off the stove. Shit. He flung his arm over her head.

Snow gear dangling from the line swayed, shredded, fiberfill puffing and exploding.

Had the Plexiglas given a distorted impression of people inside? Slowly, the long pants slithered to the floor.

Silence followed.

Alicia!

He jerked to look at her, skimming his hand up to her neck to find a reassuring pulse.

"I'm fine. Don't worry about me."

But he did. How could he not? He wanted to crawl on top of her and shield her body with his until this hell passed. She stared back at him, resignation on her face.

She knew him. She knew he would want to lead the charge as if he could fix her past for her. He thought of his own nightmarish experience he'd long wanted to put to rest…and accepted she had her own. Hers in some ways was worse, because the betrayal had come from someone she trusted.

Slowly, understanding—if not peace—rolled over him about the university siege. His faith in mankind may have been shaken, but he'd never had to question himself. He'd done his best that day.

Alicia needed to learn to trust herself again before she could fully trust him. She needed to fix her own past and win this battle on the ground.

He didn't intend to let her fight the battle alone, but damn it, she'd earned her place on the front lines. Big picture, they needed to bring these bastards down and stood a better chance working together. "We're outgunned. Our only edge is surprise since they think we're wounded or dead. They're over-armed—but overconfident. That can work for us."

"For us?" she asked, as if she couldn't believe he would include her.

"For us. Like in Cantou, we watch each other's back." *I trust you. You trust me.* And God, he hoped he'd been right to trust his instincts. For a man who'd spent a lifetime following logic, this was scary shit. "When the door opens, shoot. The gyro jets are great for tearing through a jungle canopy overhead, but their aim's not all that accurate. Hopefully we'll nail at least one of the bastards. Then we'll rush the door before the other can hide and swing around to riddle us with bullets from the back."

Footsteps crunched the snow.

"Are you ready?" he stared into her eyes and hoped that even in the faint light she could still see him, see her.

"Thank you," she said simply, didn't need to say anymore.

He understood. Thanks to Alicia, he understood so much more now.

Josh nodded, too much emotion clogging his throat and his head. He needed a clear brain.

Footsteps crunched closer. Two shadows bobbed and blended, bobbing again. Josh angled around one side of the wood stack, Alicia around the other. Staying flat on his stomach, he extended his arms in front of him, flare gun in both hands, aimed. Ready.

The door blasted open. A lone figure blocked the view. One chance.

"Fire," Josh ordered. He shot, the hiss of Alicia's gun in synchronicity with his.

Two flares blazed across the room. Reflexively, he reloaded. Only three more left in his vest.

The flares caught the looming figure in both shoulders. Howling, he stumbled back, toppled.

Falling into the second intruder. Both landed in the snow.

Luck, logic or miracle? Josh didn't care or have time to analyze. But he was mighty grateful.

"Don't move," Josh shouted to the screaming man beating at the poker-hot torches in his shoulders. The bastard was lucky the snow gear had blunted the impact and the heat had likely cauterized his wounds. "One twitch this way and we'll pin you both with another round." Josh glanced back at Alicia. "Cover me while I get their weapons, then we can pop a flare for rescue."

"Roger." She reloaded and raised her flare gun level. "I've got your back."

Her words knocked around inside his head before settling in his gut with a new rightness. He'd heard her say it before, hell, had even brought it up himself earlier. But now the words solidified and became a part of him beyond just applying to the plane or battlefield. After a lifetime of living in a world where people put up walls around him, where he put them around himself, he wasn't alone anymore.

Enemy weapons gathered, Josh launched a rescue-signal flare into the sky. An umbrella of light exploded in the midst of the purple-and-pink haze of the aurora borealis. Staring up into all those lights, he decided that it wouldn't be too far a stretch from trusting instincts to believing in miracles.

And more than anything, he wanted the miracle of forever with the wary, stubborn, incredible woman he'd married.

Alicia clicked off the cordless phone, placing it on top of a stack of packing boxes by her kitchen stove, her Christmas calls complete. Since her family hadn't been notified about her ordeal, there hadn't been any need for tears or explanations. Simply rejoicing.

Her father was celebrating with her sister and sister's fiancé. Her brother was enjoying a bachelor dinner with his girlfriend. Josh had even taken his turn speaking with everyone so she didn't have to make explanations about their breakup.

Were there even explanations to be made?

Alicia slumped against the towering boxes and stared at the starkly bare apartment walls that had yet to be warmed into a home. She'd had such plans for decorating their first place together with all her favorite colors and Pier I rattan. She still hoped to…

Except she didn't know where she stood with Josh. After their life-and-death struggle, it seemed their problems should be insignificant. But they weren't. She knew better now than to ignore troubles in hopes that they would fade of their own volition.

She couldn't delay much longer settling things one way or the other. The archway afforded a clear view of Josh starting a fire in the fireplace. Northern lights streamed through the wall-size picture window during the final hours of night.

Alaskan snow-capped mountains loomed as large and in-domitable as the man in her living room.

Long legs were encased in faded jeans, broad shoulders covered by a T-shirt and white cable sweater. Her stomach did a quick loop-de-loop.

She *would* talk to him. Soon.

First, she just needed to find the darned microwave so she could heat the carryout meal they'd snagged on their way home from base. She wasn't delaying. Much.

She sliced through the tape on a box. They'd been picked up by the military helicopter and taken to Eielson Air Force Base in Fairbanks for a once-over by the doctors. Once the flight surgeon declared them healthy with only minor frost-bite and no tissue damage, they were both released.

Sifting through the box, she uncovered…no microwave. Damn. Why hadn't she paid more attention to how the pack-ers labeled the boxes? She shuffled down to the next box and hacked it open.

A debrief with the Office of Special Investigations had taken up the rest of Christmas Eve, but well worth it. All intelligence indicated the illegal uranium mine was being used to funnel material for nukes over the Bering Strait into Russia. From there, it went to radical factions in Can-tou. The two goons on snowmobiles were already spilling vital information in hopes of immunity and new identities. Hopefully, that information would help keep things chilled in Cantou for Josh's squadron.

The plane hop from Fairbanks up to their base in An-chorage had been silent due to lack of privacy. And now they had privacy to spare during the dark of Christmas morning. Alone. Neither one sure what to say. But she had hope after the way they'd worked together at the Quonset hut in bringing down their attackers. Afterward, Josh hadn't even suggested going to his BOQ room or office.

Abandoning her microwave search, she leaned against the open box and just enjoyed staring at her hunky hubby. Josh knelt in front of the grate, adjusting the kindling on top before reaching into his back pocket for...his trusty Bic lighter. She smiled, suddenly glad there hadn't been time yet to install gas logs, this moment wonderfully reassuring in its reminder of how they'd worked together to survive the past days.

She wanted to settle in front of that fire with him and make love through the day. Years of stored hormones demanded release. But she also wanted more with Josh. She always had, but now realized she'd sabotaged their relationship from the start out of fears and insecurities, her refusal to plan for a future because making that final commitment symbolized a loss of control. Fixing things between them would be a delicate balance.

Absently scratching a moving sticker off the box, she let herself savor watching Josh in motion, the man always so sure of himself and his actions. He never seemed to need anyone.

Or did he?

Her thumb slowed on the sticker. He often joked about carrying a Scooby-Doo lunch box to his doctoral dissertation defense. Sure he got along well with people. His sense of humor earned him plenty of pals. But why had she never noticed he lacked close friendships? And he outranked almost everyone his age since he'd entered the Air Force young and been promoted early.

Alicia looked again at the solitary man blowing gently to coax the fire to life with patience and single-minded determination. He'd probably already calculated the exact wind power needed.

Beyond missing out on having a real senior prom, how many friendships had he missed out on as well? Yes, he was more than a little arrogant. Self-assured. And of course he was usually right.

Smart man that he was, he must have known on some level that he'd been pushing all her buttons, too, almost ensuring she would run. She wasn't the only one who'd kicked the legs out from under their shaky marriage.

Here they were, two combat veterans scared to death to tackle happily ever after. Two leader-loners who had to take a risk on a partnership. Partnerships came with higher stakes. Having someone to watch your back also meant having someone to lose. But if she didn't try, she would lose even more. She couldn't lie to herself anymore.

She still loved Joshua Rosen. Totally. No quitting this time.

With renewed energy and purpose, she tore into another box. Christmas decorations winked back up at her. A snow globe glistened. Santa perched on an airplane dropping packages. Her mismatched crèche waited to be assembled.

Presents and parcels were packed alongside, including a last-minute arrival she'd shoved into the box. She lifted out the package addressed to her.

From Josh's grandmother?

Alicia tore away brown packing paper and reached into the box. A wooden moose stared back up at her, antlers ready for candles.

Her eyes filled with tears. She scooped out her mismatched crèche and held it beside Josh's moose menorah from his grandmother. Somehow the two different symbols presented in their quirky manner looked so very right together.

Just the way she'd envisioned and hoped things could be for her with Josh.

She replaced both back in the box with careful hands. Shaky breaths doing little to ease her light-headed nerves, she smoothed her hunter-green angora sweater. She wasn't naive enough to believe they would never hit rocky patches again. She was scared, but then the two symbols of hope cradled in the moving box had sprung from scary times survived through trust and love.

It would take a lot of compromise and love—courage beyond a chestful of medals—for she and Josh to lower their defenses enough to be touched and healed by the power of the season.

But thanks to knowing this wonderful man who had the most endearing penchant for wearing crazy boxers, making her smile, melting her heart, she now had an abundance of trust and love to give.

"Do you need some help?"

Josh glanced up from blowing on the logs, just the sound of his wife's voice combusting a fire in him that rivaled anything in the works in front of him.

Alicia strode toward him across the white carpet, packing box in hand, crimson red velvet miniskirt begging his hands to climb right up and explore her legs. Her Christmas-green fuzzy sweater all but screamed "touch me."

Rein it in, libido.

He wanted to park with her in front of a romantic fire and she wanted to scale mountains of boxes nearly as tall as the snowy mountains outside their window. Not an auspicious start to their reconciliation.

"I'm set here." And he was, with a clear mission. Operation: Win Back His Wife—without being a dumb ass this time. Hand on his knee, he shoved to his feet. "What about you? Do you need some help with that?"

He kept his tone light. He wouldn't push her like he'd done before. If she needed time to finish settling her past, their future, then he would damn well give her plenty of space.

But he wasn't walking away.

Her black ankle boots thudded softly against the carpet as she walked past a rattan futon. "Actually, yes, I could really use help finding the microwave, but we'll get to that in a minute. First, I have something for you." She rifled through the box, setting aside bulks of packing paper, until she unearthed a gift-wrapped box, shoebox-size.

She thrust it toward him. "Merry Christmas. Happy Hanukkah. From me."

He took the box from her, the simple brush of their fingers making him long to unwrap her instead. Patience, he reminded himself. He tore through the gold foil paper and lifted open the lid. An antique brass sextant gleamed up at him. A smile spread across his face. "This is really great."

And he meant it. She'd been searching for the perfect gift for him even during the worst low point of their relationship, and that brought hope. Well, hell, hadn't he been doing the same in shopping for her?

"I thought it would look good in your office." She fidgeted with the hem of her fuzzy sweater, nerves unlike her but endearing all the same. "And when you see it, you can think about me."

"I don't need reminders to think about you." He dropped a quick kiss on her lush mouth, but pulled back before she could pull him closer or shove him away. He tucked his head into the box. "I had something for you in that stack of presents the movers packed up."

He shuffled past the snail-mail package from his grandma and lifted out the silver foil package. "Here. Merry Christmas and happy Hanukkah to you, too."

She unsealed the tape with careful precision, taking her time as if she wanted to extend the moment. The long silk scarf slithered out in a sheath of white. Her smile rivaled the gleam of the brass sextant. Her fingers traced along the personalized stitching at the tail end of the fabric. Vogue. "Oh, my God, is this ever awesome or what?"

With Alicia flair, she draped the aviator scarf around her neck, trailing it all the way down to her knees past her red velvet miniskirt.

Unexpected.

Perfect.

Worth fighting for, and more important, worth waiting for. He'd spent his life on fast-forward. Having Alicia in his life was too important to risk losing by rushing.

She stepped into his arms. "I love you, Rose-Bud."

He wouldn't rush her, but he sure would keep up as fast as she wanted to run. "I love you, too."

He met her halfway for a kiss, the fire heating the back of his legs nothing in comparison to his hot wife heating the front of him.

She wriggled closer. "Let's make a baby."

"Right now?" Not that he was adverse to making love to her, but her quick turnaround on the topic left his head spinning.

"Well, as soon as I check in with my doc, but yes."

He could feel her tremble in his arms. She was scared? Nervous? And in that moment he realized reconciling was just as important to her. Relief kicked through him.

He sketched his hands up and down her back. "I've been thinking about the two of us."

Panic flared in her eyes.

"Whoa! Hold on. This is good stuff coming up, Vogue."

She relaxed under his hands.

"I do want children. But you were right before that I was rushing, and I think that had something to do with the fact I was afraid of losing you. That's the wrong reason for getting pregnant."

Her eyes widened again, but with surprise. "I was right? And you're admitting it?"

"Yes, you were. I knew that here." He thumped his heart. "I was just having trouble getting my head to shut up long enough to listen."

"No? Really?" Her impish smile matched those funky ankle elf boots of hers. "I've been doing some thinking myself."

"And?"

"Having a plan is good, too. How about this? We know how to be friends." She tucked her hands in his back pockets and urged him closer. "We know how to make love. We just need to work on being in love and building a relationship. Let's make this next year a twelve-month gift to each other."

"You're a wise woman."

"I'm learning. This is uncharted territory for me."

"Me, too." He'd managed alone fine for more than thirty years, but since meeting Alicia, he couldn't return to his old way.

"How about this time next year we make that baby?"

Already he could see her in crazy-colored maternity clothes, could imagine the wonder of watching his baby grow inside her. "Sounds like a perfect timetable for me."

"And then the next Christmas we could work on another. And then maybe we could work on a July Fourth baby one year."

"Hey, how many kids are we talking about here?"

"Lots. I'm good at the bossy big sister-mom role. Got a problem with that?"

"No, ma'am."

"Smart man." She traced the ridges on his forehead. "And I can already hear you thinking. I don't have a problem going off active duty and flying fighters for a reserve unit once our house starts overflowing with all of those holiday babies." She bracketed his face in her soft palms. "I do make plans, Josh. I've just never had anyone to share them with before."

"You really are incredible." His mouth found hers with a wealth of friendship and respect all wrapped up in even more love flowing between them.

Eventually, she eased back, her eyes dazed. Her hand unsteady, she reached to bat at the box behind her. "I need your help now."

"As long as you want help unpacking a box of sheets for the bed. Or pillows. For the bed. Or maybe a blanket. *For the bed.*"

Laughing, she angled away to reach inside the box, giving him a glimpse of creamy thigh as her pleated miniskirt hitched higher. Dangerously high. His mouth watered.

She spun back to face him, her crèche in hand. "I'd like you to help me set this up first in our new home."

"My pleasure." Together they placed all the mismatched figurines around the barn. He laid claim to the angel, placing her smack dab on top of the star, where she could fly among the clouds like his ladylove.

Alicia scooped out another smaller box, the one with mailing wrap on it. "And this came from Nonni."

"Nonni already sent something for me?" She always mailed him the best cookies, but they were probably moldy by now. Damn.

"Actually, she sent this to me. But I thought you might want to be the one to place it on the mantel."

She lifted the lid. A dark wood antler he recognized well peeked from the tissue wrappings. His favorite moose.

"Would you please place it on the mantel, *our* mantel?"

"Of course." He took the wooden moose from her hands and placed it above the fireplace, beside her crèche.

The moment went still in one of those times a guy knows life is about to change—and in a moment he knew he would never forget. Still, he took a minute longer to imprint the image of his wife right now, the aurora borealis through the wall window bathing her feathery hair in a light festival all their own.

This was it, the start of their traditions. Quirky. Mismatched. And somehow perfect for the two of them. Life with Alicia would never be boring.

Who needed a bed when they had a fire and blanket? Josh snatched an Aztec blanket off the back of the rattan sofa and spread it on the carpet. "I wonder where we'll be next year when we're making that baby, and if we'll even get the chance to unpack the decorations then, either?"

She melted against him, his very own snow angel with whispery-blond hair. "That's one thing we never have to worry about—planning where we'll be during December."

"How so?" Tugging the ends of her scarf to draw her closer, Josh lowered his wife to the blanket while she sent one, then the other elf boot flying.

"Simple," she whispered against his mouth, northern lights streaking through the picture window and playing with the glimmer in her eyes. "I've found my life-long home for the holidays—anywhere, any day—in your arms."

* * * * *

Look for Catherine Mann's latest release,
PURSUED,
a Silhouette Bombshell, in stores now.
And watch for EXPLOSIVE ALLIANCE,
her next WINGMEN WARRIORS *story,*
coming in February
from Silhouette Intimate Moments.

HQN™

We *are* romance™

A much-anticipated, new Protectors story
from *USA TODAY* bestselling author

Sometimes love is stronger than death....

BEVERLY
BARTON

Security agent Dante Moran can't afford to fall in love—
in his line of work, emotions can get you killed. But when
he's hired to protect Tessa Westbrook's daughter, Dante is
shocked to find long-buried emotions rising to the surface....

**"Beverly Barton's 'The Protectors' series
is a number one winner."**
—*Rendezvous*

Worth Dying For

Coming in November 2004!

www.HQNBooks.com

PHBB012RTR

HQN™

We *are* romance™

There's no better gift than a new love…

A special volume of tender, heartwarming enjoyment from #1 Harlequin Romance® author

BETTY NEELS

Back in print after many years, these two classic stories celebrate Christmas as a magical time when dreams really do come true.

"Betty Neels works her magic to bring us a touching love story that comes softly but beautifully."
—*Romantic Times*

A Christmas to Remember

Available in November wherever books are sold.

www.HQNBooks.com

PHBN013RTR

#1 *New York Times*
bestselling author

NORA ROBERTS

From the master of romance—
two extraordinary tales of heartfelt reunions.

R E U N I O N

Set in a world where love the second time around
is the greatest treasure of all, these two full-length
stories are back in print after more than ten years.

December

"A storyteller of immeasurable diversity and talent."
—*Publishers Weekly*

Silhouette®
TM
Where love comes alive™

Visit Silhouette Books at www.eHarlequin.com   PSNR505TR

ᴴQN™

We *are* romance™

Their corner of paradise was beautiful...but deadly.

New York Times bestselling author

JAYNE ANN KRENTZ

writing as Stephanie James

After meeting Jase Lassiter at a seedy bar called The Serpent, Amy Shannon finds herself mesmerized. But their passion soon turns deadly when they find themselves drawn into a dangerous game of theft and deceit.

"Krentz's storytelling shines with authenticity and dramatic intensity."—*Publishers Weekly*

Serpent in Paradise

Look for this classic tale in December.

═══ www.HQNBooks.com ═══

PHJAK016TR

HQN™

We *are* romance™

A classic tale of strength, love and power from
New York Times bestselling author

DIANA PALMER

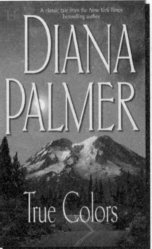

Run out of town as a penniless, pregnant teenager by
Cy Harden's powerful family, Meredith Ashe was finally
back—stronger, wiser and ready for anything. But her
planned hostile takeover of Harden Properties had
consequences she hadn't planned on. And it looked as
though in reaching her goal...she might also lose her heart.

**"Nobody tops Diana Palmer...I love her stories."
—*New York Times* bestselling author Jayne Ann Krentz**

True Colors

Available in December 2004.

═══ www.HQNBooks.com ═══

PHDP01